Jeff Sherratt

Guilty or Else

A Jimmy O'Brien Mystery Novel

Echelon Press
Publishing

GUILTY OR ELSE
A Jimmy O'Brien Mystery Novel
An Echelon Press Book

First Echelon Press paperback printing / 2009
Portions of this novel have been previously published

Echelon Press, LLC
9735 Country Meadows Lane 1-D
Laurel, MD 20723
www.echelonpress.com

ISBN: 978-1-59080-614-2
ISBN: (10-Digit) 1-59080-614-X
ISBN: 1-59080-615-8 (eBook)

PRINTED IN THE UNITED STATES OF AMERICA

10 9 8 7 6 5 4 3 2 1

This book is dedicated to the loving memory of my mother and father. Also to my three beautiful daughters, seven outstanding grandchildren and, of course, my wonderful wife Judy.

Many friends and family members have given me their support and encouragement and a number of them have donated their valuable time reading and critiquing my pre-published manuscripts. I thank you all. But I'd like to give a special thanks to four people who were instrumental in bringing about this book. My daughter, Kristin Escalante, who spent many tireless hours editing a different version of this novel. My brother-in-law, Tom Budds, a retired homicide detective with the Los Angeles County Sherriff's Department, who gave freely his expert advice in matters pertaining to law enforcement. And to Mike Sirota, book editor extraordinaire, who worked alongside me, shaping and polishing my words until we finally had a manuscript worthy of publication. I also owe a debt of gratitude to Karen Syed of Echelon Press for her belief in my competence as a storyteller, and her trust that others will enjoy reading my mystery novels.

Chapter One

They say never blame it on the weather. But I had to come up with something, a story that would explain why I was running late for Judge Johnson's command performance. Today, unlike most days in sunny California, the rain beat down in a mind-numbing torrent. These late August storms blew in from the Pacific Ocean, hung around for about an hour, dumped a billion gallons of acid rain on the smog-choked, sun-baked, paved-over landscape known as the L.A. Basin before they disappeared, leaving the freeway system and feeder roads a tangled mess.

Not that the current storm caused my tardiness. I'd overslept. But I had to place the blame somewhere. "Be here at nine a.m., exactly!" Judge Johnson demanded when he'd called my office yesterday. He didn't say why he wanted to see me, just be there on time.

My four-year-old '68 Corvette skidded into the last parking spot at the South Gate Municipal Court and I rushed into the single-story brick building. When I bolted into Johnson's courtroom, the bailiff shook his head ominously as he pointed to the Judge's chambers.

"Sorry, Judge, the traffic on Firestone Boulevard. The rain, you know," I said, peeking around the door.

"Yeah, everyone's late. Come in and sit down."

I expected a ration of crap, but instead he seemed subdued, even pensive. I took a chair facing his desk.

"I guess you heard about the murder," he said.

"Saw it on the news last night. Senator Welch's secretary, stabbed to death Saturday night. Shame." When Judge Johnson didn't say anything, I added, "Just a kid, really."

"Gloria was twenty-seven," he said in a voice barely above a whisper. Then he perked up. "They caught the guy who did it."

"Cops didn't waste any time finding the killer."

I wondered why Bob Johnson wanted to see me this morning. We weren't close or anything. Oh, we had worked together as cops on the Los Angeles Police Department years ago. He flew jets during the Korean War, mustered out shortly after the ceasefire, and joined the LAPD. I came on twelve years later after two years of police science at Cerritos Community College. Because of his military experience, Johnson rose through the ranks on a fast track and soon became a sergeant. Johnson had the chevrons. I had slick sleeves, which made him the boss of our two-man unit. But he wouldn't have demanded my appearance this morning just to talk about old times, or gab about the news.

"The cops didn't break a sweat," Johnson said. "The perp left a trail of evidence, led right to his house. Her body was still warm when they collared the bastard."

"Her gardener, wasn't it?"

"Hot-blooded Mexican. You know how they are. Violent sons of bitches. The cops and the DA figured he tried to put the make on Gloria. When she wouldn't go along…well, you saw the story on TV."

"Judge, have you talked to the senator?"

"Had breakfast with him this morning. He's shook up. Can't understand how something like this can happen right here in South Gate. It's not like we're in South Central L.A."

"Do you think the murder will have an impact on his campaign?"

Through his charisma and movie star looks, Senator Berry Welch played the game and worked his way up the system until he became the majority leader of the state senate, a kingpin in the Democratic Party. He was up for re-election in November, a shoe in. There was talk that he had his eye on the top prize in 1974: governor of the State of California.

"The press already pounced on the story. Any time violence, a pretty girl, and a politician are mentioned in the same paragraph, the news maggots crawl out of wherever they come from and insinuate all sorts of lurid bullshit." Johnson reached into a hand-carved antique humidor adorning his desk. He extracted a cigar the size and shape of a small torpedo. "Sells papers. I'm not worried. The election is still two years away." He ignited a pocket-sized, gold-plated blowtorch, set fire to the cigar, and puffed on it until the tip glowed red-hot.

"People have memories like fruit flies," Johnson said. "The story will disappear once the killer confesses. Berry, of course, had nothing to do with her death. We don't think the murder will cause problems."

I remained silent, thinking. What kind of animal would murder a young woman in the prime of her life, and why?

"Maybe there's something you can do for me. Might be good for you too."

"Sure, Bob, what do you need?"

He held out his burning cigar. "These are Cohiba cigars, Cuban, handmade for Castro. Can't get 'em here in the United States; the embargo, you know. I've got a contact. The guy brings them up from Mexico."

My eyes stung as the room filled with a blue haze, carrying with it a sweet pungent aroma. The smell of money burning. Did he want me to get him some cigars?

Johnson rolled the cigar around in his mouth. "How old are you, Jimmy? Thirty-five, thirty-six?" he asked between puffs.

"Thirty-four."

"Getting it together, are you?"

"I'm working on it," I said.

"Still drink?"

"Nope, I quit after Barbara left me."

Johnson seemed to scrutinize me while puffing his torpedo.

"You said something about a favor?"

"Heard about your divorce," he said. "Barbara's a hell of a woman. Too bad."

"Look, Bob, I'll admit I've had my problems, but I've cleaned up my act."

"How long you been off the sauce?"

"Four years now."

Johnson leaned forward. "Jimmy, I can help you out, but I've got to know I can trust you. You played ball back in the old days when we were cops. I'm not forgetting the favors." He paused for a moment. "I counted on you then, but can I trust you now?"

Being on the right side of a well-connected guy like Johnson couldn't hurt my new law practice, and I needed the business. In the six months since I started I'd only had a handful of paying clients. "Yeah, sure you can count on me."

He took another hard pull on his Cohiba. "Sometimes it's important to go along to get along."

Obviously, he had something in mind. I remained silent, waiting to see what he wanted from me.

He leaned back. "Okay, I'm going to take a chance on you."

"What do you want me to do?"

"We talked about the guy who killed Welch's secretary."

"Yeah, the gardener."

"He's broke. Hasn't got a quarter," Johnson said.

My stomach tightened. Was he going to offer me the case? "Oh?"

"This is no *pro bono* deal."

"Are you appointing me to defend this guy?"

"The government will pay you to represent him." He looked me straight in the eye. "You'll be paid, but *only* for the arraignment. The cops have an airtight case and the defendant is due to be arraigned here tomorrow. Cut a deal with the DA, maybe second degree. Plead him out, he escapes life without parole. That's it."

This could turn out to be one of the hottest cases of the year. Half a dozen well-qualified lawyers around town would love to get it. They'd probably even handle the defense without a fee. The publicity alone would more than justify the cost of a trial.

"Why me, Bob?" I said.

Johnson took a hit on his cigar, blowing the smoke toward the ceiling. "Because I'm a good guy, helping an old buddy. Now, can you handle it?"

"What if the gardener tells me he didn't do it? What if he wants to plead innocent?"

Johnson flicked the ash into his wastebasket and leaned into me; our noses almost touched. "This case is cut and dried. Understand, Jimmy? Don't try to make a career out of it. Convince the guy to take a deal and get it over with. Like I said, can you do the job?"

"Guess so," I said.

Johnson scribbled the names of the homicide detective and the deputy DA handling the case on a piece of paper.

"Here, take this. Go talk to them today. Tomorrow you can interview your new client. We'll have him here in our lockup before the arraignment. It's scheduled for ten-thirty."

I tucked Johnson's note in my pocket and left his chambers. It dawned on me as I walked the hallway of the court building that if the state had an airtight case, why would the Judge want to cut a deal? They arrested the madman who'd killed a powerful senator's secretary, a beautiful young woman. Senator Berry Welsh had the muscle to demand justice. You'd think he'd be clamoring for the murderer's head on a plate. But I'd do my job and maybe Johnson would come through and throw a bone my way from time to time.

Chapter Two

I found a phone booth down the hall from Johnson's courtroom, dialed the DA's office, and asked to speak with Roberta Allen, the deputy DA assigned to the case. The woman who answered said she'd be out to lunch until about 1:30. My next call went to the South Gate police department. When Sergeant Hodges came on the line, he said he was eating a Big Mac at his desk but would talk to me if I got over there right away.

My stomach tightened when I entered the police station, heard the familiar chatter of the two-way radio, and saw cops wandering around, some with suspects cuffed, dragging them toward the lockup. This wasn't the LAPD and it wasn't the Newton Street precinct, but it was still a police station, and I had strong feelings about the force, ambivalent memories of the job. Sure, there were some good times, some exciting times, but being here mostly reminded me of my failures, my shortcomings, and most of all, my disastrous marriage.

After checking in, a young fresh-faced officer ushered me to the Robbery-Homicide squad room.

Hodges, seated at his desk slurping coffee, looked up when I walked in. He had short hair and a bald spot. From the neck up, he looked like a monk with a crew cut. From the neck down, he looked like a fireplug with a stomach, only taller. A weary gray sport coat covered the back of his chair, hanging limp, and like its owner the coat had fought one too many battles.

Used paper cups, a butt-filled ashtray, fast food wrappers, scratch pads, chewed-on pencils, and a loaded .38 Smith and Wesson revolver littered his desk. As I approached, he stood up, wiped his hands on his pants, and holstered the gun. He wore a short-sleeved shirt and a clip-on tie with a fresh coffee stain on it. The stain improved the garish design.

"You O'Brien?"

"Yeah."

"Johnson's clerk called. Said I should talk to you, said I should cooperate." His attitude bordered on hostility.

"I need some information about the case."

"The murdering bastard's name is Ernesto Rodriguez. The evidence is overwhelming," he said.

"Tell me about it."

"You don't have to be Sherlock Holmes to figure this one out. My blind ninety-eight-year-old grandmother could've nailed the guy."

"Give me a little background. How did you solve the case so fast?"

"Look, O'Brien. They say I have to talk to you about the case. Okay, I talked. But I don't like giving you inside information."

"Sarge, I'm just trying to do my job, and you're not helping. In the morning, my client's going to be arraigned on a murder charge. I need some background. Who knows, maybe the guy's innocent."

He expanded his chest and thrust his nose in my face. I could smell the onions on his breath. "I'll give you some background. Your client's guilty, guilty as they come." Hodges stabbed a finger repeatedly on the top of his desk. "He killed a beautiful woman in cold blood, snapped her neck and cut her up. How's that for background?"

I backed up a little. "Cool it, Hodges. I'm the lawyer, not the defendant."

"I'm sick of you guys. We bust our asses to get the scumbags off the streets. Then you lawyers with the fancy suits make sure the rotten bastards go free."

I fingered my jacket. "Hey, Hodges, does this mail-order suit look fancy to you?"

Hodges didn't give me much, but what little he did tell me would put my client away for twenty-five to life–if he took the deal. If not, he'd rot in a cell for the remainder of his life at San Quentin. When Rodriguez had been arrested, he had the murder weapon in his possession, the girl's blood still wet on the knife.

At one-thirty, I returned to court building and entered the DA's office on the first floor. The receptionist said the deputy district attorney prosecuting my case had returned from lunch and would meet me in the conference room. I walked down a short hallway, glanced around the room's partially opened door, and stared at a beautiful woman sitting at a large table.

She stood and waved me in. "I'm Roberta Allen. You must be Mr. O'Brien."

She had dark hair, cut short and fashionably layered, with large, round and very deep blue eyes. Her skin, pale and translucent, was close to flawless. She wore a sensible business suit, which did little to hide her pleasing figure. I guessed her age to be late twenties, thirty tops.

I moved farther into the room, speechless for an instant. "Uh, you can call me Jimmy," I managed to say with a lopsided grin on my face. Standing next to her we were almost at eye level, but without her heels she'd be three or four inches shorter than my six-foot-one.

"Let's keep this on a professional level. Okay, Mr. O'Brien?"

"Sure, professional." We shook hands. She had long fingers with a firm grip "Anyway, I'm here about–"

"I know why you're here. However, I have to be in court at two," she glanced at her watch, "so I won't have time to go over the details, but I've prepared a file regarding the defendant. It contains the relevant facts of the case."

Roberta Allen reached into her briefcase and pulled out a manila folder. When she handed it to me, our eyes locked for a moment, but she quickly shifted her gaze to the papers that I held.

"Here are the preliminary reports. You'll get the remainder of the file later..." She looked up at me again. "...if you need it. Look the facts over and you'll see it'll be an easy conviction. It's a sure bet for the prosecution. However, in order to expedite the proceedings, if your guy pleads, we'll take life without the possibility of parole off the table. I'll recommend twenty-five to life."

"Yeah, that's what Johnson said."

"He agreed to this, in fact he suggested the deal. Who am I to argue?" She let out a small sigh.

"I'll talk to Rodriguez before the arraignment and pass along the offer, but I'll need to know more before I can recommend anything. How long is this offer going to last?" I said.

"Until tomorrow at five o'clock. After that, I'm prepared to go all out. Your client will be convicted and locked up forever, and I hope he suffers each and every day. Goodbye, Mr. O'Brien."

I looked into her face, calm, innocent and beautiful. "Like I said, I'll talk to him."

"See you in court," she said, managing to give me a weak smile. Maybe it wasn't a smile at all. Maybe it was a smirk, a sardonic expression of confidence. Maybe she knew I had never tried a murder case. Maybe she knew my biggest criminal case had been a pickpocket. The guy did a little time.

I turned and walked out of the room.

On the way back to my office, I stopped for a bite at Harvey's Broiler, a drive-in restaurant on Firestone. While I tucked into my Fat Boy burger, I reviewed the file Roberta Allen had given me. No doubt about it, just as she'd said, the case was a sure bet for the State. With evidence this tight, Clearance Darrow couldn't get Rodriguez off. Yet they wanted me to offer him a deal. Why? If this case went to trial, especially in an election year, the DA could show his office was tough on crime. The voters had a shameless passion for hard-nosed politicians who didn't coddle criminals. The DA could add another notch to his alligator briefcase, another killer got the max. All over town there would be cheering in the streets.

There had to be something missing. I rolled the facts around in my mind. Again, why me? Way did Johnson dump the case in my lap? He's a member of Welch's for re-election committee. Could it have to do with the senator's campaign? Johnson had to figure I wouldn't dig, wouldn't ask questions. He knew about my experience, probably figured I was a little naïve. He knew I needed money. But why would he assume I'd go along with the deal? Because, I'd sat on my hands and told him I would. That's why.

Chapter Three

The next day, I waited for Ernesto Rodriguez in a room the court made available to lawyers and their incarcerated clients holding pre-trial conferences. The room, a stark and unforgiving cubicle, had plain white walls and a cold, grey cement floor. A bluish light radiated from the fluorescent tubes embedded in the acoustic tile above. A metal table, bolted down, occupied the center. Two chairs, also bolted, faced the table.

At nine-thirty, the guards appeared with Rodriguez. They hustled him into a chair, and his body sagged with fatigue. The guards ran chains through eyebolts welded to the chair and locked them to the iron encircling his hands and feet. With his arms shackled behind his back, the chains hitched too tight, his torso tilted forward at an oblique angle. Fear and anger burned in his dark eyes.

I sat down across from him. "Mr. Rodriguez, I'm Jimmy O'Brien. I've been appointed by the court to represent you today at the arraignment."

Rodriguez wore a white jumpsuit with the words *LA County Jail* stenciled in India ink on the back. He had a full head of black hair, which he wore Indian style, hanging long and straight. I imagined when he wasn't in jail that he pulled it back into a ponytail.

The DA's report had a copy of his driver's license. It said he stood six feet tall, was thirty-three years old, and weighed 186 pounds.

"As you know, Mr. Rodriguez, you've been charged with first degree murder. And I'm here to help you as much as I can."

He remained silent, eyes boring holes in the steel table.

"I'm talking to you!"

"Hey, man, you're wasting your time." He spat out the words, hard and angry. "They needed somebody to hang and those *gabachos* picked me."

I ignored the remark. "Listen, I've spoken to the Judge and the DA. They've agreed to drop life without parole. You could be out in twenty-five years. That is if you plead guilty today."

With effort, he bent his neck back and looked at me straight on. "Plead? I will plead to nothing. I didn't kill her," he said through clenched teeth.

"Listen to me, damn it. Today is the last day. Tomorrow they'll withdraw the offer."

"You no *comprende*? I don't give a shit about you, the other *abogados*, or the judge. No way will I say I did it. But, hey man, tell them what you want." He closed his eyes and lowered his head.

"I can't enter a guilty plea without your consent." I placed the DA's report on the table. "Let's look at what they've got. An eyewitness saw you arguing with the victim on the evening she died. They found her blood splattered all over your pickup truck; and they found the knife you used to kill her hidden under the seat. Did they make all of that up? I don't think so."

His eyes stayed closed, his head down.

"The report says you have no alibi. She died Saturday night, the night before your arrest. If you didn't kill her, where were you when she died?

Rodriguez remained silent with no reaction.

"It says here you have a prior arrest, beat up some guy in a bar, showing a pattern of violence. Are you a violent person, Ernesto? How long ago did this happen?"

It was like talking to a zombie. All I heard was the sound of his breathing.

"Why were you arguing with the murdered girl?" I paused. "What was all that about? Tell me, goddammit. Tell me what you and the girl were arguing about."

I waited and stared at him. The chains tightened and loosened with each breath he took.

"Listen to me. I can't help you unless you talk to me."

He raised his head, shot a look filled with contempt. "*Pendejo*, you are with them. You no want to help me. You want me to lie, tell everyone I killed her. Then you collect your fee and brag to your people how you nailed another wetback."

The small hairs on the back of my neck stiffened. What he said hit a nerve. I'd pounded him hard, trying to get him to plead guilty while I just gave a cursory look at the facts. I was just following Johnson's orders. *God*, what kind of a criminal lawyer am I?

"Look Ernesto, part of my job is to let you know what the DA is offering."

He continued to glare at me defiantly. "Shit man, I did *not* do it," he said.

"But the evidence..." I stopped and thought for a moment. "Please listen to me. I have an idea. The judge handling this case wants to wrap it up. Maybe I can get you a better deal, twenty to life. How does that sound?"

Ernesto looked at me and moved his head slowly from side to side.

I took an oath to act in the best interests of my clients regardless of their crimes or their guilt or innocence. With this case, I took a few dollars to tip the scales of justice, tip them Johnson's way. A chimpanzee in a three-piece suit could have done a better job for this guy. Give Jimmy a banana; he'll do as he's told.

The hell with Johnson, Rodriguez is my client now, but the law said I had to pass along the offer. It wasn't a bad deal, twenty-five to life for a vicious murder. Okay, I did what Johnson asked me to do. I gave him the deal. Now I'll listen to what Rodriguez has to say–if he says anything. Then I'll try to figure out what's in his best interests.

"Mr. Rodriguez, c'mon, talk to me. I'm on your side."

"You say you work for me. You no want the truth. You work for the judge."

"No, I–"

His eyes challenged me. "How much you get paid to lie?"

"I'm not lying. I'm just trying to get you the best deal I can."

"I don't want no stinking deals. I don't care what they do to me. I am not going to tell the judge I am a woman killer."

"Maybe you didn't mean to kill her. Things just got out of hand–"

His nostrils flared. "You are not listening to me."

"I'm trying, but you're not saying much for me to listen to," I said. "Look Ernesto, we don't stand a chance. They have all the evidence they need to get a conviction. They'll nail you with first degree and you'll rot in prison. You'll never get out, but right now they want to settle the case."

His voice exploded. "*Que*?"

"What do you mean *why*?"

His eyes narrowed. "Why, if they have such a strong case, do they want to settle with me, offer me a chance to be free someday?"

I sat straight back in my chair. Why indeed. "That's a good question, Ernesto, and I don't have an answer for it. I just don't know."

"Here is something else you don't know, Mr. Lawyer Man. I would rather die in jail than lie and say that I killed *Señorita* Gloria. Even if they let me go, I would not say I killed her." Then in a calm voice he asked, "You have any *niños*?"

"No."

"If you did, could you tell them you are a liar and a killer?"

"I see where you're going with this, but do you want your kids to know you're rotting away in a prison cell?"

"They will know I did not kill nobody. That is *mas*

importante."

With all the evidence, he had to be guilty. But even so, he had the right to a fair trial. And I was the only person in the world standing between him and a life without hope. Was it better for him to take a deal? Should he accept a reduced charge, or was going to trial the better option? It had to be his choice, but I wanted him to understand the full consequences of going all the way.

"Are you absolutely sure you want to go to trial? We will most likely lose. Maybe it would be better if you got a new lawyer."

"You kidding me, man? All lawyers work for the judges. I will tell them I did not do it and they can do what they want to with me. I don't need no lawyer."

"Listen to me, Ernesto, you need a lawyer—*believe me* you need a lawyer. And, unless you want someone else, I'm it. If you want me, I'll work for you, not the judge or the system. But I'm obligated to tell you the deal that they're offering."

"I told you! I want no deal."

"That means you'll have to stand trial. They have a mortal-lock case, means they'll win and you'll go to jail forever. We have no evidence to present, no witnesses—nothing—we have no money. *Christ Almighty*, Rodriguez!"

Ernesto Rodriguez continued to sit there with his head down. I wasn't getting through to him. "Listen to me. The complaint says The People of the State of California versus Ernesto Rodriguez. That's twenty million people against you. How can you possibly win?"

"I don't care. I already lost. They don't give a damn about anything. I'm a Mexican piece of shit, just another spic in their eyes. But I won't lie to make them feel better when they slam that iron door on me."

There might have been some truth in what he said about the ugly specter of racial prejudice in the system. But in this case, with all the evidence pointing at him, they had the right guy.

"One last chance, guilty or not guilty?"

H shook his head violently. "Not guilty!"

I knew Johnson would be pissed, but I couldn't plead him down to second degree without his consent. If he wanted to maintain his innocence, then we would go to trial. If that's the way it's going to be, then I'd give Rodriguez everything I had. If Johnson doesn't like it, so what!

"I promise I'll do the best I can for you," I said to Ernesto Rodriguez. "I'll tell them you didn't do it, and we'll go to trial."

The voice of the deputy sheriff followed the metallic sound of the lock being turned. "It's time to remove the prisoner. His arraignment's in ten minutes."

"Ernesto, I'll see you in the courtroom."

I stood up to leave. The guard untangled the chains binding Rodriguez to the chair. He looked up at me, and his eyes softened. I think he gave me a slight nod before they dragged him away.

Chapter Four

I walked into Division III somewhat concerned about the arraignment, wondering if Johnson would explode when I announced the *not guilty* plea. Placing my briefcase on the defendant's table, I glanced at the prosecutor's station. Roberta Allen hadn't arrived.

Because of the extra security required in a prominent murder case, only one arraignment would be held in the morning session: The People versus Ernesto Rodriguez.

Two guards entered with Rodriguez handcuffed between them. They brought him to the defendant's table and sat him down next to me. He sat stiffly, turning his head, looking in all directions with wide eyes, like someone caught in a trap in a strange land.

Roberta Allen finally entered, checked in with the clerk and walked briskly to her table. She wore a no-nonsense prosecutor's outfit: a charcoal jacket and a slim skirt, but somehow she made it seem feminine. Without acknowledging my presence, she sat and arranged several documents in front of her.

My client looked like he might break in two if he bent over. I turned to the bailiff. "Can't you remove his cuffs during the proceedings?" I asked.

"We have our orders–security. You know better than that."

"I'll take responsibility."

"No way, forget it."

A small green light flashed above the chamber door, a cue to the bailiff. He moved to the front and turned to face us. "All rise. The court is now in session. The Honorable Robert B. Johnson presiding."

Johnson strolled in, adjusting his black robes as he ascended the steps to his throne. "Clerk, call the case," he said.

"Docket number 72-3852, the People of the State of California versus Ernesto Rodriguez, section 187, Penal Code. Murder in the first degree," the clerk said and took her seat.

"James O'Brien, counsel for the defendant, Judge." I placed my hand on Rodriguez's shoulder.

"Roberta Allen for the People, Your Honor," she said, then sat and adjusted her skirt.

The Judge glanced from Roberta to me. He paused a bit too long when he looked at me. Finally, he said, "Mr. Rodriguez, you are charged with murder in the first degree. Shall the court read the complaint?"

"Reading waived," I said.

"The People move to reduce the sentence, second degree, if the defendant pleads guilty today," Roberta said, half standing.

Johnson nodded at her. "So ordered." Then he turned back to Rodriguez and me. "How do you plead to the charge? Guilty or not guilty?" The arraignment: just another routine matter, all in a day's work.

The critical moment had arrived. I leaned in Rodriguez. "Last chance, still not guilty?" I whispered.

His silence answered my question.

I took a deep breath. "My client, Ernesto Rodriguez, pleads...not guilty."

Johnson leaned forward, frowning. "I'm sorry. What did you say?"

I glanced at the prosecutor's table and saw Roberta stuffing papers into her briefcase. I turned back to Johnson. "Not guilty, your honor."

The plea obviously confused Johnson. He swung his head from me to the prosecutor's table and back again. "Approach the bench," he ordered.

The deputy DA and I walked forward. Johnson put his hand over the mike fixed to his desk. "What's this all about, O'Brien?"

"Deal's off. Like I said, *not* guilty."

"You can't change the deal." He glanced at Roberta. "Didn't we agree on a deal?" Before she answered he faced me again. "You were supposed to bring in a plea."

"Rodriguez refused it."

"Just what are you trying to pull?"

Roberta jumped in. "Judge, the People made an offer. Mr. O'Brien and his client refused the deal. We're ready to go forward. We'll take the case to trial."

Johnson gave her a dismissive wave and continued to stare at me. "Have you explained to Rodriguez that he'll lose his case and die in prison? Did you tell him there's no way he can win?"

"Judge, he says he didn't do it."

Johnson's confusion turned to anger. "That's bull and you know it. I don't think you tried to get a plea, I think you saw dollar signs, six to nine months of steady work. Talk to your client again. Get the guilty plea!"

"Won't do any good. His mind is made up."

"I want to talk to him myself."

I felt my face getting hot. "You're going beyond your authority. My client says he didn't do it, and maybe he didn't. He has a right to a trial. I signed on as his lawyer. I'm staying."

Roberta broke in, cool and calm. "Your Honor, Mr. O'Brien has agreed to represent the defendant. I suggest we set a date for the prelim."

Johnson looked at Roberta one more time, then sighed. "All right, O'Brien, it's your case. Don't come back later and try to get released and don't think you'll get any money from the county. You won't get a lousy dime. If Rodriguez wants you, you're stuck."

I turned to my client and watched him stand with his

head bowed. I hoped he was praying silently for a miracle. He had to know the consequences of his decision. Going to trial, murder one, no money and the deck stacked against him. A sure trip to oblivion.

"Trial is set for sixty days from today in Norwalk Superior Court," Johnson said, biting his words. "Preliminary hearing in ten days, also at Norwalk. Does that suit the People, Miss Allen?" She nodded. "Okay, court's adjourned." Johnson picked up his gavel.

I figured I'd push it a little. "Wait a minute, Judge, let's keep the date open." Without consulting Rodriguez I said, "My client waives time. It'll take longer to be properly prepared."

"You will be in Norwalk Superior Court in sixty days ready for trial. Is that clear?" Johnson raised his gavel, ready to slam it down. "And, remember, not a dime from the county. I'll see to it."

"Judge, I want to discuss my client's bail–"

"Bail denied. Now get the hell out of my courtroom." He banged the gavel. "Court's adjourned."

He jumped up and bolted from the room. Any ideas I had about getting future favors from Johnson left the room with him.

The guards started to march my client back to the courthouse cell, where he would wait for the return bus to the central jail. I asked them to hold up for a moment.

"Ernesto, I'll see you downtown tomorrow. In the meantime, I want you to think about everything you did on the day before you were arrested. Go over in your mind every second of that day. We need to fill in the blanks. And for God's sake, don't talk to anybody. And I mean about anything."

The guards pulled him away. In mid-step, he turned his head and looked back over his shoulder. "*Su muerte no era a mi mano*," he said in a voice choked with emotion. She did not die by his hand.

24

Roberta walked hurriedly down the aisle toward the exit. I caught up with her just as she reached the rear of the courtroom. "I need to see you, go over the case, evidence, autopsy report, stuff like that," I said.

"The judge was pretty hard on you just now. I won't make it any harder." She pushed the doors open. "I'm tied up the rest of the day and I'm due in court in the morning. You open for lunch tomorrow?"

I looked at her face and inhaled, exhaling slowly. "Where and when?"

"The Regency in Downey. Twelve-thirty?"

"Fine," I said. "I'll take care of the reservations."

"See you tomorrow."

She rushed through the doors, down the hall, and glanced back at me. Did I imagine it? Or did she give me warm smile before she disappeared around the corner.

Chapter Five

I cruised east on Firestone Boulevard, drove over the Long Beach Freeway bridge and heading to my office, a two-room storefront on Second Street in the neighboring city of Downey.

Rita Flores, my law clerk and secretary, worked at her cluttered desk in the outer office, which doubled as our lobby. Bills, junk mail, and personal mementos cluttered her desk. A small stuffed bear with a big red paper heart pinned to it rested close to the phone. Pictures of her mother and her boyfriend sat next to the bear along with a white rose from an *anonymous* admirer–the young salesman at the business next door. I didn't know what the bear was all about.

"Hey Rita, do me a favor, call the Regency and make reservations, lunch tomorrow, booth for two."

Rita, in her final year at Western States Law School, had been with me for six months. With her petite and shapely figure and innocent face, she appeared young and naïve and acted a little ditzy at times. But Rita was bright, one of the few Hispanic women in the school, and the only one to graduate in the top ten percent of the class. She studied night and day and had taken the bar exam a month ago. The results would be published later in the year.

"Okay, Boss. Hey, you had a call while you were gone, told him you weren't here." She looked at me with a playful pout on her face. "But he wouldn't leave a message."

"That's fine, Rita," I said.

"Probably trying to sell you something. More insurance, maybe. Sheesh, we can't pay the bills now. I'm glad he hung up."

Rita flashed me one of her winning smiles. She had

dimples in her cheeks, and rich dark hair flowing softly to her shoulders. I never asked her about her age. I wouldn't, and anyway the new employment rules disallowed asking personal questions. She looked nineteen, but she had to be at least twenty-three or twenty-four.

"Yeah, I'm glad too, Rita. But it might've been a client..." We shook our heads in unison. "Nah," we said.

I watched the swing of her hips as Rita turned and walked to her desk to call the restaurant. I hoped she passed the bar on her first try. Not many did, but if she passed, I figured she'd leave me afterward. I enjoyed her company, her youthful exuberance, and her full of life personality, but no way could I match the offers that would come her way. With corporate law, the pay and benefits would be excellent. Who knows, maybe someday she'd make partner and be a role model to for other young Latinas. I moved into the other room, my office, and put on some coffee.

"Jimmy, the Regency wants to know what time you and your... Wait, are you taking a date?" Rita shouted from the other room. "Hey, good for you. Anyway, what time are you and your new girlfriend having lunch tomorrow?"

"It's business! Tell them twelve-thirty."

After she finished the call, Rita came into my office. "The coffee smells good. I'll pour you a cup. Too bad about your date. You should find someone–"

"Rita!"

"Hey, you're a good-looking guy. Don't give up; someone will come along."

I reached for the phone. Dialing, I said, "I not looking for anyone to *come along*. I want to get settled before I...never mind. Don't you have some junk mail to file or something?"

Rita left. I took a sip of coffee and called Sol Silverman at Rocco's Restaurant on Florence Ave. Sol, a licensed private investigator, information broker, and consummate horseplayer had been my friend since my days on the LAPD.

Although Sol had a full suite of offices upstairs in the same building as the restaurant, he conducted most of his business downstairs. He even had a private phone installed at his exclusive booth in the rear of the main dining area.

When he invited me to join him for lunch, I didn't mention that I desperately needed his help with the Rodriguez murder case. Without Sol and his staff's assistance I didn't stand a chance. His investigation and security company, the best in the business, commanded extraordinary fees. But, I'd drop a few hints while we ate and see if maybe he'd volunteer, *pro bono*.

Rocco's long and narrow dining room, two steps up from the bar area, had red leather booths with white linen covering the tables. An ornate chandelier hung from the ceiling, which cast the room in a dim glow. I walked in through the heavy, carved double doors. André, the *maître d'*, escorted me to Sol's booth.

Sol put his hand over the mouthpiece of the phone he held. "Thanks André," he said and waved at me while continuing with his conversation.

A tall drink rested in front of him. Knowing Sol, I figured it had to be Beefeater's Gin and tonic, his choice before sundown. In the evening, he switched to straight Beefeater's on the rocks. Something about not really drinking during the day.

He hung up the phone and stood to greet me. Sol was actually taller sitting down than standing up. His chest and stomach were huge, but his legs were short and skinny. He had a large head perched directly on top of his torso without a noticeable neck. His crop of frazzled salt and pepper hair darted out in all directions. Most startling were his eyes: deep, dark and penetrating. They could bore right into your brain searching for some truth that might be in conflict with your words. He wore a ring with a diamond on his pinky, and a solid gold Rolex that looked like it weighed five pounds circled his wrist.

Sol bought his suits from Sy Devore in Hollywood. His tailor here in Downey altered them. Benny tried his best for Sol–marking, measuring, cutting the material, adjusting everything you could adjust, and sewing it all back together– but to no avail. Sol still looked like Omar the Tent Maker had fitted him, that is, if Omar made his tents out of worsted virgin wool with pinstripes.

He reached out and shook my hand. "*Vos tut zich*? How you doing, Jimmy?"

"Okay, Sol, I guess. Your luck still holding at the track?" Sol had The Racing Form spread out on the table next to his drink. I didn't know whether it was his ability as a handicapper or the inside information he had at his fingertips that financed his lavish lifestyle.

"Luck has nothing to do with it, dear *boychik*. Genius, sheer genius, that's why I win." He slid into the booth. "Sit down and tell me what's up."

"Sol, I need some help." No use playing games. I decided to come right out and ask.

"Money, you need money?" He reached into his coat pocket and pulled out a short stack of hundred-dollar bills. "Here, take what you need, pay me back when you get the chance."

The fantasy of catching up on some past due bills, or maybe picking up a new suit flashed through my mind, then just as quickly disappeared. I'd never ask to borrow money, and I knew he wouldn't turn me down if I did. But now I had to ask him to help me professionally, without pay, which was just as hard for me. Maybe harder.

"Thanks for the offer, Sol. You're a good friend, but what I really need is your help with a case I have to defend."

He gave me a knowing smile. "I heard about it. Got in a brawl with Johnson. Took on a murder case. Chutzpah, *bubbee*, you've got chutzpah, I'll say that."

Before I could respond, one of Rocco's long-legged

waitresses waltzed over to take our order. We both asked for steak sandwiches, coffee with mine, an extra order of deep fried onion rings for Sol.

"You heard about it already?"

"My spies tell me everything. You should have such spies."

Sol had spies everywhere–not spies in the traditional sense like the CIA or James Bond, but more like a loose network of informants in the right places.

Background people were his spies–secretaries, clerks, janitors, typists, and at the courts, maybe the court reporter, a clerk or two, and a few bailiffs. His spies worked at City Hall, the DA's office, restaurants, and bars. Waitresses, bartenders, and receptionists in public buildings fed Sol a continuous stream of intelligence. Sol was a merchant, his stock was information, and the spies provided the inventory.

"Will you help me, Sol?" I laid it on the line, waited, and held my breath.

He pulled a gold pen from his pocket and looked down, saying nothing. I watched him mark his Racing Form, drawing little circles and underlining words that must have been important. After a few seconds, he raised his head and picked up the phone. "Please forgive me," Sol said. "We'll talk, but important business first. I'm gonna put a nickel on the daily double."

Sol placed a call to Dwayne, the bartender at the Regency, who held the dubious honor of being Sol's favorite bookmaker. Sol placed his bet–five thousand on the daily double at Del Mar.

Long Legs brought our food. While we ate, I didn't mention the murder case. Sol's rule number 47: no business while food was on the table. We talked about the horses, then college football. Sol said USC would go undefeated this year. With Anthony Davis and Sam 'Bam' Cunningham, John McKay's team couldn't lose. I told him not to bet on it. He said he already had.

"Now to Jimmy's *tsores*," Sol finally said after the busboy removed the dishes, and the waitress brought him another drink and refreshed my coffee. "If I help you with this case, is your client worth the effort? Did he kill the girl?"

A fair question. Why would he help me set a murderer free? He deserved a candid and straightforward answer. "I don't know. He says he's innocent, but the evidence against him is solid." I placed my hands on the table, palms down. "Even if he did it, I'm still morally and, in fact, legally bound to provide the best possible defense. There might be mitigating circumstances or other factors that need to be explored." I paused and looked into his eyes. I wanted Sol to understand how I felt. "Then again, maybe he didn't do it. But if I don't do my best, Rodriguez will die in the gas chamber."

Sol listened while sipping his drink. "Reasons, do you have reasons to think he might be innocent? You have evidence on your side?"

"No, and he's been violent in the past, a bar fight. He's not talking other than to declare his innocence. But I'm worried. I'm not sure he's guilty, at least guilty in the first degree. I have a feeling inside me that won't go away."

"Can you win cases with feelings, Jimmy? I don't think so. This sounds like one of those *there's-no-evidence-so-pound-the-table* defenses."

"Sol, there's a couple of things that just aren't kosher. How could the cops have known about Rodriguez so fast? What turned them on to him? They just showed up at the break of dawn and arrested him. Another thing: why is Johnson in such a rush to close the case?"

"Why is that important? If they get him to plead, the case is over."

"Seems to me, if the DA feels that they have an open and shut case, they don't have to bargain. They'd know that they'd win in a heartbeat."

"Ah, maybe you're reading too much into that. Maybe Johnson just wants to take the easy way out."

Our discussion continued for quite some time. I told Sol all the facts I had so far, including my upcoming meeting with Roberta Allen, the deputy DA. He asked lots of questions, and I answered, *yes*, *no*, or mostly, *I don't know*. I explained my defense plan. It wasn't much, but it was all I had. I wouldn't stand a chance unless I developed an alternate theory of the crime. Meaning, I had to come up with one or more suspects who could have murdered Gloria Graham, a basis for reasonable doubt.

"I'm a gambler, Jimmy, and I know a long shot when I hear one," Sol said. "And besides, maybe your client's guilty."

"I'm his lawyer, guilty or not." I paused and looked into Sol's eyes. "I need your help."

He shook his head. "*Oy vai iz mir*," he moaned, and then exhaled in an exaggerated fashion. "Of course I'll help. Have I ever turned you down?"

"I've never asked before."

"So, that's my fault?"

I chuckled and drew up a contract of sorts on the back of a cocktail napkin. I paid him a dollar for his services. With that, he would be covered under the attorney-client privilege and attorney work-product doctrine.

On his way out, Sol handed the dollar to the busboy.

Chapter Six

The air conditioner in my Corvette rattled once, then quit as I inched along on the Santa Ana Freeway. The radio played a Beatles number–"Twist and Shout." I didn't twist, but I shouted, and it felt good. In the lane next to me, a Peterbilt truck belched heavy black smoke. All at once, it made a gear-grinding spasm and lurched forward to close a two-foot gap that opened behind a pink Caddie convertible driven by a bleached blonde lady with grotesque makeup. The drive to the new Los Angeles County Jail, in downtown L.A., would take over an hour.

The rain vanished and now it threatened to be another hot and smoggy day. The eight a.m. newsbreak predicted a stage-three air quality alert over the entire area except, of course, for the Palos Verdes Peninsula. The smog knew better; Palos Verdes had an ordinance against that sort of thing.

I circled the jail parking lot, looking for a place to park. No luck. But I found a spot on Vignes Street, two blocks away. I trudged up the small rise and entered the building at the visitors' sign-in door. I walked through a chain-link gate and into a small hall. The gate behind me closed, and the one in front of me opened with a buzzing click. At the counter, I presented my attorney's bar card and driver's license to the deputy in charge.

"I'm here to confer with my client, Ernesto Rodriguez," I said as I signed the logbook anchored to the counter's shelf. "I'm his lawyer."

The deputy looked at my credentials, raised his head, and studied me for a moment. "Here," he said as he tore a page from a pad and handed it to me. "Fill this out." He pointed to an uncomfortable looking hardwood bench that ran the length of the wall across from the counter. "We'll call you when we take the prisoner to the conference room. You can talk to him there."

I perched on the narrow ledge, crossed my legs, and used my briefcase as a desk to fill in the blanks on the Visitor's Interview Request form. A few minutes later, I gave it back to the guard. Ten minutes after that, an unarmed deputy sheriff approached me. "Are you O'Brien, the lawyer here to see Rodriguez?"

I glanced around the area, up and down the bench. Only three other people were visible. To my right, about three feet away, a spaced-out Mexican kid in baggy clothes slouched, staring at a bug on the floor. To my left, farther down, slumped a grubby old white guy with a red carbuncle nose. His head was tilted against the wall, his face skyward, his mouth a gaping hole. He snored, rattling when he inhaled and whistling when he exhaled. A tall black guy, built like a pool cue, stood at the counter. He had to be over six feet tall, but couldn't have weighed more than ninety pounds. A bright green and yellow bandana sheltered his head and large gold rings hung from his ears. His flat chest was covered with a tight fitting black knit tube, which he tucked into a flowered free flowing skirt. He wore dainty pumps on his feet. His lipstick clashed with the three-day stubble covering his pockmarked face. The guards called out to him, "Hey, Olive Oyl, show us your titties–c'mon pleeeze, Olive Oyl."

The deputy sheriff walking toward me and calling my name knew I had to be the lawyer in the room, briefcase and all.

"Yeah, I'm O'Brien. Here to see my client," I said to the deputy as I stood.

"Can't take your client to the conference room. He's on psych watch."

"Psych watch, why?"

"I don't know...orders, the brass thinks he's a suicide

risk."

"A suicide risk? You've seen my guy, what do you think?"

"Hey fella, it's not up to me."

"I've got to talk to my client." I glanced at my watch. "I'm meeting the deputy DA in a couple of hours. I need some answers."

"I'll take you to his cell. You can talk to him through the bars. But you'll only have fifteen minutes. And I'll have to search you first. Rules."

After he patted me down, the guard behind the counter buzzed us through the door leading to the bowels of the jail. "Stay close to me, don't wander off."

"Yeah, like where would I go?" I said under my breath.

We arrived at Rodriguez's cell, a six-by-eight foot concrete cubicle outfitted with a stainless steel toilet, metal bunk, and a sink without a mirror. It occurred to me, he'd spend his life in a place like this. I wondered what it would be like to do time, locked up in prison. Just one look at the other cells on the block, all jammed with prisoners, and I knew the answer. It would be like moving into my bathroom and inviting a few of strangers off the street to come and live with me for, oh say, the rest of my life.

"Are you going to let me in the cell, so I can sit and take notes?" I asked the guard.

"Stand on the outside. You're not going in there."

"You have a chair?" I already knew the answer.

He didn't respond. "Remember, we're watching you."

"Watching what?" I said. "Are you listening too, are there hidden mikes around?" He ignored the remark and wandered away.

In the cell, Rodriguez, slumped on his bunk, stared at the floor with his hands folded on his lap. "Listen up," I said. "I don't have time for games–no more silent treatment. You're going to tell me exactly what happened." I opened my briefcase and took out the police report and a yellow tablet. "I want to hear more than 'I didn't do it'. You're going to answer my questions, or I walk. Is that understood?" After Johnson's exhortation, I couldn't walk, but I didn't think he knew that.

He came over to the bars and grabbed them with both hands. He nodded.

"Okay, tell me what this is all about."

He removed his hands from the bars and flexed his gnarled fingers. "I am good with plants. I work hard to send my children in Mexico some money. My son, Panchito, he is the oldest, will start high school next year." A shadow clouded his face. He must've just grasped the thought that he might never see his son again. "I can't pay you–"

"We won't worry about money right now. We'll work out something later." I reached inside my jacket and pulled out a pen. "Tell me everything that happened. Start with Saturday. Tell me in your own words. Tell me about the argument, everything."

"*Nada*, No argument."

"The women across the street…" I glanced at the police report. "Mrs. Wilson, she's a retired school teacher. She'll make a good witness." I mumbled the last part more to myself. "She says you two were arguing."

"I go to *Señorita* Graham's…Gloria's–she say *es* okay to call her Gloria–to work once a week, mow the grass, trim the bushes. But she hired me extra to fix up her backyard. *Caracoles*, it needed too much work."

The victim's name was Gloria Graham, like the '40s movie star, but without the 'e' at the end. From her picture, I noticed she had a striking resemblance to the actress, very pretty, but a little hard around the edges.

"You were working in the backyard when she got killed?"

"No way, man. I started early Saturday, eight o'clock, put in a new lawn, planted three palm trees, flowers. All day I work. At six I was almost done, picking up tools to put in my truck. She come out of the house to see. '*Es* okay, Ernesto,' she said. But she wanted me to move the trees. She wanted to see them from the kitchen, she said."

"That's when the argument started? You argued about trees?"

"No argument, man. She wanted me to move the trees–I move the trees. No problem."

"Mrs. Wilson, the lady across the street, said that she went to bed at ten, after the *Bob Newhart Show*, but first she looked out her window and saw your truck in the driveway." I glanced at my notes. "The back of the pickup truck was hidden by the house, but the front end stuck out and she could see it clearly. She didn't take down the license number, but she described it: broken headlight, dented fender. She had the color right."

"*Es muy* dark at night. How could she see?"

"Good point Ernesto, but were you still there at that time?"

He dropped his eyes, "No, *señor*, I was not there."

"She said–"

"Hey, man, let me finish. Okay?" He paused for a second, trying to gather his words. "I work until dark on the trees. Dig them out, dig new holes to plant them. I come back *mãnana* to finish. Miss Gloria came out of the house, had a package or something. I go to wash up, and she invited me into her kitchen for a cold *cerveza*. I drank one, went to my truck to go home, but the battery, it was no good."

"You were in her house?" The police report said nothing about his prints being in the house or on a beer bottle. "How long were you in there?"

"Twenty minutes, half hour. I dunno."

I scribbled on my tablet, trying to juggle the police report, my briefcase, and write at the same time. I figured it would be a miracle if I could read my notes when I got back to the office.

Needing to establish a time line, I glanced back at the report. She died between eleven p.m. and two a.m. "Okay," I said. "You worked until dark, say around eight, had a beer and stayed until at the latest, nine. Then what?"

"I walk home. Waited. Then I went out, got a battery, come back to *Señorita* Gloria's house, started my truck. The cops grab me when I got back home again."

This story had more holes than Ben the Bum's T-shirt. "Hold it Ernesto. You walked home? Isn't that a long way from Gloria's house?"

He shrugged. "Ah, four, five miles, not far."

"Then later you left your home and got a battery somewhere? All the stores are closed in the middle of the night. Where did you get the battery?"

"Midnight auto supply."

"Midnight auto supply—you *boosted* a battery?"

"*Ah chingado*! I did not steal, I borrowed it."

"Explain."

"I waited 'til two o'clock, everybody sleeping by then. I walked, had pliers, jumper cables. I found a truck just like mine, *pero* newer, took the battery, carried it to Gloria's house. Jump started my truck—"

"You jump started your truck?"

"*Si.*"

"Where's the battery you stole, if you didn't put it in your truck?"

"I told you, I borrowed it. I drive back to where I *borrowed* the battery and put it back in the guy's truck. Then drive home. The cops, they were waiting." His eyes begged me to believe him.

"What about the blood on your truck, the stuff under the seat? The body in the backyard?"

"In the dark, I don't see no blood, and I don't look under no seat. I don't go into the backyard. I did not even get my tools out of the yard. Anyway, I was coming back on Sunday to finish the job, clean up the yard, fill in the holes where I moved the trees, you know. But right then I had to hurry. I had to get out of there and put back the battery that I borrowed."

"Okay, let me get this straight. You say that about the time of the murder, you were at home. Then later you walked the streets looking for a battery to steal. That's your alibi?"

"To borrow—"

"And nobody saw you?"

"When you borrow things in the middle of the night, nobody is *supposed* to see you."

I jotted some more notes. I had a lot more questions and wanted to go over his story again, but the deputy approached and tapped my shoulder.

"That's it. Let's go. You're out of time. The interview is over."

Rodriguez's knuckles turned white as he twisted his hands on the bars. I studied his tired face. "Hang in there, Ernesto. We'll beat this thing together."

"*Si, amigo*," he said.

I shoved my notes in my briefcase and snapped it shut.

The guard placed his hand on my shoulder. "This way to the real world, buddy," he said, leading me away.

Obviously, Rodriguez wasn't a suicide risk. They'd brought him to that cell for a purpose. I wondered how long it would take for the clandestine tape recording to make its way to Roberta Allen's desk.

Chapter Seven

I drove to the Regency and turned into the curved blacktop driveway that ran under the restaurant's white Greco-Roman portico, waved at the parking attendants, and pulled into a spot on the east side of the building. Although I rarely frequented the Regency–too expensive for my budget– they knew me from being here on occasion with Sol. Everyone in Downy knew Sol and went out of their way to treat him like royalty.

Marilee, the hostess, stood at her pulpit located at the entry to the dining room, greeting new arrivals as they strolled in through the double doors. I caught her eye.

"Emilio will take you to the back booth in station five, Mr. O'Brien." She gave me a wink. "When Miss Allen arrives we'll bring her to your table."

At precisely twelve thirty-five, Roberta Allen arrived with Emilio in tow. She slipped into the seat directly across from me, set her briefcase down and picked up and examined her spoon. Finding an imperfection, she polished it with her napkin. She placed it back on the table, rearranged the silverware into a straight line, and then turned to the waiter. "I'm pressed for time. Emilio, bring me a chef's salad, please. Roquefort on the side and iced tea." She turned to me. "Did you order, Mr. O'Brien?"

The barbequed ribs sounded good, but what the heck. "No, I didn't, Miss Allen, but I'll have the same." Emilio scribbled on his pad and hurried off.

She reached across to shake my hand. "What do you say we skip the Miss and Mister routine? I'll call you James and you can call me Bobbi. Deal?"

I shook her hand. "Deal. But, Bobbi, call me Jimmy."

"Jimmy and Bobbi, sounds like a couple of grade school kids at recess." She smiled.

"Golly gee wilikers, wanna play marbles?" I said.

She laughed. "Hopscotch?"

"As long as we don't play dodge ball."

The laughter stopped. "What do you mean?"

"Are you going to hold out, not give me everything you have?"

She flicked an invisible bit of something off the table linen and leaned forward. "Like what? I'm not holding back."

I was referring to my suspicion that my interview with Rodriguez had been recorded and the tape given to her. But I had no real evidence, so I figured I'd let it pass–for now.

"Jimmy, there is something new that just came across my desk this morning."

"I'm listening."

"The police can prove Rodriguez was in the house. His fingerprints were found on empty Coors bottles in the kitchen. He drank several beers, wanted to party–she didn't, and he killed her." She announced this like it was a fact carved in granite and handed to her on the mountain.

"He worked hard all day, had one beer to relax, then he left," I said.

She leaned back, rolled her eyes, and gave me that *oh brother* look women do so well. "If that's your story, stick to it. It'll be a short trial."

"Bobbi, a wise man once said, 'It ain't over till it's over.'" The wise man was Yogi Berra, but I didn't think she knew who he was. "We'll see how it plays out."

"I'm sure we will." Bobbi opened her briefcase and extracted a file about two inches thick; half a dozen rubber bands held it together. "Here are copies of the reports, photos, everything, all the evidence so far." She handed me the file.

"This is everything?"

"I told you I'd give you all I had. Now, quit being a jerk."

I sat the file on the table and started to unravel the rubber bands. "Are the cops looking at anyone other than Rodriguez?"

"When you study the file, you'll see the police were very thorough, meticulous. All the facts pointed to your guy."

"Look Bobbi, I can sense you're a straight arrow, least I hope so, and I appreciate your cooperation. And I'm sure if you win, you don't want the decision overturned because of lack of disclosure, but I wouldn't be able to handle any last-minute surprises. A ghost in the machine, so to speak."

She didn't respond, so I continued: "I'll make you a deal. I want to win fair and square." I paused when the busboy filled our water glasses. "I'll play it strictly on the level and you continue to play it straight with me. Okay?"

A smile played on her lips. "I'll go by the rules. But, I'll make you another deal, as well."

"Yeah, what?"

"You quit quoting Yogi Berra, and I won't quote Oliver Wendell Holmes."

Emilio appeared, pushing a small cabinet on wheels. It had our food on top and shelves underneath containing various culinary regalia. He picked up a fork and with it he crumbled a hunk of cheese in a large bowl, splashed in a shot of red vinegar, some olive oil, and sprinkled a pinch of coarse salt over the mixture.

"We only use sea salt." He kept talking while vigorously working the bowl. "*La Baleine, Sel de Mer*, it comes from France," he said with a phony French accent.

Why France? I asked myself. Is the ocean saltier over there? Guess so, the French must know their salt.

Finally, Emilio served the salads. Bobbi daintily forked a piece of lettuce, and nibbled on it. I sipped my iced tea. "How did the cops find my client so fast?" I asked. "Or for that matter, the body? She was killed around midnight, and they busted Rodriguez at about five a.m. It was still dark out."

She rearranged her bread plate, placing it on her left.

"Anonymous tip. The call came in around four in the morning. Male voice, didn't give his name. Didn't want to get involved. Told the police where to find the body and who did it."

"What?" I exclaimed. "An anonymous tip? Don't you find that weird? A murder is committed and the solution falls out of the sky, in the middle of the night, before the body had time to cool down." My hand started to shake. I had to put the tea down; the ice cubes were clinking. "I don't believe it." That never happens. Only in the movies."

"No, it happens all the time. Some nearby resident or passerby doesn't want to be identified. Maybe the person has an outstanding warrant, sees something, and calls it in."

"Hey, the cops must've canvassed the neighborhood. Did they find anybody with an outstanding warrant, a hold, or anything to hide?"

She speared a crouton, and held the fork in front of her face. "I would've told you about it if they did. It doesn't matter anyway; we have the killer in custody, locked up, with an overwhelming amount of evidence stacked against him."

Marilee came to our booth with a plug-in phone. "Mr. O'Brien, you have a call. Would you like to take it here at your table? The caller said it's urgent."

I looked at Bobbi. "Do you mind?"

"No, of course not."

Marilee plugged in the telephone.

"Jimmy, I've got news. Big news." Sol, who else? "I know you're having lunch with the Ice Princess, doubtless she's at the booth with you right now. True?"

"Yeah." Muffled racetrack noises echoed in the background. I heard the announcer call, "*And there they go...*"

"Did the race just start?" If Sol had a bet riding he wouldn't talk until it ended.

"I'm not down on this one–maiden fillies, *meshugas*."

I was eager to hear the news, but I didn't want Bobbi to know I was talking to Sol. I turned my head and said in a low voice, "What's up?"

"Jimmy, I'll be brief. I know you can't talk in front of Miss Rigid Frigid, and they have a policy about phones here at the track. All outgoing calls are taped. Bookmakers, you know–a plague on society..."

"C'mon, tell me."

"What?"

"You know. What you called me about."

"Oh, you mean the news I heard."

"Yeah, of course."

"Okay, hang on to your seat..." Sol paused for dramatic effect. He always did that. "It seems Senator Goody Two-Shoes Welsh was *shtuping* the vic, having an affair with her. The info comes from a tipster, whose identity shall remain undisclosed. But I'll tell you this: the tip came from an extremely reliable source." Then he whispered, "She was a long-lost friend of Gloria Graham."

"You just whispered the person's identity."

"I wanted you to know."

"Yeah, but–"

"But, what?"

"You said the phones... never mind. But, are you sure she's on the level?"

"It wouldn't surprise me a bit. I've known Berry Welch a long time. He's always on the prowl, looking for someone to jump. Maybe it's an occupational hazard, these power-mad politicians."

I glanced at Bobbi, sitting across from me. She reached into the butter bowl and removed one of the foil-wrapped pats. With her polished fingernails, she delicately removed the wrapper and put the butter on her bread dish. She pretended not to eavesdrop.

Sol's news shook me to my core, but I had to play it cool. "Uh huh," I said to him as he continued to ramble on about Welch's sexual peccadilloes.

"Jimmy, I gotta go. Angie and Burt just arrived. You

know, Burt as in Bacharach?" Sol said. "Their table is next to mine. They've got a horse in the Crosby Stakes, and I need some info." He shouted away from the phone, "Hey Angie, baby–" and the line went dead.

While I was on the phone, a busboy had zipped over and scooped up the dishes, including my untouched salad.

I turned back at Bobbi. Her face held a mischievous smile.

"You look a little perplexed," she said. "Something you ate? Or perhaps it was Silverman's message?"

"Whose message?" I said.

"Sol Silverman, the investigator. The guy who's helping you with the case."

"Silverman? Helping me? Bobbi–"

"C'mon, Jimmy. Everybody knows you retained him. Not a bad move, if I may say so."

How did she know about Sol so fast? Maybe she had spies too. Maybe everyone had spies. Christ, maybe I was the only one who *didn't* have spies.

"You spying on me?"

Bobbi laughed. "You should be so lucky."

I was a little unnerved that Bobbi knew about Sol and wondered what else she knew about me, or the case. I quickly ran through my mind the jailhouse discussion with Rodriguez. Was there anything we said during the interview that she could use? Not much. Everything we discussed would just help our side.

It would be a violation for the sheriff's deputies guarding the jail to turn over to the DA anything overheard or recorded during a lawyer/client conference. But I knew it happened from time to time. Even if the information gleaned in this manner couldn't be used in court, it could help the prosecution plan their trial strategy. Sometimes, the deputy DAs had integrity and refused the proffered information, but that was an uncommon occurrence.

Bobbi had beauty and brains, but I wondered about *her*

45

integrity. Would she play it straight? "Remember, Bobbi, we're going to be square on this, no tricks. Right?"

"No tricks, he says, and coming out of the gate, he goes running to Silverman."

"I'm not saying I did, but hypothetically, so what?"

"He knows more tricks than Rex the Wonder Dog."

"Just a minute ago you said if I hired Sol it'd be a smart move."

"Jimmy, you're going to need all the help you can get. But, my friend, I'm still going to pound you into sand." She flashed a half-second smile. "No offense."

"None taken," I said. "But with Rex the Wonder Dog on my side, how can I lose?"

The County picked up the lunch tab. I offered, but Bobbi insisted on paying. She said she had an expense account. We left the restaurant together; she went her way, and I went directly to Angelo's Fat Burger for a real meal without the pompous bullshit. I asked the fry cook where he got his salt.

"From the bag in the backroom," he answered.

I figured I'd survive.

Chapter Eight

"Gotta go, the boss just came in–yeah, me too." Rita hung up the phone.

"That your boyfriend?" I asked.

"Yeah, how'd you know?"

"Just a guess. Listen, Rita, I'm going to work here a while longer. There's no need for you to stick around."

"Thanks, Boss. By the way, a reporter from the *L.A. Times* called." She scoured her desk for the message. "Richard Conway. Wants information on the Rodriguez case." She handed me the slip of paper with the number on it.

I knew it would only be a matter of time before the story broke. "The *Los Angeles Times*," I said. "That's big time."

"Are we gonna be famous, Jimmy?" Rita winked. "A little publicity for the firm?"

"I don't know." The press could be a big help if I could pull it off, but I'd have to be prepared, have snappy one-liners at my fingertips, and know the case thoroughly, backwards and forwards. One slip and the newspapers would crucify me. The trial would be over before it began.

"Shall I get him one the phone for you?"

"Let's wait on this, if he calls back, tell him I'm not in."

She placed her hand over her heart. "You want me to *lie* to the press?"

"Cut it out, Rita. Just tell him I'm not here, okay?"

She looked disappointed. "Seriously, you don't want to talk to him? The PR could help."

"Not yet, but I'll hang on to the number." I stuffed the pink message in my pocket. "I'm sure we'll use him before it's over. I want to be prepared, that's all."

I walked into my office and moved to the desk, carrying

the Rodriguez file. At this point, I had nothing to offer the media, but I was eager to dig into the file. Perhaps it contained hidden information that would help me point the finger at Welch. Without evidence, speculation about the senator wouldn't fly. Even Sol's news couldn't be used at this point. I'd need more than rumor and innuendo before accusing him in the press of having an affair with Gloria. I'd need hard facts to support my theory that Gloria threatened to go public, and when she did, he killed her.

I cut the rubber bands and spread the work on my desk. Photos of the dead woman jumped out at me. Lots of them. I looked them over carefully. The vivid color photographs were an assault to my eyes. The file contained dozens of clinical photos taken at the morgue. They would be used to back up the autopsy. The file also held horrendous pictures shot at the murder scene. Her once pretty face was battered almost beyond recognition, its frozen expression one of silenced terror. Her dull eyes stared directly at the camera. Large glossy pictures showed where sharp steel had sliced her torso, almost cutting her in two. Obviously, the murder wasn't the result of a robbery gone wrong. It was personal, an act of revenge. If Welch did it, he must've hated her. Maybe he hated all women. But there was one thing I knew for sure: Rodriguez didn't fit the profile. Couldn't the police see that?

"I thought you'd be working late so I made some coffee." Rita entered, carrying a steaming mug. "I hope it's okay. I never made just half a pot before." Her vibrant face brought me back to the living world, where I wanted to stay. I put the photos back in the file. "Thanks, Rita. I'm sure it will be fine." I took a sip and felt my toes curl.

"Is it too strong?"

Strong, she asks. The coffee made Big Foot look like a wimp. "No, it's fine," I said. "You know, Rita, when you're a lawyer you won't have to make the coffee any longer."

"Oh, boss, you're always kidding around." She smiled. "I don't have to make it now." She turned and walked away.

I heard the front door slam, Rita had left for the day, and I edged back into the file.

Senator Berry Welch and his wife had flown to Sacramento on the Thursday afternoon two days prior to the murder. They flew as guests of a guy named Andreas Karadimos, owner of the Acme Refuse Corporation. They flew in his Citation business jet. Riding in the plane with the businessman, the senator and Mrs. Welch were Judge Johnson and his wife. Another couple–Thomas French, the attorney, and his wife–traveled with them. The only other person on the plane that day had been the pilot.

The group flew to Sacramento to attend a thousand-dollar-a-plate Welch re-election dinner, which was held Saturday night. The group returned in the same jet after gathering for a Sunday morning brunch, which had been held in the Senator's suite at the Sacramento Inn.

I leaned back in my chair. Welch's alibi was ironclad. Saturday night at the time of the murder he was four hundred miles to the north at the Sacramento Inn doing the money shuffle with a couple hundred of his supporters, glad-handing, backslapping, and for all I knew kissing babies, or maybe even making them.

Damn, the killer *had* to be Welch. No one else in the report had even the slightest motive to murder Gloria. But how could I prove it? Juries hadn't bought the premise that a person could be in two places at once. I doubted I could convince them otherwise.

I stood, stretched, and walked to the window. Night crept over the horizon. Cars whizzing by on Lakewood Blvd. clicked on their headlights and the neon sign atop the Broadway in the Stonewood Center blazed red against the darkening sky.

Sitting at my desk again, I continued to study the file. I needed to know more about the victim–about Gloria–but there wasn't much in the report. She'd been born in Kansas and had family there. She moved to L.A. after high school.

While attending UCLA, she'd met a guy who became her boyfriend. They both majored in political science, but split up when the guy hit the big time, assistant to Congressman Chet Holifield. The cops found out about him from Gloria's co-workers. They called him, but he had an ironclad alibi. He'd been even farther away than Welch had been at the time of the murder. The ex-boyfriend was in DC working the phones on the day of Gloria's death, raising money for Holifield's campaign. He was making calls from the congressman's office, phoning rich guys who did business with the government. The telephone company had the records.

The file contained Gloria's phone records, as well. Only two long distance calls were made from her house on the day of the murder, one at three-eighteen in the afternoon to a Kansas number, and another to the Sacramento area at four fifty-three. I called the Sacramento number. An operator at the Sacramento Inn answered. I hung up. The call must've been made to Welch. If so, other than Rodriguez, Welch would've been the last known person to speak with her. I combed the files, going through them over and over. Several more hours flashed by. Still nothing to crack Welch's alibi.

My stomach rumble. I glanced at my watch: eleven p.m. I realized I hadn't eaten anything since the Fat Burger at lunch–except Rita's coffee that I'd chewed on earlier.

Luigi, the owner of Luigi's Italian Deli on Paramount Blvd., greeted me as I came through the door. "Hey *Goombah*, whaddya know, whaddya say?"

"I don't know much, and I'm saying less," I said.

I grabbed a table up front and plopped down in a chair. Being here felt good. My migraine was waning, and I liked Luigi. There was something genuine about him, and his food.

"You wanna eat, my friend?"

"I'll have a pizza. The one with the little fishies. And a Coke."

"You got it." He turned his head and shouted to his wife

in the back, "Hey Momma, one number six pie. It's for Jimmy, double the anchovies."

"You and Maria working late tonight?" I asked.

"Yeah, the night guy, he didn't show. I stayed. Momma won't go home without me." He leaned in close. "*Donna Bella*, they're all after my bod," he whispered. A furtive grin filled his face. "Momma has to protect her interests."

The *bod* that all the beautiful women lusted after stood about five foot-six, weighed in at around two hundred-fifty pounds, and waddled when it walked.

"Yeah, Luigi, she can't be too careful."

I glanced around the deli and looked out at the parking lot. There weren't any other customers in the place, but there were two cars in the lot: mine, and a blue Buick sedan. I thought I saw a shadow inside the car. The shadow moved. Someone sat behind the wheel.

I called to Luigi, wiping down tables across the room. He waddled over. I pointed to the Buick. "Hey, Luigi, is that a customer out there?"

He looked out the window. "Dunno, but I'm getting ready to close."

He went outside and spoke to the guy in the car. Shortly after, the engine started and the Buick pulled away slowly.

Luigi came back in and went directly to the kitchen. A few minutes later he emerged and walked to my table, carrying the pizza and Coke.

Curious about the sedan, I asked him, "What did the guy in the car say?"

"He was trying to decide if he wanted to come in and eat, but I told him he'd better hurry and make up his mind, that I'm closing soon." He sighed. "It's been a long night."

"I can take the pizza home if you want to close up and leave," I said.

"Nah, stick around. Momma's gotta count the drawer and tidy up."

The *bod* waddled to the front entrance, flipped the sign

to read 'closed' and locked the door.

I started in on my meal. The banner out front said it was world's greatest pizza. I had no reason to doubt it. But I couldn't eat the whole thing. They say breakfast is the most important meal of the day. Might as well start the day right; I'd have the leftover pizza in the morning.

It was around midnight when I carried the half-eaten pizza to my car.

Downey tucks itself in about nine every night. By nine-thirty the stores are dark and the streets quiet. By ten most of its citizens were home watching the *Wacky World of Jonathan Winters* on TV, howling at his stunts. By eleven they were all asleep. At twelve the crickets chirped.

When I zipped past Mathews & Son gun shop on Paramount Ave., next to the deli, I saw the Buick from Luigi's lot parked there. I hung a right on Florence. But when I turned on Fifth Street, the street where I lived, something flashed in my rearview mirror. I wasn't alone. I glanced back. The flash became twin beams. I continued down Fifth, past my apartment building, and made a U-turn. Flipping off the lights, I pulled to the curb, killed the engine, and waited.

The Buick accelerated and blew past me. I turned to see its crimson taillights fade. I sat in my Corvette surrounded by darkness and silence.

Was I becoming paranoid, a little jumpy, seeing boogiemen in the shadows? Maybe the Buick was a coincidence, some guy going home after a night out. Of course, that had to be it. What's the matter with me? Is the pressure of defending a murder case getting to me already? I started my car, left the lights off, and edged toward my apartment.

Chapter Nine

I lived in a monument of sorts to the 1970s musical taste of American. The Carpenters, the singing duo–Karen and her brother Richard–had a ranch-style house north of Florence Ave. in Downey. The house came fully equipped with a built-in washer and dryer, and a professional recording studio.

Unlike most of the musicians and singers I'd met during my drinking days and others I've read about, these youngsters seemed to have their heads screwed on straight. They took some of the profits from their hits and bought half a block on Fifth Street, tore down the pre-war tract houses and built two apartment buildings. They named the buildings after a couple of their blockbusters.

I lived–or at least slept–in the apartment building known as "We've Only Just Begun." My bedroom window looked directly into my neighbor's window across the street, "Close to You." I'd rented the one-bedroom unit the same week that I had hung out my shingle. I thought the name was a good omen. The song title matched my high hopes.

The apartment came unfurnished and mostly stayed that way. In the living room, an old armchair faced a black-and-white TV. The chair had been part of my divorce settlement. Barbara didn't want the chair, or me, but I loved the big ratty old thing. It was warm, comfortable, and cozy to come home to at night. I could talk to the chair. It rarely talked back.

I put the leftover pizza in the refrigerator, my prized possession. Luigi got it for me wholesale from a commercial restaurant supply in Norwalk. It was overkill: the unit was too large for me but too small for a restaurant. The only things in it right now were the pizza, three cans of Coke, and several boxes of my laundered white dress shirts, folded and pressed.

In the bedroom a box spring mattress–no headboard or frame–took up most of the space. I didn't have a chest of drawers, hence the shirts in the fridge. It was a good idea. In the winter, I had to remember to take a shirt out before I showered to warm it up a bit, but in the summer, it was great. I left the shirt in until the last minute. Very refreshing.

I didn't know what time it was when I nodded off, but when I awoke I was still engulfed by the big armchair with the file opened in my lap. Sunlight streaked in through the living room window, and the sounds of morning traffic rumbled around me. I looked at my watch: seven-eighteen. I showered, got a shirt from the refrigerator, gobbled a pizza slice, and headed for the office.

My heart almost stopped when I walked out the front door of my apartment. The blue Buick, the same one I'd seen the night before, was parked across the street about twenty yards away. I stared at it for about fifteen seconds. A big guy with a buzz cut sat in the driver's seat reading a newspaper. I debated walking up to guy and asking him why he was stalking me. But then I thought he's probably a private eye keeping tabs on my neighbor, Poppy Jasper. She had several boyfriends, all of them married, or so I'd heard. If it was the same car I saw last night, then the guy had probably mistaken me for his client's husband. If this were a movie my character would jot down the guy's license plate number, and in the last reel he'd turn out to be the mad-dog killer. I chuckled and walked to my Corvette.

But when I drove past it, the Buick pulled out and followed me. What the hell? I turned on Downey Ave. The car stuck with me and remained three car lengths behind. Enough is enough. I had to straighten out his mistake. I veered to the curb, parked in front of the Meralta movie theater, and started to climb out of the Vette.

I flagged the driver of the Buick, figuring he'd stop as well. But the car crawled up next to me without pulling over. The driver pinned me as he passed and pointed his finger like a gun. Our eyes met, and he mouthed the word "Bang." This guy was no P.I looking to snag a wayward husband. No, the ugly son-of-a-bitch knew who I was. I sensed it. Something in his eyes told me he knew he had just shot Jimmy O'Brien.

When I reached the office it was 8:30 and Rita hadn't arrived yet. It was just as well. My hands shook a little when I made the coffee. Guys shooting you can do that, make your hand shake a little–unless they use real bullets, of course.

While waiting for Mr. Coffee to complete its cycle, I sat at my desk, picked up the telephone, and called Welch's district office in South Gate.

"Good morning, Senator Welch's office. May I help you?" The voice conveyed a polished warmth, no doubt to convince the constituents that the Senator cared.

"My name is O'Brien, I'm the attorney representing–"

"Yes, we know all about you." The tone dropped about eighty degrees. "What do you want?"

"I need to speak with the Senator. I understand he's back in town."

The phone clicked, silence, then it clicked again. "I'm Paul Tidman, the Senator's Assistant to the Chief of Staff. What can I do for you, Mr. O'Brien?"

"I need to speak with Senator Welch. It's urgent."

"I'm sure your call is urgent and most likely related to Miss Graham's unfortunate demise. You're the attorney representing the accused, are you not?"

"I am."

"Well, first of all the Senator isn't in, and secondly, I've been instructed to inform you that the Senator's personal attorney, Mr. Thomas French, here in Downey, will be handling all matters relating to the tragic event."

"Let me get this straight, are you saying that Welch hired a lawyer?" My heart rate increased. "Does he feel he needs an attorney, has something to hide?"

"No, of course not, strictly routine. The Senator is

extremely busy doing the People's business. Your business as well, Mr. O'Brien. Surely you can see he just can't drop all his important work any time someone such as yourself calls."

"I don't give a damn what he's doing. I have to speak with him."

"Come now, Mr. O'Brien, even you must know how valuable the Senator's time is."

I didn't like this guy's condescending line of bullshit. "Look Tidbit, or Titman, or whatever the hell your name is, *damn it*, this is a murder case, and the Senator has information I need..." I took a breath and tried to cool off. I realized I was talking to a messenger boy, an assistant's assistant. "Look Mr. Tidman, tell Welch that if he doesn't call me I'll get a subpoena, drag him in–"

"Good day, Mr. O'Brien." The line went dead.

I looked up Thomas French's phone number. I didn't know him personally, but I knew *about* him. Seemed like an okay guy; a family man, usher in his church, and he belonged to all the community service clubs–Rotary, that sort of thing. His name was constantly in the local paper, giving speeches, presenting awards, promoting the community, and raising money for worthy causes. He was a do-gooder deluxe, a real boy scout. I wondered how he found the time to practice law.

Rita walked in just as I was about to place the call to French. She had on white Bermuda shorts and a loose-fitting blouse with cheerful flowers printed on it, bluebells or bluebonnets, some kind of blue flowers. With no clients to speak of, I didn't insist on a dress code. Anyway, she looked bright and fresh with her perennial smile intact.

"Good morning Boss. Shall I make the coffee?"

"No Rita, it's been made, but I've got something for you to do right now."

"Okay."

I took a number-ten envelope from my desk and handed it to her. "I want you to take this to the mailbox on the corner and pretend to mail it."

"What this all about?" she asked, flipping the envelope over in her hand.

"Rita when you get to the mailbox, look around to see if you spot a blue Buick parked somewhere close by."

"Jimmy, what's the story?"

"Just look for the car, okay?"

"Sure, but I'll save the envelope; money's tight, you know." She winked.

"That's why you're the money manager around here."

While waiting for Rita to return, I made the call to Thomas French's office. He probably wasn't there. He'd be out helping little old ladies cross the street.

A female voice answered. "Law office. May I help you?"

"Mr. French, please. Jimmy O'Brien calling about a matter involving his client, Senator Welch."

"Mr. French is away from the office." Her voice turned cold, like a wind from the north. Her lips must be purple.

"I'll leave my number. Please have him call me back. It's important. I have a hearing in a few days and I need to discuss an urgent matter regarding his client."

The frosty voice said French was in court and would check his messages during the break. But *if* he called me back, it wouldn't be until court adjourned, in the afternoon.

French might not know anything about Welch's affair with Gloria Graham. Even if he did, I doubted that he would be willing to discuss it. He would only tell me facts already in the police report. I needed to go eyeball to eyeball with the Senator himself to see if he'd blink when I mentioned his romance with Gloria. But if I handled French right, maybe he could arrange a meeting. I figured I'd have to hound him until he answered my calls.

Rita returned, humming a pleasant tune I didn't recognize. She came into my office and handed me the envelope.

"I saved the envelope," she said, smiling. "But I didn't see anything out of the ordinary."

"You didn't see a blue Buick?"

"Let me see–there was a pick-up truck and a bug, you know a V-dub. I think it belongs to the guy in the State Farm office next door. And two or three other cars parked close."

"How about a blue car, a sedan? Maybe some guy sitting in the driver's seat?"

"Well, yes, but it was down by the corner. Some big guy sitting behind the wheel," Rita said. "He was giving me the eye. I just figured he liked the way I looked."

"I'm sure he did," I said.

Rita turned to leave, then stopped. "Is this trouble, Jimmy?"

"No, of course not. It seems I've picked up a tail." I leaned back in my chair and tried to appear unconcerned. It didn't make sense to worry her. "Someone's trying to intimidate me. That's all," I said. "If they were pros, out to do harm, we wouldn't have seen them or the car."

"Jimmy, this is giving me the creeps."

"Rita, forget about it."

"Are you sure?"

"There's nothing to worry about." Okay, so I lied.

I needed answers. After Rita went back to the outer office, I sank into my chair and tried to think. Why was the guy in the Buick tailing me? Who'd care enough about a small-time murderer to send thugs out to scare me off? Another thing bothered me: why did Johnson pick me to represent the accused in the first place? And why'd he get so upset when Rodriguez wanted to plead not guilty? There had to be answers and there was one man who could give them to me.

"I'll be gone for a while," I told Rita as I blew by her.

Chapter Ten

With the blue Buick trailing three or four car lengths behind, I drove west on Firestone, heading to the South Gate Municipal Court. I parked and walked directly to Division III, Judge Johnson's courtroom. I pounded on his chambers door. His clerk stuck her head out. "Judge Johnson is busy at the moment, Mr. O'Brien."

"It's imperative that I speak to him right now."

Johnson shouted from behind the door, "What do you want, O'Brien?"

"Bob, I need to see you, *now.*"

"You want to see me, *ex parte*? Have you notified the DA's office?"

"This is off the record."

"Look, Jimmy, I'm busy. I'm preparing for hearing. It's coming up in an hour."

"It will only take a minute. It's about the Rodriguez case."

"All right. But I can only give you five minutes."

Johnson sat behind his perfectly organized desk, not a paper or file in sight. He wore an expensive, yellow alpaca sweater. The clerk shook her head slowly as she left the room, carrying a stack of papers.

I sat in one of the tufted leather chairs facing his desk. "Nice sweater," I said, glancing at the golf bag leaning against the wall in the corner.

"You've got four minutes left," he replied with a hard look on his face. I figured he was still steamed over my inability to bring in the guilty plea.

"You give me what I want, and it won't take that long," I said.

"You let me down. We were friends, I trusted you, tossed you a bone, and you let me down."

"I'll get straight to the point, Bob. Something's not right about the Rodriguez case. I've got thugs following me around. Rodriguez is a *gardener*, for chrissakes, not a mob boss. Who gives a damn about him? And, by the way, why'd you pressure me to get a guilty plea anyway?"

"Calm down, Jimmy. Nobody pressured you. I tried to help you out, give an old buddy a break. That's all.

"C'mon, Bob. You wanted a guilty plea for a reason, and you forced the deputy DA to go along with it."

He rose from his chair. "Who are you to come busting in here–"

"I'll tell you who I am," I said, my voice rising. "I'm the patsy you conned into taking the case."

He stood and looked at me for a moment. Then, before saying anything, he sat down again. "Are you going to calm down and listen to reason, or are you going to continue to make a fool of yourself?"

"Something around here smells and you know it." I paused. "Tell me this, Bob. Are you protecting Welch?"

"That's absurd. Welch didn't kill the girl. He told me he was in love with her, dumb shmuck. But the cops had the killer, and Welch was running for re-election. The campaign couldn't stand a scandal."

"Welch wanted the case wrapped up nice and tight. Didn't he?"

Of course he wanted it wrapped up, wanted a conviction before the muckrakers and his political enemies tore into his hide and blew it all out of proportion." He leaned back in his chair and studied my face. "Surely you can understand his position, and mine as well. I'm up for reelection too, and I'm on Welch's campaign committee, for *chrissakes*. But my obligation to the bench comes before politics. I didn't do anything wrong."

"Nothing wrong? You have a conflict, and Rodriguez

got the shaft–"

"Whoa, slow down. Welch has an unimpeachable alibi, four hundred miles away at the time of the murder. I was with him in Sacramento at his fund-raising dinner. Everybody was there having a good time, great entertainment–Robert Goulet, and a comedian, Foster Brooks. The guy was hilarious, did a drunk routine–"

"I don't care about the dinner or the show. I want to get to the bottom of this. Maybe Welch didn't kill her, maybe he did; don't ask me how. But I'm saying there are other factors to consider. I think the cops made a rush to judgment. Rodriguez was a very convenient fall guy."

"Look Jimmy, I went to law school and took the same courses you did. Even the one where we learned, 'When you're up a creek, lay the blame on someone else.' It was called *Reasonable Doubt 101*. You'd better come up with something other than what you're implying. No jury is going swallow a line of bull like that."

"Yeah, what about the class we also took, *Don't Frame an Innocent Man 101*. You sleep through that class, Johnson?"

Johnson shook his head slowly. "You always were pig-headed, even when we worked together on the P.D."

"I'm not being pig-headed. I just want–"

Johnson interrupted. "Shut up and listen to me."

"I'm listening, but it better be good. Why am I being followed? I don't like getting threats."

He stood and walked around the room. He glanced at the photos on the wall, pictures of him shaking hands with politicians. He focused on the one with Governor Reagan for a couple of seconds before turning to me. "You're in deep shit, Jimmy, but you wouldn't listen. You had to be a big hero, didn't you? You're in over your head."

"I know I am. I've never defended a murder case, but I'm going to give it all I got."

"That's not what I mean."

"Oh?"

"Big players are involved. They mean business. They don't want you messing where you don't belong. You could get hurt."

"What are you telling me? You're going to throw this case because some bigwigs are leaning on you? *My God*, Johnson!"

"No! No, you got it all wrong. Rodriguez will get a fair trial. I'll see to it. But, I'm just telling you what I overhead. Certain people don't want you snooping in their private affairs. Stick to the facts. Don't go on a fishing expedition."

"Who are these guys?"

"They're not Boy Scouts."

"I don't give a shit who they are. I'm going to defend Rodriguez to the best of my ability. And if it takes me places where these *big players* don't want me to go…well, so be it."

"Brave talk, Jimmy." He shook his head again. "I'm sorry I got you into this mess."

It was ten-thirty when I arrived back at my office. The Buick sedan followed me at a discreet distance. I entered through the front, went straight to the back door, exited the office and walked to the rear parking lot. Moving back around the corner of the building, I spotted the sedan parked curbside about ten feet down the street pointed in my direction, but the guy in the Buick hadn't spotted me. I doubled around the block and crept up behind the car. On the back of my business card, I scribbled the license number.

I rushed back to the office and hurried to my desk. Rita had left a note: "*Went to the stationery store to get some legal forms!!!*" She put three exclamation points and one of those smiley faces at the end of it. I wondered why the forms were important enough to rate three exclamation points. One exclamation point was nothing. She put exclamation points on the shopping list: *Coffee!*, *Paper towels!*, stuff like that. Two would be more of a big deal, something like my car insurance was overdue, but now three? Why were forms so important? Rita would let me know when she returned. But first, I had to get a hold of Sol. I grabbed the receiver and punched in his office number.

"Is he around, Joyce?"

"He's still at Del Mar, but I can get him a message."

"I've got a plate number, need an ID."

"No need to bother the boss, I can handle it. Won't have the information until this afternoon. It's almost eleven now. Our DMV contact would be out to lunch. He'll run the plate when he gets back, around three."

"Thanks. Call me when you get the name, okay?"

I leaned back in my chair, laced my hands behind my head, and put my feet on the desk. All I had to do now was wait until Joyce called back, then I'd find out who was following me. With a name and Sol's help, I'd find out why.

The front door opened. "Jimmy, I'm back. I've got the forms."

"What forms?"

"Discovery forms. I'm sure you want me to fill them out and file them with the DA as soon as possible."

"For the Rodriguez case?"

"Well, duh."

"Oh, yeah. I was just going to ask you to do that."

Rita smiled and walked back to her desk. In a few minutes the phone rang. She shouted from the other room, "Miss Allen's on the line."

"Hi, this is O'Brien."

"Jimmy, I just received a call. Thought you might want to talk about it, but you probably already know what I'm referring to."

Why would she call me? Is there something I should know? "Yeah, sure. I know what it's about."

"Do you want to discuss it? That is, if you know what I'm talking about."

"Of course, I know."

"He called me too, and I thought maybe we could figure out a plan, how we're going to handle the press. I don't want this case tried in the newspapers."

I pulled the pink message slip Rita had given me from my pocket. The one about the reporter from the *Times* wanting information. "Conway called you, too?"

"Yeah, that's what I want to talk about. When will you be available?"

"Let's talk about it over a bite. I owe you lunch," I said.

"I don't know about that. Two lunches in a row…"

"It's the only time I have available." I enjoyed having lunch with beautiful women, even if it was only business, but she hesitated. "Unless you want to see my picture in the paper, I suggest we meet and agree on the ground rules. The media is going to be all over this. I don't want us arguing in public, either."

"Okay." She sighed. "Shall we meet at the Regency again?"

"It's my turn to pick the place. How about Chris 'n Pitt's?" I said.

"Oh my God, Chris 'n Pitt's. Sawdust on the floor and all that." She didn't sound too thrilled. Her voice had a cringe to it, but I thought I heard a small laugh behind the cringe.

"Yeah, I see you know the place. I'll see you there in a half hour." I hung up before she could bail on me.

Chapter Eleven

Chris Pelonis had painted the exterior of his Chris 'n Pitt's restaurants to look like log cabins. He said the paint job reminded people of honest-to-God country barbecue. It reminded me of painted stucco. The dining room floors, as Bobbi had said, were covered with sawdust, and you ate your huge slabs of baby-back ribs with all the trimmings while seated at wooden picnic tables. The waitresses' costumes— gingham blouses, Levi mini-skirts with white piping, and cowgirl boots–went with the country western music that hee-hawed in the background. I did a little two-step up to the hostess's station and put my name in for a table.

Bobbi came through the front doors and gawked in disbelief. She ventured a little farther into the waiting area. As soon as she spotted me, she shook her head slowly, giving me a mock scornful look. Then she started laughing.

I went to her side. "Howdy, ma'am."

"I hope you're not going to do that cowboy shtick all through lunch."

"A little cowboy shtick, but mostly lawyer shtick."

The hostess called my name and showed us to our table. Bobbi ordered a small salad with blue-cheese dressing, no Roquefort. I had the barbecued beef sandwich that came with about a pound and a half of French fries.

While we waited for our food to arrive, we talked about the implications of granting interviews to the press. "It'd be a circus," I agreed.

I figured if the DA's office wouldn't release information favorable to their case, then I wouldn't counter. Handling the media took special skills I knew I didn't possess, at least not yet. Famed lawyers, such as Melvin Belli, were masters at manipulating reporters. But even for them it could backfire, and when the media turned on you it could be brutal. Belli, late in his career, after ranting continuously about several of his ex-wives, became known as Melvin Bellicose. Yeah, it would be best if Bobbi and I agreed to avoid the spotlight as much as possible. One less thing to worry about.

"So it's a deal? We both offer *no comment* to the media hounds," I said, shooting my hand across the table.

"Deal," Bobbi said with a smile, taking my hand in hers. Our eyes locked for a moment. "Jimmy, you seem like a nice guy. I want you to understand something."

"Oh?"

She removed her hand and continued: "I just want you to know I play by the rules, no tricks or fancy footwork. I'm a professional and take my responsibility seriously. I won't be underhanded with you. I want the system to work and justice to be served, that's all."

"That's all I can ask."

The food arrived. Bobbi silently picked at her salad. I took a few bites of my sandwich, grabbed a napkin from the stack on the table, and wiped my hands. "There's something else on your mind," I said. "Want to tell me about it?"

"My superior says that she'd still be willing to accept a plea. One last chance."

"We'll pass on the offer. I want to make myself clear. Rodriguez did not kill her."

"They all say that." She shook her head. "The prisons are full of innocent people."

"In this case it's true."

"This is your first murder case. I'll give you some advice–"

"Forget it. I'm not going to see an innocent man go to prison."

"I'm sorry to say this, but with you as his lawyer he's lucky the Supreme Court put a hold on the death penalty last July."

"That's a crummy thing to say."

"No offense, Jimmy, but you are inexperienced."

"I'm experienced enough to know an innocent man when I see one."

"Have it your way."

Bobbi took a sip of iced tea, stirred her fork slowly around in her salad. "You should think it over. He could be out in twenty-five years if he accepts."

"Twenty-five years in prison for a crime he didn't commit. I don't think so." I took a sip of coffee and stared at Bobbi over the rim of my cup.

"What? Why are you looking at me like that?" she asked.

I debated whether I should tell Bobbi the information I had about Welch sleeping with Gloria Graham. As a matter of pure tactics I was better off keeping my knowledge of the affair to myself. Surprise was one of the most effective trial strategies, and I knew enough to understand that most criminal lawyers would never tip their hand in a situation like this. But, I had no evidence to take to trial, no defense whatsoever, just rumors and innuendos, which wouldn't be admitted. I needed proof. I needed the police to do a full investigation of Welch. Maybe the authorities could somehow break his alibi, and If Bobbi reopened the case–with her powers of subpoena and full investigative staff–at least I'd know if I were on the right track. But could I trust her? I had to be sure that she was more concerned about justice than victories in the courtroom.

I wouldn't mention being tailed and what Johnson had said about heavyweights being involved. I needed more information about them: who they were, how they were connected, and what all of the cloak and dagger stuff had to do with the case. I'd keep it under wraps. If all else failed, I'd have something for the trial.

"Bobbi, can I talk to you, ah… one-on-one, straight out?"

"You mean man-to-man, don't you?"

"C'mon, you know what I mean."

"Jimmy, what's on your mind?"

"A few minutes ago we spoke of justice."

"Yes, go on."

"Can I trust you?"

"That's entirely up to you, but what I've been trying to explain–"

"I know what you said, but–"

"Let me finish." Bobbi looked down at her salad. She paused, as if to prepare herself for what she was about to say. "In all my cases, I feel deep sorrow for the victims of the crimes. I feel for them just as I would if the crime happened to me. I want–no, make that *demand*–justice, retribution for what happened."

She pushed her plate back and folded her hands on the table. "I'm not concerned with racking up convictions, getting my name in the papers, or scoring points with anyone. I'm not running for office, nor do I ever intend to. My only concern is that the perpetrators are punished for their crimes."

"What about the times when the police arrest the wrong man?" I asked. "You know it happens."

"You know better than to ask that, Jimmy. There would be no justice if that were the case. The guilty person would go free. That's why just adding more convictions to my resume does nothing for me."

"If you feel so strongly about justice and retribution–and I assume you mean that the punishment should fit the crime– why were you willing to accept a plea from Rodriguez at the arraignment?"

"That wasn't my choice. Johnson had set that up with my superior and I had to go along. But thanks to you, it doesn't matter now. Your client will get his trial and he'll be convicted."

"You just went along?"

"Yes. But it's never been my goal to speed up the process and alleviate the court's burden. As Thomas Jefferson said, 'Delay is preferable to error.'" Her smile returned. " I had to work that in."

"In other words, if you had any doubts, any at all about my client's guilt, you'd reopen the case. Is that what you're saying?"

"In a heartbeat," she said. "However, it would have to be convincing. Why, do you have something that casts doubt on his guilt, something tangible?"

Bobbi's sincerity moved me. I had no question about her sense of fair play. She wanted to see the guilty man convicted as much as I did. I just had to convince her that Rodriguez wasn't her guy. I decided to confide in her and take my chance. I hoped that I wasn't letting her beauty rule my judgment. It was hard not to.

"I have evidence that Senator Welch was having an affair with the deceased," I said. "It wasn't in the police report. It could provide a motive."

Her eyebrows arched. "Is that true? Where did you hear that?"

"Gloria Graham told a friend of hers that she was sleeping with a politician. We could corroborate her statement, motels, restaurants, places where Welch and Gloria were seen together, that sort of thing."

"So what if he was? That doesn't prove anything. If all the bosses who slept with their secretaries killed them, we'd have a whole lot of dead secretaries lying around. No, sorry, that in itself doesn't change anything."

"Gloria's girlfriend will tell her story. Reasonable doubt," I said.

"You'd bring up this *so-called* affair without a shred of evidence other than some girl's story and possibly ruin a man's reputation–"

"To save an innocent person from life in prison, *hell yes*. Besides, if Welch wasn't sleeping with her, then he has nothing to worry about."

"Yeah, sure. You'll tell the media Welch is an adulterous

murderer. You going to tell the newspapers he kicks his dog, too?"

"Didn't know he had a dog."

"I thought we agreed not to discuss the case with the press."

"I'm not running to the papers, but it'll come out in court."

"You know how the media is," Bobbi said. "They'll print the story, make a big hullabaloo. Later when the truth comes out... Well, the retraction will be on page forty-seven."

"Look, Bobbi, I'm just saying it's possible that he was having an affair. And it's possible, just possible, that in the heat of passion, he might've killed her."

"That's extremely unlikely."

"It's a lot more logical than your motive. Rodriguez, her gardener, all of a sudden losing control."

"Welch wasn't even in town at the time of the murder." Bobbi shook her head. "All the physical evidence points to your guy. He had a motive–even if you don't buy it–means, and opportunity. The police arrested the right guy."

"That's not all," I said.

Bobbi leaned closer to me. "You have more?"

"Yeah, it was the Senator who pressured Johnson to wrap this up, get a plea, and close the case."

"Johnson told you that?"

"Not right out, but it fits. I'm sure he did."

"Perhaps Johnson was just trying to get you to accept a plea so he could clean up his calendar."

"Believe me, Bobbi, it was Welch. He pressured him."

She drew back; it only took a moment for her disposition to harden. She grabbed the napkin off her lap and threw it on the table. "You could be right and I should've known better."

"Don't be angry with me. I'm just telling you what I know to be true."

"I'm not mad at you. It's those damn politicians. They used me, wanted me to speed the process so it won't muddy up their campaign."

"I think the police should reopen the case, take a hard look at Welch."

"Jimmy, get real. It's just politics, doesn't change anything. The case is closed."

"It changes everything."

"The case is closed, period," she said through clenched teeth. But almost immediately her expression softened. "Jimmy, listen. Welch was in Sacramento at the time of the murder."

"If I show how he could have slipped away from the party, flew here–"

"You show me evidence that Welch was in Southern California at the time of the murder, I *guarantee* we'll reopen the case. But you have to provide me with ironclad proof. Talk to Welch, see what he has to say."

"He's not talking to me. I've tried."

"Try harder."

We said good-bye in the parking lot; no sign of the Buick. It was after three o'clock when I walked into the office. Rita wasn't around, so I called the answering service.

Mabel, the owner of the one-person business, came on the line after several rings. "This one's from Joyce, at Mr. Silverman's office. It says, 'I have the license plate ID for you. The car is registered to Hartford Commodities.' The message goes on and on. Do you want me to read the whole thing?" she asked.

"Mabel, what's the matter with you? Of course I want you to read the whole thing."

"Okay, here goes. It says, 'I've checked with the Secretary of State's office in Sacramento. They show that the sole trustee of Hartford is an offshore corporation called Triple A Financial, Inc. I am trying to find out its address, the company's local correspondent bank, and the person who signs on the account. Might take a while. Someone is trying to hide the ownership.' Signed, Joyce," Mabel said.

I had the phone tucked between my shoulder and chin, scribbling the highlights of the message on the back of the Edison bill.

"The next message is from some guy selling insurance. Do you want me to read that one too?" Mabel asked.

"What?"

"A guy selling something."

"No, that's okay." I hung up the phone.

There was no message from French. I kicked back and stared at the wall, wondering what to do next. Welch wouldn't talk to me and now French wasn't returning my calls. I opened my desk drawer and pulled out the police report. The name Andreas Karadimos popped out at me. I figured it was about time I talked to him. He had flown Welch and his friends to Sacramento on the weekend of the murder, but I also remembered his name from the past.

I didn't want to call him and get the brush-off, as I did from Welch and French. But I trembled at the thought of barging in on him unannounced. Karadimos owned a garbage collection company, and I'd heard rumors about him. They say he was ruthless and tough, one nasty son of a bitch.

His company, Acme Refuge, held all of the residential trash collection contracts with cities in the southeastern area of the county. His blue and white trucks were a common sight on the streets. Not only did Acme Refuge have the neighborhood business locked up, their roll-off bins could also be seen behind virtually all of the commercial establishments in the area. Garbage collection at these locations wasn't covered by city contracts as the household accounts were. Business owners could select a refuge company of their choice. That is, if they could find one, other than Acme, willing to service them.

A few years back, when I was a cop, I bumped into a classmate from my days at Cerritos College. We both majored in police science. Tommy was now a homicide detective with the sheriff's department.

Over drinks, he told me about a case he was working on that involved Acme Refuge Company. It seems that a rival trash company had tried to land some of the larger commercial accounts in the southeast area. A trash war of sorts broke out and Acme eventually won control of the region when the owner of the rival company committed suicide.

Tommy said that he tried to look further into the case, but his hands were tied by the brass downtown. His suspicions had been aroused when he read the autopsy report and discovered that the deceased had shot himself in the head–twice.

I'd given him a questioning look.

"Maybe the first shot didn't kill him. Maybe he tried again." Tommy shrugged.

Chapter Twelve

I drove to Cudahy, a smokestack community about five miles west of Downey. Railroad tracks crisscrossed as they sliced through the landscape. I waited on Firestone at the Union Pacific crossing as a slow moving freighter crawled across the boulevard. Continuing on, I drove a few blocks farther, turned right on Atlantic Ave. and waited again for the same train as it moved along the diagonal. It crept behind factories that populated the area, dropping off boxcars along the way.

Acme Refuge Company's yard, about ten acres square, was located on the southern edge of the industrial commonwealth of Cudahy. A twelve-foot-high fence made from corrugated metal and topped by sharp razor wire surrounded the facility.

I parked my car on the outside and hiked to the doublewide gate that closed in the middle. A chain, locked with an industrial padlock, encircled the gate where the two halves came together. A hand-lettered sign hung on the fence: "KEEP OUT–THIS MEANS YOU." I looked around for a buzzer or a doorbell, something like that, but didn't see one. The chain hung loosely and when I pulled on one side of the gate and pushed on the other, it opened slightly and left a gap large enough for me to squeeze through.

I stuck my head through the opening and glanced around. The sound was deafening. Machinery screamed, trucks growled, and a Caterpillar dozer's blade screeched as it heaved garbage into a huge pit. The only people I saw were far away, busy at work. They didn't seem to notice me. I pulled my head back out and looked up and down the street, nervous just standing there. It might be considered trespassing, but I figured I'd slip through the gate, find the office, and maybe Karadimos would talk to me if he were there. I turned sideways and with a little effort squeezed through the opening in the gate.

On the north side of the yard, in front of a row of twenty-five or thirty garbage trucks, stood a small stucco building. It looked like an old tract house that had been picked up, moved, and plopped down at its present location without concern for the building's integrity. Cracked plaster covered the exterior, windows were broken, and the pitched roof sagged in the middle like a swayback horse. Someone had taken a paintbrush and splashed the word OFFICE over the front door. An area had been scraped smooth next to the building, probably parking spaces set aside for the office workers. No cars were there.

A thick, obnoxious stench hung in the air and I practically had to dog paddle through it as I made my way to the office. It took a couple of minutes to reach the door. I knocked lightly, waited, and knocked again. No answer. I put my hand on the knob. Glancing around the yard–nobody was looking in my direction–I twisted it and sighed. Maybe down deep I really didn't want to go in, but I gave the door a little shove and it opened.

I didn't know if I'd learn anything and wondered if breaking in would be worth the risk. I wasn't even sure what I was looking for, but I had to look anyway.

Slipping inside, I shut the door behind me and jerked the knob to make sure it was closed and locked. Then I turned and scanned the room. Defused light streaked in from the dirty windows illuminating dust particles floating in the air. The dust swirled, forming intricate patterns in my wake as I moved through the office.

Battered pieces of junk served as furniture. The back seat from an old car stood in for a couch. At the far end of the room, in front of two banged-up filing cabinets, sat a scarred wooden desk.

No art or personal effects hung on the walls, no family pictures, citations, or anything like that. But someone had nailed a giveaway business calendar to the wall. It advertised a company called Executive Aviation, located at Long Beach Airport. The calendar had a picture of an airplane on it, a Lear Jet flying among puffy cumulus clouds. The page hadn't been turned in a while. Although it was August, the Lear Jet was the plane of the month for April.

I rushed over to the filing cabinets and tugged on the drawers. Locked. I turned and checked the desk. I saw nothing of interest on top of it, just an ashtray overflowing with cigar butts, a half filled cup of cold coffee with a dead fly floating on the surface, and a few pieces of paper that looked like lists of garbage routes.

A shadow filled the room. Something outside moved across the window. I flattened myself against the wall. Trembling slightly, I glanced out the filthy window that overlooked the yard. A truckload of rotten cantaloupes rolled past the window. I watched as the truck dumped the slimy melons into several gray metal bins. But, thank God, I didn't see anyone coming toward the office.

I turned from the window and moved rapidly back to the desk to see if I could spot anything that might shed light on the Sacramento flight. I opened the top center drawer. It held some pens, a few pencils mostly with broken tips, and a dozen or so unwrapped cigars. I quietly closed it and opened the narrow drawer to the right. A .45 automatic sat on top of a small stack of invoices. I wanted to examine the papers, but I didn't want to touch the gun and leave my prints on it.

As I stood there frozen, staring at the gun, I heard a car door slam. *Christ*, I thought as I shoved the drawer closed.

Quickly scanning the room, I spotted another door to my left. I was almost through it when the front office door burst open. I slipped into the next room, a small kitchen. Dark green oilcloth covered the windows.

I heard voices coming from the room I had just left,

three men talking shop.

Damn, I had to figure a way out. I sidled along, inch by inch, my back to the wall, feeling with my hands in the dim room. Perspiration soaked my shirt and my heart pounded in my chest. I thought, what a fool I'd been. If caught here, the charge would be breaking and entering. At best I'd lose my law license. I didn't want to think about the *worst* that could happen.

Finally, I reached the back door. I knew the kitchen had to have one, and I felt a moment of relief as I twisted the knob slowly and it turned. I gently pulled and prayed that the hinges wouldn't squeak as it opened. I needn't have worried about the hinges; the door wouldn't budge.

I pulled harder; nothing. Panic set in. I yanked on the door with both hands. Sweat gushed from every pore of my body. No use, the door wouldn't open. It must be dead bolted, with no key in the lock. Definitely a building and safety code violation. Perhaps, if I were caught here, I could make a deal with these guys. They'd let me go and I wouldn't turn them over to the building inspector. That ought to bring them to their knees.

I stood as still as I could, breathing slowly, in and out. I hoped they couldn't hear the drum beating in my chest. After a few minutes, I moved along the wall back toward the door to the front office. I figured I'd wait them out. The light was too dim in the room to read my watch, but I knew it must be close to five. Wasn't five quitting time? The freeways were jammed at five, people heading home. But that was just dreaming. No telling how long I'd have to wait, and every minute I waited was a minute closer to being caught.

I was now close enough to the door to hear the voices. One guy did all the talking; he spoke with a nasal wheeze. It had to be Karadimos, the boss, because all he did was bellyache. I could hear two other guys, both grunting. Karadimos continued to rant, complaining about the lack of payment from a number of his deadbeat customers. He bitched about the ineffective collection efforts of the two guys in the room.

"God damn it, I want that money. Explain the situation to 'em. Hell, use a little finesse; try the two-by-four approach."

"Okay, boss." The other voices said in unison.

"All right then, get on it tomorrow," Karadimos said. "Anyway, the men must be through unloading the stuff. Let's go check it out."

I didn't hear the front door open, but I heard it slam shut. I didn't know if all three guys had left, but I couldn't wait around any longer. I had to make my move. Peeking through the opening, I didn't see anybody in the office, so I made a dash to the front door, where I stopped. I didn't hear a car drive off. They could be standing right outside the office.

I opened the door about an inch and looked around the edge. Nobody in sight. I slipped into the yard and crouched down behind a black Mercedes, my pulse racing. I took a couple of deep breaths, then glanced over the hood of the car. The three men walked with their backs to me toward the bins of rotten cantaloupes.

I duckwalked along the side of the Mercedes and stopped at the rear bumper. I eyed the expanse of wide-open land between the yard and the gate; no cover. But I couldn't stay here. Maybe I'd draw less attention if I just stood and calmly strolled across the yard to the exit.

I was wrong. Halfway there someone shouted, "Hey, who the hell are you?"

I spun around. Two guys came rushing toward me, a heavy guy wearing a dirty tan jumpsuit, and another guy who looked a little like Elvis Presley. He had a pompadour and bushy black sideburns; he even had on the same kind of gaudy peach-tinted sunglasses the King used to wear. "Whaddya doing snooping around here?" the big guy said, shoving me in the chest.

"I'm not snooping. I came to see the owner."

The heavy guy shoved me again, this time hard. I stumbled back a little, but quickly regained my balance. "You touch me again and I'll knock you on your fat ass," I said.

I didn't know if I could knock the guy down, but I was pissed. Amazingly enough, my threat seemed to work, because he backed off a little.

"Leave him alone, Willie," Elvis said to the guy in the jumpsuit. "We'll take him to the boss." He pointed toward the office. "Let's go, O'Brien."

I tensed. *Jesus H. Christ*, these guys know who I am. "Who's O'Brien?" I tossed out the question like I was asking a stranger for the time of day.

"Knock it off, asshole. We know all about you," Willie said.

"Yeah, the boss's been waiting for you to show," Elvis added.

I walked back toward the office, the two guys crowding each side of me. The door wasn't locked. I opened it and went in.

"You like wandering in my yard, O'Brien? Sticking your nose where it doesn't belong? Keep it up, shyster, and you'll find out who you're messing with." Karadimos was about the size of Rhode Island, but not nearly as pretty. He stood behind the desk panting like a rabid hyena. Someone had turned on the air conditioner jammed into one of the windows, and it pumped full blast. The room was cold, yet Karadimos's face glistened with a sheen of moisture.

"I need information about Senator Welch," I said.

Karadimos charged around the desk and stopped when he was close enough for me to feel his hot breath on my face. He moved fast for a man his size. "You stay away from him! I got money in his campaign and I don't want you messing around."

"I have to talk to him, that's all. He might know something about the Graham murder."

"Listen, punk, I don't want you screwing around with

any of my politicians. I bought 'em, I own 'em, and I intend to keep 'em in office where they can do me some good–you hear me?" Karadimos jabbed his finger in my face. "It's a disgrace what people like you will do to tarnish the reputation of our public servants."

I didn't say anything. Karadimos returned to his desk and snatched a Kleenex from a dispenser. He wiped his forehead and threw the tissue on the floor.

"Come here." He pointed his finger at a spot on the desk. "I want to show you something."

I took a step forward and looked down at what he pointed at: a tiny fruit fly, probably from all the rotten cantaloupes outside. "Yeah, what about it?"

The insect moved slowly across the surface of Karadimos's desk. He peered down at it. "The fruit fly has a life expectancy of three days," he said.

"So?"

Karadimos took his thumb and ground it out in an exaggerated fashion.

"This one didn't make it." He looked up at me. "Get my drift?"

Chapter Thirteen

After leaving Cudahy I felt drained. I wanted to get home fast to shower and scrub the scent of the meeting off me. It wasn't the odor of the trash yard that bothered me; I needed to purge the stench of Karadimos and all that he stood for.

I opened the door to my apartment and heard the phone. Running to the kitchen, I caught it on the fifth ring.

"Ah, Jimmy my boy." It felt good to hear Sol's friendly voice. "I knew I'd catch you at home. A single guy like you should be out and about, having a little fun on a Friday night, prowling those discotheque joints, maybe."

"Nah, I don't get out much anymore," I said, while rummaging through a counter drawer with my free hand.

"Why not call that good-looking DA you've been seen breaking bread with? I hear she's between guys. Chewed up the last one and spit him out."

"Are you kidding me?" I found a leftover chocolate donut in the drawer next to a pair of pliers and took a bite. "She's the prosecutor on the Rodriguez case. It would be unprofessional," I said while munching on the dry but tasty donut.

"I'll have her home number for you by Monday," Sol said, laughing.

"Aw, Sol, you're something else." The fantasy of a date with Bobbi flashed through my mind…a pleasant fantasy.

"Hey, Joyce phoned me at the track. Told me about the tail, guy in a blue Buick. She said she gave you the plate I.D. What's up?"

I told him about the car tailing me for the last couple of days, and my hunch that Karadimos had something to do it.

"Andreas Karadimos, the garbage guy?" Sol asked.

"Yeah, but there's more. I went to see him..." I recounted my meeting with Karadimos. I didn't tell Sol how stupid I'd been for breaking into the office, but I told him that I felt I was being threatened.

"I know Karadimos," Sol said. "He's a bad actor. Has a lot of *gelt*, but dirty hands–and not just from handling garbage, if you get my meaning."

"I'd like to know about his connection to Welch."

"Listen to me, Jimmy. Karadimos is dangerous. If you're going to butt into his affairs, you'd better get some protection."

Sol was dead serious and it wasn't like him to exhibit anxiety. I couldn't think of a time when I heard him speak with an edge in his voice like this–unless, of course, he was talking about the IRS. "How serious is he about his threats? Does he follow through?" I asked.

"That *yentzer* is very serious. I've heard stories... Step lightly and watch your *toches* with this guy, Jimmy."

"I've got the preliminary hearing coming up in a week. I can't let that son-of-a-bitch slow me down."

"Boychik, he won't just slow you down; if you're not careful, he could stop you in your tracks–dead."

The dry donut felt like lead in my stomach. "Karadimos is that bad, huh?"

"I gotta be straight with you. He's as bad as they get... Wait a minute! I just had an idea. Yeah, it might work." Sol paused for a moment. "Don't let that fat-ass Greek worry you, Jimmy. It'll be okay." His voice held a hint of his usual confidence.

"Christ, Sol, what are you saying? Don't let him worry me? You just said–"

"Jimmy, my boy, keep cool. I've got something in mind, but I've got to make a few phone calls. Anyway, here's why I called you tonight: I want you to get down here tomorrow to meet a guy, a politico–a pro. He could shed some light on

Welch and his campaign. You'll have some fun too. Clear your mind for a day."

"Joyce said you're at the Del Mar race track."

"You got it. I'm staying at the La Costa Resort. Meet me at ten-thirty in the hotel lobby. We'll take the limo to the oval from there," he said.

I sighed. Maybe Sol was right. A day off couldn't hurt. "I'll see you there."

"And Jimmy, one more thing."

"Yeah?"

"Until I work out my plan, lock your door."

Chapter Fourteen

Saturday morning I jumped on the I-5 freeway at Lakewood and shot south. The speedometer needle swung through its arch, hovered at seventy for a while, then edged upward past eighty, fluttered, and settled in at eighty-five. I popped a Beatles tape into my eight-track, the "White Album." "Back in the U.S.S.R." and "Rocky Raccoon." I beat my hand on the steering wheel to the rhythm of the music. "*Why don't we do it in the road…*"

The Corvette screamed past the San Clemente turn-off, past the Western White House, and continued along the coast. Then at Oceanside, I rewound the tape and started it again. "*Rocky had come equipped with a gun… To shoot off the legs of his rival.*" It was good.

I parked my Corvette in the lot at La Costa, walked past Sol's limo sitting under the archway in front, and entered the hotel. Sol reclined in one of the club chairs clustered around the lobby, studying *The Daily Racing Form.*

"Jimmy my boy, *shalom.*" Sol stood to greet me. He wore a lightweight white summer suit, a pink shirt with a blue collar, and a cream-colored tie. The suit coat fit in the shoulders, but I doubted he could button it.

"Thanks Sol, great view." The lobby overlooked the resort's Olympic-sized pool.

He turned and glanced out the wall of windows. "Yeah, I think a… Wow! Check that out. Is that bikini legal?"

"Holy cow!" The girl made Raquel Welch look like a boy.

Without turning back to me, Sol continued: "I'm glad you could get down here today, Jimmy…" He paused until the geezer with his arm wrapped around the young beauty's bare waist walked out of our view. "The guy who's going to join us later at the track is…" Sol put the *Racing Form* on a nearby table and pulled a paper scrap from his pocket. "Philip Rhodes, he's a political consultant, works with the Democrats. I don't know him. But I'm told he's sharp as they come. His public relations firm handled Cranston's senatorial campaign. And get this: he'll be handling Welch's 1974 campaign."

"He must know about the fundraiser last week," I said.

"Sure. But I don't know how much he'll tell you about the Senator. Not in his best interests to rat him out, you know." Sol stood. "But hey, let's go. Time to head to the oval."

"How'd you get the guy to come down here, anyway?" I asked as we strolled outside to the waiting limo.

"I called Chuck Manatt, the Democratic Party state chairman. He owed me a favor. And when Manatt tells a politico in his party to do something, they do it. Plus these guys are *shnorrers*, always looking for a hand-out for their clients."

As we approached the limo the chauffeur opened the rear doors. We climbed into the backseat. The limousine pulled slowly away from the hotel. A small refrigerator stood nestled between the black leather seats. Sol removed a bottle of chilled champagne and opened it with a festive pop. He grabbed a flute glass from another hidden compartment and filled it half full.

"Too bad you quit drinking, Jimmy. This is supposed to be a good stuff. Never had it before." He examined the label. "Krug, *Rheims,* 1962. Sounds okay." he said. "Bought ten cases. A guy I know from the track needed some cash in a hurry."

"He bet his money on de bobtail nag?"

"He should've bet on de bay."

"Doo-dah."

"Oh! De doo-dah day." We laughed.

Just south of Batiquitos Lagoon, we turned left onto the

I-5 from La Costa Ave. and continued on toward Del Mar.

"Yesterday you said you might have a plan to keep Karadimos off my back while I check out Welch," I said as Sol took a sip of the champagne. "Said you were going to make some phone calls."

"Hmm, not too shabby." He raised his glass up to the light streaming in from the window, examining the pale liquid as if he were Pierre Cartier appraising a diamond. "Hey, look at the little bubbles."

"Sol, the plan?"

"Yeah, the plan." He took another sip. "I left a few calls, need to talk to some people I know. They'll get back to me," he said, still studying the glass. "In the meantime, be careful and remember, your phones are probably tapped. Is the Buick still shadowing you?"

"No, I haven't seen it since the meeting."

"That means they're not being obvious, but they're still watching you."

"Why would Karadimos hassle me?" I said. "It's just a political campaign, for chrissakes."

"Karadimos does a lot of business with the government, legit and otherwise. He plows a lot of cash into certain campaigns and not all of the money is spent on the election."

"What happens to the money that's not spent?"

Sol took another sip. "You know, this stuff's not half bad."

"What about the money?"

"I didn't pay that much–"

"Not the champagne, Sol. The political contributions."

"Oh yeah. The candidates keep it, of course," he said.

"They keep it? Then what's the difference between a bribe and a contribution?"

"I'm afraid, not much. The leftover money isn't supposed to be touched until the candidate retires from office." Sol held his arms out. "But do they check?"

"So let me get this straight. Karadimos is giving money

86

to political campaigns, buying influence. Nothing illegal there. Lots of people do that. But with Welch he gives a lot more. Makes me think he's involved with the Senator in something deeper."

"People have disappeared trying to investigate Karadimos's business. And I mean his *legitimate* businesses. Jimmy, if you started messing with his illegal stuff..." Sol took another sip of the champagne. "...let's just say Karadimos might get a little irked."

Chapter Fifteen

We exited the I-5 at Del Mar and swept into the valet parking at the racetrack. A deep blue sky arched above and a refreshing breeze blew in from the nearby ocean. No smog, gorgeous weather, with the temperature in the low seventies; perfect. The weather *had* to be perfect; this heavy-moneyed crowd wearing outfits that cost more than my car wouldn't have it any other way.

Sol scattered cash, giving money to the parking attendants, and to a guy at the security checkpoint who said, "Good morning" in a pleasant sort of way as he stamped our hands. I also saw the folded $50 bill he slipped to Goldie, the *maître d'* of the Terrace Garden, as he escorted us to a table with a direct view of the finish line.

Goldie wore a dark suit, white shirt, and knit tie. His coal-black hair formed a widow's peak low on his forehead and was plastered down and swept straight back. All the hair needed was a blaze of gray streaking through it and he would be perfect to play Count Dracula in a B-flick made by Ed Wood. When he smiled–which was probably often with people handing him money all day–his front tooth, the gold one, glittered.

Goldie left and was replaced by our waiter. Sol ordered a Beefeaters and tonic, I ordered black coffee. Within minutes, a tall, well-built guy with a deep tan approached our table.

"Hey Sol, whaddya say?"

"Vince, good to see you. Sit. Got anything on the next race?"

"Nope. Maxie the tout isn't around, but I'm gonna go with the four horse." Vince held up the *Racing Form*. "I handicapped it myself."

"Oh..." Sol said, and sighed.

"What? You don't think I have a chance?

Sol ignored the question. "Vince, I want you to meet Jimmy O'Brien." Sol turned to me. "Jimmy, say hello to Vincent James. Used to play Dr. Riley on TV, remember?"

Vince had dark brooding eyes, was impeccably dressed, and it looked like he retained a very expensive barber. "Yeah, sure. How you doing?" I said.

He gave me a passing glance and then put his binoculars up to his eyes, aimed at the tote board in the infield. He leaned closer to Sol without lowering the glasses. "I have a message for you," he said quietly.

"Oh yeah, what?"

"I went to a party last night, mutual friend's house." Vince set the binoculars on the table and took a fast look around. "The man said you were trying to reach him."

"You were at Sica's house?" Sol asked.

"Yeah, not so loud. I hung around a while. He likes me to show up at his parties. I'm kind of a decoration..." He lowered his head for an instant, and then brought it up. "What the hell, he helps me out from time to time."

"Sure," Sol said. "He figures celebrities like you add a lot of class. Which you do."

"Thanks. Anyway, he said for you to call him." Vince slid a scrap of paper across the table. "He'll be at this number at one-thirty today. Said not to call from the track. Use an outside payphone."

Sol picked up the paper and put it in his jacket pocket. It was ten minutes to post time and the horses were on the track. Vince jumped up and headed for the pari-mutuel windows to place his bet. I noticed that Sol's *Racing Form* remained unopened on the table.

"You're not going to handicap the race?" I asked.

"Nope, not betting this race or the daily double." Sol sipped his gin and tonic. "We got a system working, my boy." He glanced from side to side and leaned forward. "You're going to make some money today. But we can't let anybody in on it," he whispered.

"System? What kind of system? Don't they have a saying about gamblers with systems?"

"That they do, but this one works. It'll only be for one race, later in the day, but we'll clean up." Sol's eyes sparkled and he gave me a mischievous grin. "How much money did you bring?"

"Only a couple of hundred, but it's all I got and it's gotta last."

"Don't worry about it; this is money in the bank."

"How does it work?"

"Not now, Rhodes is going to show up any minute. But I'm going to need your help to pull it off."

"Sure, Sol," I said, but I worried about betting the last of my money on a *sure thing*.

Vince returned a moment later with a stack of pari-mutuel tickets about an inch thick. "I bet five large. Ran into the Arab downstairs, lent me the money." He glanced at a nearby table. "But I have to sit with him and his friends. See you around, Sol."

"What's the story with Vince," I asked, after he left again.

"He's not a bad guy," Sol shook his head. "Used to be on top of the world. But unfortunately he got the gambling bug and now owes his soul to the mob. They take all his TV residuals, leave him enough to live on, but he has to borrow money to gamble. Don't loan him a dime, Jimmy. He'll never pay it back."

"He gave you a message, something about a guy named Sica. What's that about?"

"Later, this is probably Rhodes coming." Sol nodded toward the aisle behind me.

I glanced over my shoulder. A tall man about forty, wearing a business suit and spit-shined, wingtip shoes strode confidently toward our table with Goldie at his side.

"Excuse me, are you Mr. Silverman?"

"You're Philip Rhodes?"

"Yes. But please, call me Phil."

Sol offered him chair and he sat down. He ordered a single malt Scotch on the rocks, and after a few minutes of chatter we got down to business.

"So, I understand you handled Senator Cranston's winning bid for the senate seat," I said.

"Yes, and we'll be managing the governor campaign for the Welch organization. Some powerful people want us on the team." He paused for a few seconds when the waiter brought his drink. "It's still very hush-hush. We haven't announced it yet. We won't let it be known until after he wins re-election to the state senate."

"We won't say anything," Sol said.

Rhodes took a sip. "Anyway, Charles Manatt asked me talk to you gentlemen."

"I need some background on Welch," I said. "I'm the lawyer defending the man accused in the homicide of his assistant."

"I don't know much about the murder, but I don't think it will be an issue in the current campaign. We plan on running polls in the next few weeks."

"Going to run strictly on the issues?" I asked.

"Of course. Welch's political record will play well with the demographics." His face took on a somber expression. "But we've heard rumors of his profligate behavior."

"Profligate behavior…" Sol looked at me and winked. "Yep that's Welch. He's been known to profligate a lot."

Rhodes turned and glanced at Sol. "Ah, well I mean–"

Sol laughed, and Rhodes eventually joined in. "I guess he's a real big profligator, all right," Rhodes said.

The bugle call interrupted our conversation, signaling that the horses were approaching the starting gate for the next race.

"You gonna place a bet, Phil? You a gambling man?"

Sol asked.

"I don't know anything about the ponies, and besides, I'm not much of a gambler."

"Well it seems to me your business is one big gamble. Spend two or more years on a campaign and it all comes down to one day in November."

"That's true, Sol. But I get paid, win or lose. However, I'd be out of business if I lost too many." He tapped the table a few times with his fist. "Knock wood, we've been fortunate, we rarely lose."

The bell sounded. Eight horses, with jockeys clad in colorful silks and clinging low on their backs, charged out of the gate. The race began, and even though we hadn't made a bet, we stopped our conversation for the minute or so it took the horses to circle the track. The number four horse–Vince's nag–finished second to last.

The waiter appeared at our table. "Bring another round, Joe. But skip me," Sol said, then turned to Phil. "I have to leave for a little while to make an important call, but feel free to order lunch."

"Thanks Sol, but I won't be able to stay much longer. I have an appointment this afternoon down in San Diego. Possible donor; could be very fruitful."

Sol dashed off and I had to get the discussion back to Welch before Rhodes disappeared. I needed to get to the point, no finessing or beating around the bush. I wasn't going to get anywhere by trying to cajole the information out of him. He would open up, or maybe not. But I had to ask the questions burning in my brain.

"Phil, do you know anything about Welch's connection with Andreas Karadimos?"

He shook his head. "Karadimos is a powerful figure in party politics, spreads his money around freely and he's garnered a lot of influence, but there are other power brokers out there as well," he said, glancing around nervously. "Karadimos is very powerful."

"You didn't answer my question. I'll rephrase it: do you think his influence with Welch has crossed the line? How much cash did Karadimos lay on the line?"

His face tightened. "Why, the unmitigated gall. Who do you think you are, asking me a question like that?"

"Come on Phil, you've studied Welch's voting record, examined the committees he's served on. You're a pro. You'd see something if it was there."

The waiter returned with our drinks. Rhodes picked up his Scotch. "I think you're out of line with your implications, Mr. O'Brien."

"Didn't Manatt tell you to talk to me? Manatt's the party chairman and you do want funding from the central party, don't you?"

Rhodes tossed back his drink. "Manatt can go fuck himself." Rhodes slammed the glass on the table and left.

I sat alone at Sol's table knowing I'd hit a nerve with Rhodes. I pissed him off, sure, but indirectly I got the answer I was looking for. If Welch were on the level, he would've said so. I shifted my gaze to the table with the three Arabs laughing it up with Vincent James, the idealistic, honorable TV doctor. Is everything a veneer, an illusion, a deception? Yeah, I got what I came for. I smiled. Shine a light in the sewer and watch the rats scramble.

Chapter Sixteen

Sol returned from making the call. We ordered lunch. I had a club sandwich, coffee. Sol ordered a cold prime rib sandwich and a gin and tonic. He purposely didn't tell me about the call. I was dying to find out but figured he'd clue me in when the time was right. Instead, we discussed my meeting with Rhodes, and his abrupt departure.

"So Rhodes just got up and left?" Sol asked.

"Might have been something I said."

"What did you say?"

"I asked him if his squeaky-clean candidate took bribes."

"Think it upset him?"

"Might have."

Sol grinned. "Well, some people are just too sensitive." All of a sudden he stared intently over my left shoulder. "Hold it!" he shouted.

"What?"

"Jimmy, get ready to make some money. I think it's on."

"What do you mean? What's on?"

He grabbed the racing program, flipped it to the fifth race. "Yes, this is what we've been waiting for." He slapped the pamphlet on the table and quickly glanced around. "Okay, Jimmy, look at that table, one down and two over to your right." He indicated a table behind me. "Do you see it?"

I turned and looked. "The table with the three good-looking ladies?"

"*Jesus*! Don't be so obvious. Quit staring."

I turned back to Sol. "What about them?"

"Did you see the blonde, the girl with the big purse–Hold it! She's getting up. Hurry, follow her; she'd recognize me. If she gets in line at the $100 betting window, come and get me, fast. If she goes to the $2 window, forget about it."

The blonde's chiffon skirt swayed in a fascinating rhythm as I followed her out of the Terrace Garden and into the cavernous barroom. She stopped, coolly glanced around, focusing on me for a moment. I moved toward the bar and sat down, taking a quick look out of the corner of my eye.

Apparently satisfied that I was nobody, she started walking again. Heads turned as she waltzed past the other male patrons drinking at long bar. Then she veered left at the wide corridor that led to the betting area.

The blond stopped at the $100 window. I turned to get Sol and saw him lurking behind a column next to a potted rubber plant.

He rushed up to me, wiggling his fingers. "C'mon, Jimmy, gimme your $200."

"It's all I got. I need the money to defend Rodriguez–"

"Gimme the goddamn money! Hurry!"

I pulled the bills out of my pocket and reluctantly handed them over. "Okay, are you sure..." I started to ask about the bet, but he was gone.

I wandered back to our table and waited. I'd given him all the money I had, money to pay some bills, money I needed to defend Rodriguez. The two hundred I gave to Sol was supposed to last until I could arrange for a loan on my car, which would take a while. I had no clients other than Rodriguez, and defending a murder rap would take not only a lot of money, but all of my time.

My eyes wandered around the Terrace Garden. Everyone was decked out in expensive clothes, dressed to the hilt. They obviously had plenty of cash to toss around. They wouldn't even notice the loss of a couple hundred. That was just tipping money to these people. They were full of smiles and falling all over themselves with laughter. What a happy crowd. I knew money couldn't buy happiness. I thought everyone knew that, but I guessed that these people hadn't gotten the memo. Ignorant fools, thinking they were happy, probably going through their whole lives thinking they're happy. It's sad. They'll die without ever knowing they weren't happy.

Sol had returned and slipped into his seat. Handing me a couple of pari-mutuel tickets, he said, "We're down on the number three horse, Street Dancer, ridden by Jorge Torres."

I stared at the tote board. "The favorite is the eight horse. He's even money." I wondered if Sol knew what he was doing. "But we've bet on Street Dancer?"

"Yeah, the morning line on Street Dancer was twelve-to-one. A long shot. But now he's six-to-one. I only bet five, I didn't want to drop the odds any farther."

"Hundred?"

"Thousand. Your two hundred won't affect the odds, but if I made a big bet the odds would drop off the chart, would look funny."

I looked at the program. "Windy's Daughter is ridden by Eddie Cruz. It's the heavy favorite, Sol. Do you think Street Dancer is a better horse than Windy's Daughter?" Not that it mattered; he'd already bet our money on Street Dancer.

Sol chuckled. "You know better than that. Windy's Daughter is a great horse, better than the one we bet on. But the jockeys decide who's going to win the race, not the horses."

I didn't want to mention anything about the ethics of fixing horse races. Not with my two hundred on the line.

The horses pranced around on the track, wound up and fidgety, and soon they were set to go. The grooms shoved the last one into the starting gate. Taking a deep breath, I wondered if it would do any good to cross my fingers.

The bell rang. My pulse quickened. The racehorses jumped from the starting gate.

The public address system bounced the announcer's voice around the grounds, broadcasting the horses' positions as they stormed down the track. Street Dancer was third around the far turn. It looked like Torres was pacing our horse well, but Windy's Daughter was running first and running easy. They maintained their position down the backstretch and around the near turn until they entered the final straightaway.

Thundering down the homestretch, Windy's Daughter held the lead, but our horse improved his position, second by a length. About one hundred yards from the finish, Street Dancer started to slow, bobbing his head. It was obvious that the better horse, Windy's Daughter, would win the race. I would lose my money. My mind spun;, maybe I could sell my car, move to a cheaper place...

Then it happened. Cruz inexplicably stood in the saddle and tightened the reins.

A guy at the next table jumped up and screamed. "Look at that! Cruz missed the finish line. Thought he won the race. He's done that before. *God damn*!"

At that moment, Torres gave Street Dancer his way and let him run. His powerful muscles rippled, and the thoroughbred's synchronized legs were a blur as the magnificent animal charged at Wendy's Daughter. He took the lead. And before Cruz could recover, it was over. Street Dancer won the race by a nose.

A deep resounding roar like an eight-point earthquake erupted from the fans. I bolted from my seat and looked out into the infield. My eyes and the eyes of 30,000 other fans were glued to the tote board. I waited for the official declaration that Street Dancer had won.

After a minute of dead silence, an aftershock rose from the crowd; my stomach lurched. The word INQUIRY flashed bright and red before my eyes. I turned to Sol. He was studying the dessert menu.

"They have a crème brûlée here that'll knock your socks off. Where's the waiter?" he said.

"Crème brûlée–dessert–what the hell! What about the inquiry?"

"A mere formality, my boy. Sit down, you worry too

much."

"It was no accident. Cruz stiffed the race," I said.

"Of course he did. That's why we didn't bet on Windy's Daughter," Sol said.

"How'd you know he would–"

"The good looking blonde is Cruz's new wife. When she shows up with the big purse, it means the fix is on. The purse is full of money."

"Okay, but how'd you know to bet on Street Dancer?" I asked.

"The teller at the $100 window is my friend, tells me which horse Cruz's wife had bet on. Besides, The Cruiser only does this when Torres is riding in the same race."

"Do they do this often?"

"Nah, only once in a while. Maybe a couple times during a meet. Then six months will go by before they do it again, at a different track."

"So today was the day, but you figured it out before his wife left for the window."

"Sure, everything fit. Eddie Cruz was the heavy favorite. Torres was in the race, a long shot, and the blond was here with her big purse. Didn't you notice the purse didn't match her outfit? Anyway, when Cruz's wife started to leave the table with the purse, I knew the fix was on. Everything fit and it worked."

"Except for the inquiry."

"Well, Eddie the Cruiser was a little too obvious. The horse, Windy's Daughter, wanted to run and win the race."

Sol made eye contact with the waiter. He came over and we each ordered the crème brûlée.

A low murmur from the fans rumbled through the warm afternoon air. The sign on the tote board had changed from INQUIRY to OFFICIAL. Street Dancer was declared the winner and paid six to one. I jumped and shouted. By then I was a nervous wreck. But we won! My two tickets were worth over $1,400. I could keep my car and have money to defend Rodriguez, after all.

After I calmed down, I asked Sol about the inquiry. "It took a while for the stewards to decide who the winner was," I said.

"Nah, there was nothing to decide. Who knows, maybe they're in on the deal. Disgraceful..." Sol shook his head. "But, remember, most of the people bet on Cruz and the stewards wanted a cooling off period, that's all. Didn't want the crowd to riot, would be unseemly."

I glanced around and saw people with angry faces ripping betting tickets to shreds. "But these are powerful people. Don't you think they'll be a little pissed?"

Sol smiled. "That's tough," he said, as we got up to go cash in our tickets.

Chapter Seventeen

We glided in the big limo back to La Costa. The stereo played a ballad by Mel Tormé. I gazed out the window while Sol sipped champagne, unusually quiet. I thought about my day at the races and the money I'd won. What a day.

The limo rolled onto the curved cobblestone driveway at the entrance of the resort. Guests in pairs strolled in and out of the wide, heavily carved doors leading to the lobby. The visitors seemed carefree and relaxed. A few couples, dressed in tennis whites, swished their rackets through the air, talking about their killer serves and dynamite backhands, no doubt.

I stood in the driveway next to the limo. Sol climbed out and one of the parking guys went to get my car. I was ready to get started on my trip back to Downey, back to reality.

"I had a great time. Thanks, Sol."

"Sure," he said. "By the way, Joe Sica has agreed to help you with Karadimos. All you have to do is say the word. That was my phone call today."

I froze with my mouth half open. Joe Sica was the godfather of organized crime in Southern California. The leader of what the media referred to as the Mickey Mouse Mafia.

I started to thaw. In fact, I started to sweat. "What? The mobster? Jesus Christ! I don't want to be mixed up with those guys. They help me and I'll owe them–forever."

"Calm down, Jimmy, my boy. Let's go in the hotel. We'll talk it over in the bar. I need a drink and you can have coffee or something."

"You hook me up with Sica and I may start drinking again."

"Don't make a decision about Joe until you hear me out."

100

It was after six. High rollers back from the track filled the lounge. The happy hour was in full swing. A jazz trio belted out the old standards. A singer who sounded a lot like Billie Holiday sang "Body and Soul." The crowd stopped lying about their winnings and listened. She was that good. We found a table in the back, away from the people.

"Why? Why would you want to set me up with an animal like Joe Sica?"

"Because, I don't want to see you get hurt. Karadimos is worse than the Mafia, a lot worse, and you need help to stay alive."

"What can I say?"

"Nothing, just hear me out." Sol stopped talking when the waiter came to take our drink order, a Coke for me, and Beefeater's on the rocks for him. It was after six, time to start his real drinking. The wine, champagne, and gin and tonics earlier in the day didn't count.

"I called Joe while you were talking to Rhodes. There's bad blood between the Mafia and Karadimos's new gang, and you know the saying: 'the enemy of my enemy'..." His voice trailed off as he searched my eyes for an answer.

"I appreciate what you're trying to do, but I won't get involved with those guys."

"You won't be involved. They'll just kind of watch over things. Help out when you need a little protection. They know the territory and they know how Karadimos operates."

"No."

"*Goddammit*, they can protect you. If you aren't concerned about yourself, think of your client. You'd be no good to Rodriguez, dead..." Sol paused, set his drink on the table, and leaned into me. "...or maybe you wanna quit the case."

"Aw, *Christ*, you know I'm not going to walk away. But why do you say Karadimos is worse than Sica? Am I going from the frying pan?"

"Look Jimmy, I know these guys–

"Mobsters are your buddies?" I asked in a sarcastic tone.

"You know better than that. I'm surprised at you. I don't do business with them directly. I work for their lawyers. Like I do for you and your clients...except they pay me."

"Touché," I said.

"Well, sometimes I *do* get involved with Sica. I go to his restaurant." He picked up his Beefeaters and took a sip. "He's got the greatest seafood bistro on the planet. He comps me, everything on the house." Sol's face brightened. "Hey, Jimmy, I'll take you there. You won't believe the abalone–"

"Sol, please."

"Okay, but listen to me, you've gotta trust me on this."

"You know I trust you, but these guys are Mafia. *Christ almighty.*"

"Let me tell you how I met Joe Sica." Sol looked around carefully, then lowered his voice. "It was a few years back. The Feds had him dead bang on a tax rap. He was going down, five years minimum for that. But they were also going to nail him with a laundry list of other charges having to do with drugs..."

The waiter came back with our drinks on a serving tray. When he left, Sol continued with his story, telling me about how he worked for Sica's lawyer, Sidney Grossman, and somehow managed to prove that Sica wasn't involved with drug trafficking. Sica pulled a nickel for the tax rap. He'd just recently been released.

"So Jimmy, if he'd been convicted on the drug thing, he'd still be in the joint. He owed me one, and I called in the favor."

Chapter Eighteen

Just beyond Capistrano Beach I turned off the I-5 and took the longer route back to Downey, the highway running along the coast. The Spaniards, late in the eighteenth century, originally cut the road through the hills at the edge of the ocean and named it *El Camino Real*, the Royal Road. We paved it over and renamed it Pacific Coast Highway. Maybe the tranquility of the scenic drive would help alleviate my anxiety.

I drove into a cutout, a view spot on a high steep bank overlooking the ocean, and stared out at the sea. The sun was slipping below the horizon, its golden path glittering on the water. Huge breakers were rolling in from the south swell caused by Hurricane Estelle down in Mexico. The wind blew, carrying with it the salt-tinged fragrance of the Pacific. I stood at the edge of the bluff thinking about the greed and corruption of organized crime. I thought about the destruction, violence, and lives ruined. I thought about my discussion with Sol.

Sica had hinted to Sol that Karadimos was involved in activities that were not compatible with the Mafia's traditional businesses. The Mafia's code of silence prevented Sica from telling Sol specifics, but he let it be known that a territorial gang war was brewing between the mob and Karadimos. I asked Sol if he had any idea what the war was about. Sol said he didn't know, but Sica summed it up in one word, "Bad news." I pointed out that *bad news* is two words. Sol winked mischievously and said, "Yeah, but it's not smart to argue with the godfather of the California Mafia."

I realized Sol's concerns about my safety were real. Before we left the bar at La Costa, he convinced me to at least meet with Joe Sica. If he wanted to keep me alive for his purposes, so be it. As Sol had said, there was nothing illegal or unethical about staying alive. If Sica called, I'd hear him out, but wouldn't ask for any favors.

The wind shifted. The golden path disappeared with the sun, and darkness crept over the horizon. I walked slowly back to my car.

When the phone rang, I was home drinking my second cup of coffee and working my way through the Sunday morning *Times*. The comics always came first, then the sports page. If I had time after that, I'd read the rest of the paper.

"You O'Brien?"

"Yeah."

"I'm Joe Sica. You'll meet me at Alfred's Pasta House on Atlantic Ave. in South Gate. You'll be there at eleven this morning."

Before I could answer, he hung up.

I looked at my watch: ten minutes after ten. I hopped into the shower, dressed, hit the road, and pulled into the parking lot with five minutes to spare.

I shouldered my way into the restaurant, packed with people. A jukebox blasted fifties rock and roll. The sensuous aroma of Italian cooking drifted in from the kitchen as waiters dashed from table to table with heaping plates of manicotti, lasagna, and veal parmigiana. Three bartenders poured drinks as fast as they could set the glasses on the bar.

The loud and rambunctious crowd consisted mostly of well-groomed Italian men, with a few women who looked like Vegas showgirls thrown in for color.

"Who's dat bum singing?" I heard someone shout.

"Ricky Nelson," someone else shouted back.

"Get ridda dat crap. Put on Frankie," the first guy yelled.

Within seconds, Frank Sinatra's smooth baritone voice crooning *My Way* floated in the air. The place erupted with a clamor of approval: "Sing it Frankie," "Way to go kid," and

"I'm doing it my way, too." Fat guys with their arms in the air danced, weaving and swaying almost in time with the music. Quite a scene.

A tall man who looked as if he spent a lot of time pumping iron approached me. "You O'Brien?"

"Yeah."

"The boss is in the office. Follow me." He looked me over. "Are you packing?"

"Packing what?" I asked.

"No weapons in here. Not allowed."

This was like a bad B movie. "I don't have a gun."

I felt the eyes of the patrons on my back as we walked through the dining room toward the office. Iron Man knocked on the door.

"C'mon in," a voice answered.

We walked into the small unpretentious office. An older guy about seventy but fit and trim nodded at me. He wore a checkered sport shirt, buttoned at the collar. The old man sat in a chair with his feet on the desk. Except for his nose, which looked like it had been broken a few times, he could have been someone's gentle and loving grandfather.

"I'm Joe Sica," he said. "Just so you know who you're dealing with, I'm the *capo crimini*, the godfather around here. I control the territory. Sit down."

"You have grandkids?" I asked.

"Yeah, why?"

"You have that look," I answered.

"What look?"

"Like a grandfather."

"I'm the godfather."

"Hey," I said. "Do the kids call you Grandfather Godfather, or Godfather–"

He gave me a blank stare. "You through with that shit?"

I realized this guy was nowhere near the benign elderly gent he resembled. His eyes were as hard and cold as a chrome-plated rock. "Ah, yeah, guess so." Maybe I should watch my mouth.

"You're a lawyer," he said.

"Yeah."

"I'm kinda like a lawyer too," he said. "And we have laws." He reached into his desk drawer and pulled out a .38 caliber revolver. Bouncing the gun in his hand, he said, "In my business, *la pistola dettava legge*, do you understand?"

"I think I get the idea." The B movie took a turn for the worse.

He put the gun back in the drawer and took out a cigar box. He opened it, looked in, fumbled around, and pulled out a dollar bill. He handed it to me. "Here, take this."

I took the money. "What's this for?"

"A lawyer is an officer of the court," he said. "Supposed to tell the cops things they hear. I just paid you a fee, a retainer, now everything you hear or see is privileged, can't tell nobody."

What he said was not exactly true. If he were really my client, and told me about a crime he was planning to commit, then the privilege wouldn't hold. I'd be obligated to report what I heard. However, this was not the time, I thought, to debate the finer points of legal canons.

"You're not really hiring me, right?"

"Nah, Sol Silverman says you can be trusted, but I wanna cover the bases. *Capish*?"

"I understand."

His dark, cold eyes met mine. "Get this straight. You know nothing, from nothing, about nothing. Am I clear?"

"I get the point."

Sica snapped his fingers. Iron Man sprang to attention. "Yo, Boss."

"Vito, go get Big Jake. Bring him here."

Vito split, and Sica turned to me. "We'll talk about the Karadimos thing when Big Jake shows up."

"Okay."

"You want something from the bar."

"Nope, I don't drink."

He looked at me. I looked at him. We both remained silent. We just sat there staring at each other.

After a short interval, I decided to say something to fill the void. I wanted to ask him if the mob had anything to do with the Kennedy assassination, but I though this was not the time for that either.

"You've got a jumping joint here," I said. "The place is packed."

"Nah, this is a bust-out. Know what I mean? You know about a bust-out?"

"Kind of a going-out-of-business sale?"

"No, this place has been out of business since the previous owner–who owed me money–decided to leave town. Unexpectedly."

"Oh," I said.

"We take over the restaurant and throw a party for our friends and associates, a little R 'n R for the boys. We order booze and food from the previous owner's suppliers on his credit. What we don't use here for the party, we sell to other places that we do business with."

"Sounds kind of penny-ante for guys like you."

"We're not businessmen. We don't do everything just for money. Gotta have a little fun."

I thought about what they did for fun. Run some guy out of business, destroy his life, and then throw a party in what's left of his establishment.

"Fun?" I asked. "What about the ex-owner of this place? Is he having any fun?"

"Sentimental bullshit."

"Yeah, maybe so. But his life is ruined, dead for all I know, while you and your men are laughing it up in his place of business."

"Hey kid, it's what we do." His eyes got hard and he reached into the drawer. I started to sweat. Was he going to pull out his *pistola*? Jesus Christ, me and my big mouth. Why can't I just shut up?

He pulled out a handkerchief and blew his nose. Then he said, "The owner came to us. Needed money. He knew the rules going in, knew we weren't humanitarians. We lived up to our end of the deal. He didn't." Sica shrugged his shoulders. "Whaddya want from me? Do I look like Mother Teresa?"

I didn't see any rosary beads. "No, you're too tall, but maybe a little in the face."

"Wise guy," he chuckled. "But you got guts. I guess you're okay."

The clamor from the dining room stopped, as if someone hit the eject button on a tape deck. Sica jumped to his feet, went to the door, opened it a crack and peeked out. "It's no big deal, but we've got company. When they come in here, don't say anything."

"Who–"

"Just don't say anything."

He went back to the desk and sat on the edge, striking a blasé pose. The office door opened. Two men wearing conservative three-piece suits entered the room. One of them had a small notebook in his hand, the kind that would fit in the inside pocket of a suit coat. He was scribbling in the book. The other guy moved slowly around the office, looking things over, fingering the desk and riffling the paper on it. Sica sat there, calmly staring at the ceiling.

"Okay Joe, what are you *goombahs* doing here, another bust-out?" the suit without the notepad asked.

"We have a legal right to be here. The owner gave me the keys, told me to watch the place. Nobody invited you. Now get the hell out. You're bad for business," Sica said.

"Where's the guy who owns this joint?"

"He's on vacation."

The suit asking the questions pointed his head in my direction. "Who's he?"

"Nobody," Sica said.

108

"Who are you?" he asked me.

"I told you he's nobody." Sica planted his feet on the floor. Expanding his chest, he said, "Now, unless you got a warrant get the fuck outta here."

The two men casually glanced around. The scribbler put his notebook away and they both strolled out of the room.

When the door closed after the men left, Sica asked, "You park your car in the lot?"

"Yeah, why?"

"They got your plate number. They'll run it, find out who you are."

I didn't need that. Just by being here I was digging a deep hole. Maybe I'd already dug it too deep to climb out of when this thing is over. Sica must have felt my concern.

"Hey kid, it's no big deal. The FBI gets their kicks outta hassling me. That's all."

The noise, laughter, and Sinatra's voice, louder than before, resumed. Someone shouted, "The Feebs have left the building."

A few minutes later, the door banged open. The biggest, meanest looking guy I'd ever seen stood in the doorframe staring at me. He must be the muscle in this organization, the guy who hangs the rats on hooks. He could do it one handed.

"Hey, boss," he mumbled, nodding at me. "Who's the prick?"

Chapter Nineteen

Big Jake looked tough, like he could knock down a building. It was easy to see how he got his name. I didn't know about the Jake part, but the *big* part was obvious. He was massive. I guessed nearly four hundred pounds. He stood at least six-foot five, his legs were short for a man this size, but his arms were longer than normal. If he'd had a lot of hair, which he didn't, they'd call him Big Jake the Gorilla. I didn't ask him if he wanted a banana.

"We gotta help this guy," Sica said.

"If you says to help, den we help," Jake said.

"O'Brien's a lawyer, having trouble with Karadimos."

"What kind of trouble?"

"The usual shit."

"I'd like to stomp Karadimos, smash him like a cockroach."

"We help him..." Sica did a hand waffle. "He helps us. Might get rid of Karadimos that way."

"No shit?" Jake said.

"Yeah, you don't think I want to help this guy because I like lawyers. I hate the bastards." Sica looked at me. "No offense, O'Brien."

Yeah, sure. "None taken," I said.

"Let's go, Jake. We're taking a ride. You too, O'Brien. I don't want to talk in here. Know what I mean?"

Sica's gold-colored Cadillac Sedan DeVille was in the lot. The car looked brand new, not a scratch on it. The paint gleamed and the white sidewall tires still had the little rubber tidbits sticking out from the tread. The only problem: this model was five years old.

When I started to open the front passenger door Sica said, "Jake won't fit in the back seat." Sica and Big Jake climbed into the front. I opened the rear door and got in. The interior was as pristine as the exterior.

"Joe, you sure keep this car in great shape," I said, making small talk.

"It's been in storage while I've been away."

"Where you been?"

"Joe's been a guest of the Feds," Jake chortled. "Just got out–he's been rehabilitated."

"Very funny, Jake." Sica started the car. "Let's get down to business." He backed out and we headed north on Atlantic.

"O'Brien, I'll give you a little background," Sica said. "Karadimos wormed his way into my territory. Took some of my action. He's outta control, gotta be stopped."

"I thought you guys had ways of handling situations like that."

"He's too strong politically. I'll tell you right out, if I had my way, he'd already be a new reef off San Pedro. He's so fat he'd be a navigation hazard, have to mark him on the Coast Guard charts." He smirked. Jake laughed. It was probably a good idea for Jake to laugh at Sica's humor, kind of like Johnny Carson and Ed McMahon.

"I was going to have him taken care of. Had to get the okay, went to the council, all four godfathers from California. They said no. I'd have to find some other way. That's where you come in."

"Me?" I asked. "What do I have to do with this?"

"Silverman said you figure Welch had something to do with the bimbo getting whacked. Maybe he does. If Welch is involved, then so is Karadimos. Welch won't take a dump without Karadimos giving the okay. You take Welch down, he'll drag Karadimos with him." He looked at me in the rearview mirror. "Maybe you're fulla crap. Who knows, but we'll take the chance."

We cruised up Atlantic and after about three miles,

turned right on Florence Avenue and headed toward Downey. We turned left into the Don's Market parking lot on the corner of Paramount and Florence.

Three Downey police cars were parked in front of Dave's Donuts, adjacent to the grocery store. Joe and Jake got out of the car. I followed. Six cops sat at tables in front of the donut shop. They looked us over as we approached the take-out counter. A sergeant, with three hash marks on his sleeve, stood.

"Hey Joe, what's happening, my man? Haven't seen you in a while," he said.

Joe went over to the cop, made a fist with his hand, and tapped him playfully on the shoulder. "Been outta town, Mike. But hey, buddy, nail any bad guys lately?"

"Nah, nobody this morning. It's Sunday, all the bad guys are in church. But someday I'll nail you. Big collar like that and the brass'll make me a lieutenant."

"Aw, Mike, always the kidder."

We went to the window. Sica and I had coffee. Jake ordered a dozen jelly donuts with a large Pepsi. Joe also bought donuts, five dozen assorted. He gave them to the sergeant.

"Here, Mike, take these to the boys at the station."

"It'll take more than donuts to get you off when I hook you up," Mike the cop said.

"Consider it a down payment," Joe said.

We pulled out of the lot and headed back the same way we came. Jake gobbled donuts, Sica drove, and I sat in the back thinking about the tightrope I was walking. I'd have to be careful. It would be easy to fall off and land on the wrong side.

"Jake, put the goddamn donut down and listen to me," Sica said. "I want round-the-clock protection on O'Brien."

"How long we gonna baby-sit this guy?"

"Until I say stop. And listen, you better not screw up like last time. Anything happens to him, you'll be in deep shit."

Screw up like the last time? What the hell was that about?

"Aw, Joe, I can handle a pussy like Karadimos."

"It's his soldiers I'm worried about." Sica flicked his head in my direction. "Their out to punch the counselor's ticket. The Greek stole a few *soldatos* from Buscetta. I know those guys. They're vicious, scary bastards."

"Don't worry about it, boss. Ain't nobody I can't handle. If those guys tries anything, I'll cram my fist down their fuckin' throats, rip out their fuckin' hearts, and eat them raw while they watch." Jake turned and looked at me over the seatback. He took an immense bite out of a jelly donut. Purple jam squished out and ran down his face.

My stomach was already doing somersaults listening to Sica speak casually about how Karadimos planned to have me whacked. But now the sight of Big Jake eating donuts made me want to puke.

Chapter Twenty

I got up early Monday morning, had coffee, and took off for Long Beach Airport. I drove south on Lakewood Blvd., blowing by the massive Douglas Aircraft factory as I headed for the private aviation service center, Executive Aviation Company, on the south side of the field. Turning right on Spring Street I saw their sign bolted high on the side of a modern concrete building adjacent to runway 25L. I pulled into the parking area in front of the buff-colored structure and went to the reception counter in the lobby.

I remembered Executive Aviation's calendar hanging in Karadimos's office and figured that his business jet could be hangared there. If so, I might be able to find out if the jet plane had been flown back from Sacramento on the day of the murder.

I walked through the lobby and followed a sign pointing the way to the maintenance office. I went through a door and walked into the large, spotless, well-lit hangar. Floods high in the ceiling beamed down on five or six jets parked in the building. The airplanes were magnificent, all regal and sparkling, poised to propel you across the skies at a moment's notice, streaking through the air at a velocity faster than a bullet shot from a high-powered gun. I strolled around and between the planes, running my hand over their glossy surfaces.

My reverie–Ace O'Brien of the Skies–shattered when I heard a shout.

"Hey you, what are you doing in here?"

I turned toward the shout. "Looking for the maintenance manager."

"That's Fred Vogel. He's in his office. Back there," the

voice said.

I looked where he pointed, saw a glass-enclosed cubicle at the back of the hangar, and moved toward it. Inside, I saw a man sitting at a desk, talking on the phone while he puffed on a Marlboro. I could see the distinctive red and white flip-top box on his desk. I knocked on the door. He hung up. "Come in!" he yelled.

I entered. "You Fred Vogel?"

"That's me. How can I help you?" He squinted at me with one eye.

I didn't think he'd give the information I needed to just anybody who walked in off the street, so I had to get clever. I pulled my insurance man's business card out of my wallet and handed it to Vogel. "I'm Mr. Biddle. Here on official business."

He handed the card back. "You'll have to see Mr. Damski, he's the GM. He's in charge of stuff like buying insurance."

"No. That's not why I'm here. You see, I'm doing a survey on..." I took an old phone bill out of my pocket and pretended to study it. "One Andreas Karadimos. He's applied for a large life policy, double indemnity for accidental death. I understand he keeps his airplane here and my company wants to be sure that it's safe to fly, well maintained and all that." I had Vogel's attention and I almost started to believe the story myself. "I'm sure you can understand why we have to check on these things. Do you know this Karadimos person?"

"Karadimos, insurance? What's this all about?"

"I want to see the logbooks for Karadimos's plane."

"What are you trying to pull?"

"Nothing. I'm an insurance investigator, doing my job."

"What kind of horseshit are you feeding me, anyway?

"Look, Mr. Vogel... May I call you Fred?" I'd try the friendly approach, first name basis. Always works. Turn on the old charm and smile. "I really need to check the flight logs."

He stubbed his cigarette out in a rusty piston sitting upside down on his desk, and stood. "Listen to me, Mac. I don't know who you are. I don't give a damn what you want. Just get the hell outta here."

So much for the charm. "OK, the name's O'Brien. I have to see about a flight that Karadimos took to Sacramento."

Vogel picked up the Marlboro box, opened it, and fiddled inside it with his finger. "This is about the girl's murder, ain't it?"

"Yeah," I said. "How'd you know?"

"Word gets around." He dropped the empty red and white box on his desk and with one swift stroke smashed it like a bug. "You're not a cop or you would've shown me your buzzer right off the bat. Besides, the cops were already here. You a lawyer or something?"

"Yeah, I'm defending an innocent man."

"Why should I help you? I already told you the cops have been here. They checked the logbook to see if the plane flew back that Saturday. No flight was made on that day." He patted his shirt pocket a few times, the one under his nametag.

"I want to check it myself."

"You got a cigarette?"

"No."

"You want to see the logs, go get a court order. Now beat it. I'm busy."

I could issue a subpoena, but Karadimos would find out. Records could be changed and the logbook could disappear.

"Listen, Fred, a subpoena would take time." I laid a twenty on his desk. "I'd have to pay a filing fee. Why should the county get another fee?"

He looked down at the double sawbuck for about a nanosecond. His hand shot out like Wyatt Earp drawing down on the Clantons. The bill was gone without a trace. Thank God for the horserace Saturday. I had a little cash to spread around.

"Yeah, the bastards will nickel and dime you to death," he said.

Fred pulled a leather-bound binder from a bookcase behind him. Spreading it out on his desk, he flipped through the pages.

"Here it is." He ran his finger down a column. I glanced over his shoulder. "See, the jet left LGB a week ago last Friday. Flew directly to SAC. Total time from engines start until shutdown is recorded."

He took a pencil and paper out of the drawer and began to figure. "One-point-one hours, that's okay. The Citation cruises at four hundred-twenty miles per hour, Sacramento is about four hundred miles away, lets see...climb out...landing. Yeah that's it." Vogel kept working the numbers on the paper. "Returned Sunday, point-nine hours...a little tail wind. Total time two hours."

"No flights on Saturday?"

"None–you sure you don't have a smoke?"

"I quit," I said. "Was there only one pilot on this flight? No copilot?"

"Nope, no copilot. That's the good thing about the Cessna Citation. The plane's single-pilot rated."

"What if the pilot didn't log the flight?" I asked.

"That's against the rules. It would be a federal violation."

"Yeah, I guess a murderer wouldn't want to piss off the FAA. Could get in big trouble." I shook my head. "How do you check to make sure that all flights are logged?"

A smirk surfaced on his face. "The hours on the Hobbs Meter in the plane wouldn't match the hours in the logbook." His tone was sarcastic. "I know what you're thinking, but the cops checked that too. Sorry, pal."

"The Hobbs Meter is some kind of hour meter, records the time of the flight, right?"

"Yep."

"Could someone monkey with it? Change the time?" It

didn't seem to me that unhooking an hour meter would be a big deal. Used car dealers unhooked and rolled back odometers all the time.

"Look, O'Brien, your twenty-dollar service fee didn't entitle you to my time for the rest of the day. Now be a nice guy and take a powder."

"Vogel, my ass is on the line. Now, goddammit, couldn't someone just roll back the meter?"

"I guess they could. If they knew what they were doing. Yeah, it's possible." He thought for a few seconds. "Wouldn't work though–there's an additional Hobbs Meter on the plane, hidden."

"What do you mean, hidden?"

He sat down, folded his hands on the desk. "Karadimos has the plane on lease-back to us, means we can rent the jet out by the hour. We rent it to various charter companies, split the profit from these flights with the owner, Karadimos. We installed the other meter to keep these charter boys honest. Nobody's cheated yet."

"Did you check the secret meter after the Sacramento flight?"

"No, of course not. We don't check the meter after the owner uses the plane. He's not renting it. He owns it," Vogel said.

"Let's check it; can't hurt."

"I told you I'm busy. Now get the hell outta here." He started to climb out of his chair.

I laid another twenty on the desk.

His eyes focused on the bill for a moment before he ripped it from the desk. Then in a flash, he opened a drawer, took out a flashlight, a note pad and a screwdriver.

"Wait here." He darted out of his office.

I watched him through the glass window. He rushed to the starboard side of a blue and white Cessna Citation and with the screwdriver, he popped open a little trap door under the wing, bent over, peered inside, and wrote on the pad. He was back in the office in less than three minutes.

"Okay, sport," he said. "I think it's a waste of time, but it's your nickel."

He ran his finger down the open page of the book and stopped at the last entry. I peered over his shoulder again.

"One thousand-sixty-seven hours, total time on the plane." He glanced at the paper in his other hand. His jaw dropped. He looked up at me. "One thousand-sixty-nine hours," he said. "Two hours. I'll be damned. Two hours not logged."

We stared at each other. Vogel scratched the back of his head. I thought about the extra two hours, the exact time of a round trip to Sacramento. It would be an awfully big coincidence if the plane flew exactly two hours, off the books, on any other day than the Saturday of the murder. "When was the last time the logbook and the hidden meter matched?"

Vogel dashed to the gray metal cabinet next to the bookcase and pulled out a file.

"The weekend before the Sacramento flight. I remember that particular charter. Had to stock the plane with extra booze. The group was a bunch of Mormons flying to Cedar City, Utah for a family reunion."

"Any flights after that?" I asked.

He was a little more humble and I was a whole lot more elated.

"No... Guess not."

"Who's the pilot? And where can I find him."

Vogel glanced at the book. "He's not one of ours. Works full time for Karadimos, but we keep copies of the licenses of all the pilots who fly out of here."

He looked at me and laughed. "You should know about that. It's an insurance regulation, *Mr. Biddle*."

I don't know why, but I laughed too. "What's the pilot's name?"

"Ron Fischer. I'll you get his address and phone

number."

I left the hangar and ran to my car. It took me five minutes to find a payphone that worked. I didn't want to use the telephone in Executive Aviation's lobby; too many eavesdropping ears. There was a phone booth at the Union Oil gas station on the corner of Lakewood and Spring Street. The door wouldn't close, and the booth was filthy, sticky stuff on the handle and fast-food wrappers scattered about. But I got a dial tone when I picked up the receiver. I put a dime in the slot and dialed Fischer's number. An operator came on and told me to deposit another nickel. I did, and asked the operator to stay on the line. I wanted to make another call if no one answered. After six rings, I gave the operator my office number. Rita answered on the first ring.

"Oh Boss, I'm glad you called. We've got trouble." She sounded frantic.

"What's the matter?"

"Someone broke in here, probably during the night. Whoever it was trashed the office. It's a mess. Papers and stuff tossed everywhere. Jimmy, someone went to a lot of trouble. Who'd do such a thing?"

I immediately thought of Karadimos and his thugs. But maybe I was getting a little paranoid. Could've been anybody: kids looking for a couple of bucks, a burglar, or some guy down on his luck, trying to made a living the hard way.

"Did you call the police?" I asked Rita.

"No, I was waiting for you to call. And there's some big fat guy here. He's sitting at your desk. His name's Jake, says he knows you. He's kinda scary."

Big Jake? Oh Christ, you'd think they would've told me ahead of time that he'd be coming to the office. This could be a problem. "Jake's okay. He's on our side," I said with a sigh.

"Do you want me to call the police about the break-in?"

"Did they take anything, the typewriter, stuff like that?"

After a short pause, she said, "Who'd want to take this junk?"

"Yeah, you're right."

"Just the file on your desk."

"What are you taking about?"

"The only thing missing."

"What! The Rodriguez file is gone?"

"I was going to file it away for you, but now it's gone."

"Don't call the police and don't clean up yet. I'll be at the office in twenty-five minutes." The file hadn't really held much–police report, crime scene pictures, and some notes I'd jotted down, my thoughts about the case, but Karadimos didn't know that...until now.

My heart sank when I saw the mess. Everything broken, destroyed. I tiptoed through the junk, stopping once to pick up a framed photo of the old 1951 Los Angeles Angels minor league baseball team. The frame was shattered and the autographed picture had been torn. Maybe I could glue it back together somehow. My dad had given me the picture on my thirteenth birthday along with a cap and jacket. It wasn't much, but it's about all I had to remember him by.

Rita wasn't at her desk, but Big Jake stood by the window, looking out. "Hi Jake, big mess, huh? Where's Rita?"

"I sent her for some donuts and a bottle of Jack Daniels."

"How long ago did she leave?"

He wore a blank look on his face. "'Bout fifteen minutes ago. When your visitors came. I didn't want her around while they were here. She's a foxy little babe."

"What visitors?"

"A couple bruisers. Karadimos sent them here to discuss a few things with you. They mistook me for you. Imagine that."

A knot formed in my stomach. "What'd they say?"

"Not much. I explained to them who I was and what I'm doing here."

"Then they took off? Just left?"

"Yeah, they were in a hurry. The guy that could still walk had to get the other guy to the hospital, fast."

"Jesus, you beat them up?" I said. "Two of 'em?" I looked at Jake. *Christ*, there wasn't a mark on him.

"I told you, I had to explain to them guys who I am. Don't think they'll be back."

He pointed his thumb over his shoulder to my inner office. "There's a little blood in there. Couldn't be helped."

I moved toward the office door, but stopped. "Hey Jake, did the visitors say anything about the break-in? They must have noticed the mess."

"They didn't have no time to notice nothin' but my fists."

This wasn't the random act of vandalism that it was supposed to be. When Rita told me that the only thing missing was the Rodriguez file, I thought I knew who had sent the thugs. But why would Karadimos send thugs to scare me off the case during business hours, if he'd sent them to trash the office during the night? Could someone else also want me off the Rodriguez case?

Chapter Twenty-One

Rita had returned and tried to create some order out of the chaos. Jake sat at my desk while I rummaged through the debris looking for the checkbook and my old tax returns. I'd carefully put the torn baseball picture in my car. I didn't care about the rest of the stuff.

I gave some money to Rita. "Go over to the All American Home Center and buy a rake, the kind you use for leaves, and rake up this trash and toss it. Okay?"

She stood with her hands on her hips. A little lock of hair–a curl–slipped down on her forehead. She looked cute as she glanced around the room. "Yeah Boss, we can start all over. Your filing system was no good anyway."

"When you leave, call Mabel at the service. Ask her to take the calls. I'm going out with Big Jake. We've got to talk."

"Do you don't think whoever did this will come back?"

"Nah, they got what they wanted. They won't be back."

I told her she could have the rest of the day off after she got rid of the junk. "Thanks Jimmy, but I'll stay and tidy up a bit before I leave."

Jake moseyed out of my office. "Hey, O'Brien, gonna gab all day? I want to chow down. Let's go."

The four-hundred-pound muscle machine needed fuel but I had a lot to do and really didn't want to go to lunch. However, I needed to talk to him about our deal. He suggested Marmac's, the prime rib joint on Florence, behind the Union Oil gas station. I agreed, but insisted on separate cars. I left and Jake followed close behind.

A banner hung across the front: *Marmac's. All You Can Eat Buffet–Prime Rib–$3.95.* I pulled into the parking lot and Jake pulled in next to me. We walked in together.

Inside, patrons formed a swarming, slipshod line in the hallway leading to the dining room. The line led to the buffet station and it grew longer by the minute. Customers picked out their food cafeteria style before passing into the dining room. By noon this place would be packed.

"Coming through. Get outta the way. Hey pal, move it." People stepped aside as Jake pushed past the line into the dining room. I followed in his wake.

We moved to a roped-off area and sat at a table reserved for eight customers. One of the roving cocktail waitresses, dressed in a plain black skirt and white blouse, spotted us. She rushed to our table.

"Hey, guys, you can't sit here. This area is closed. You'll have to move."

"Sweetheart, bring me a double Jack Daniels on the rocks, tall glass. What do you want, O'Brien?"

"Now wait a minute. sir!"

"Coke," I said.

A $20 bill appeared in Jake's hand. He waved it in front of the waitress's face.

"Well *helloooo*, Mr. Jackson." She snatched the cash. "Yes sir, double Daniels on the rocks and a Coke." Her teeth flashed. "Now what else can I get for you fine gentlemen?"

"After you get the drinks, get me a big plate of beef, rare, extra portion." Jake gestured in my direction. "You gonna eat, O'Brien?"

"I had a late breakfast." I lied about that, but I couldn't eat with Jake. Thinking about how he wolfed down the donuts killed my appetite.

The waitress did a little curtsy and left to get the order.

"We've got to talk," I said.

"So talk."

"No offense, but you can't hang around me all the time."

"Say it like it is. You don't like us, don't like what we do, and you'd get a bum rap hanging with wise guys."

"Yeah, my credibility would suffer. I can't be seen with

you all the time. It wouldn't look right to certain people for me to be constantly seen in your company."

"Change of plans, gotta clear it with Joe."

"Talk to Joe, okay?"

"I'll call him right now. Watch my food when it comes."

Like someone would steal *this* guy's food. "Sure, I'll watch it."

He left to find a pay phone. While he was gone, the waitress brought the order. Jake's plate was heaped with slabs of semi-raw meat. The sauce dripped over the edge, creating a rust-colored stain on the white tablecloth.

Jake soon returned, grabbed a fork and a small butcher knife. He hacked off a couple hunks of meat and shoved them in his mouth. He chewed, swallowed, and started to cut off another big piece.

"Here's the deal," he said. "Two things. First, we're doing Silverman a favor protecting you." He talked and ate at the same time. He finished chewing, grabbed the drink, and downed half the glass. "Second, you do your job, maybe Karadimos will be outta business."

"That's right, I think—"

"Hear me out," he shouted, his mouth half full of rare prime rib.

"Okay, sorry."

He looked at me sideways and set the cutlery down with a bang. "So anyway, we're not going to get in your way..." He tossed back the rest of the Jack Daniels.

"Good, and if I need you I'll call—"

He swallowed. "You don't call *nobody*, goddammit."

"Okay, I won't call."

"I ain't gonna hang around all the time no more. I ain't no lousy bodyguard, but when it gets serious, I'll be there. He lowered his voice. "And believe me; you'll be glad I came."

He leaned back and belched.

Chapter Twenty-Two

We left the restaurant. I said goodbye to Jake in the parking lot. He grunted something. We each got into our cars and drove off. I headed east on Florence. Jake followed for a couple of blocks. I didn't see his Caddie in my rearview mirror when I turned right on Woodruff Avenue.

Karadimos's pilot, Ron Fischer, lived on Newville Ave. in a two-story apartment building. The street was lined on both sides with pastel stucco, box-like structures dating back to World War II. The building that Fischer lived in had splotches of gray plaster showing through its pink color. It looked like somebody had painted the building with strawberry Kool Aid, one coat.

After parking at the curb in front, I climbed the outside stairway and walked along a railed balcony to unit 6. I rapped on the door, no answer, knocked again but still nothing.

I went down the stairs and walked to a rickety carport in the back. The parking area was divided into sections with numbers. Parked in stall number 6 was a dirty, white El Camino. Two other cars were parked in the carport, a beat-up red Pinto with no hubcaps, and a twenty-year-old Ford station wagon.

I found the manager's unit and knocked. A drowsy old guy opened the door. "You here about the apartment? It's rented." He started to shut the door.

"No, wait," I said. "I'm looking for Ron Fischer."

He held the door half open and looked at me with red-rimmed eyes.

"His car is back there." I nodded my head toward the parking area. "But he doesn't answer his door."

"Yeah, so what?"

The old guy's TV blared inside, a soap opera. "I need to find him."

"What's this about?"

"Official business."

He scratched his rib cage. "You some kind of bill collector?"

"No, I just want to know if you've seen him around."

"Hey fella, I mind my own business. As long as they pay the rent and don't cause a ruckus." The manger closed the door.

"Mister, you looking for Ronnie?" a hushed female voice asked.

I turned. A twenty-something woman with dyed blond hair stood before me. The dye job needed a retouch. "Yes, I am. Do you know him?" She had a dynamite figure, but a rather plain face. A trip to the dermatologist would help.

"We're kinda friends," she said.

"Have you seen him lately?"

"No, and I'm worried. I haven't seen him for about a week."

"He's a charter pilot," I said. "Maybe he's on a flight."

"I don't think so. I have a key to his apartment..." She paused. Her eyes seemed to focus on something faraway. After a moment she continued: "He always takes his flight case when he's on a charter. It's still here."

"You two are pretty close, huh?"

"Sorta. We go out sometimes."

"When was the last time you saw him?"

"Last Monday, or maybe it was Tuesday, I dunno." She held up a blue bag, which had the words *dirty duds* stenciled on it. "I was going to the Laundromat. I do his wash too. What are friends for, huh?" She glanced down.

"You do his laundry?" I wanted to keep her talking.

"Yeah, it's no big deal."

"Sure, no big deal."

"Last week I went to his apartment to get his stuff.

Ronnie rushed outside and left. He walked right by me, didn't even say goodbye."

"Where'd he go?"

"Got in a cab and took off."

"You don't know where he was headed?"

She glanced at her open-toed sandals. A moment later she looked up at me. Her mouth quivered. "No, I don't know where he went. But I think something's wrong."

I glanced at a monarch butterfly, its wings doing a slow flutter as it rested on the flower box in the window of the apartment next door. I didn't tell the girl I also thought something was wrong, very wrong.

"Two guys came looking for him later that day," she said.

My head snapped back to her face. "Two guys? Do you know who they were? Seen them before?"

"No, but they were mean lookin'. One guy had a jagged scar on his face, you know, like he'd been in a knife fight. And the other guy...he was mean too. I could tell."

"Maybe they were cops?"

"No way. I'm a...ah...modern dancer at the Kozy Kitty on Pioneer Boulevard. I know cops when I see them. They're our best customers."

So she was a stripper. She had the body for it, that's for sure.

"Did you file a missing person report?" I asked.

"No, Ronnie wouldn't want the cops looking for him." She hesitated a moment then continued. "He's been in trouble before. It's behind him now, but he's got a thing about cops."

"Do you have a picture of him? Might help me find him."

"He had a thing about having his picture taken, too. One time I brought a Polaroid camera with us when we..." She shook her head. "No, I don't have any."

I gave her my card—the real one, not George Biddle's—and asked her to call me if he turned up. I told her I was working on a case and Fischer was a witness. She didn't ask and I didn't tell her what the case was about. She gave me her number, said her name was Tracy, and asked me to call her if I found out anything about him. I said that I would.

I hurried back to my office to make some calls. When I arrived, Rita was gone and the place was clean. Everything was put away and the office seemed to be in order. She'd done the best she could on the bloodstains in my office, but I could still see a few rust-colored spots on the carpet.

Picking up the receiver, I remembered the warning Sol had given me about the phones being tapped. I set it back down.

It was almost two o'clock and I hadn't eaten all day. Foxy's on Third St. had a good hamburger and the place was spotless. I'd grab a bite at the coffee shop and make my calls from their pay phone.

I drove to the restaurant, entered, and sat at the counter. The waitress arrived and I ordered a burger and fries, then went to the pay phone.

"Joyce, I've got to talk to Sol. It's important."

"He's not in," Joyce said. "But I can get him a message."

"Tell him I'm at Foxy's here in Downey. I'll wait for his phone call."

I went back to the counter and polished off my meal. Helen brought me another cup of coffee. While waiting for Sol to call, I wrote facts about the case on a paper napkin.

Fact one: Welch was having an affair with the victim. Fact two: the plane was flown back on the day of the murder. Fact three: Welch pressured Judge Johnson to wrap up the case. I looked at what I had written and reflected on it. One problem: Welch had a hundred or so witnesses who were with him in Sacramento at the time of the murder. Another thing: why was Karadimos pushing me so hard to stop the investigation? If Welch were guilty, why wouldn't Karadimos just drop the Senator from his payroll and replace him with the next stooge that came along? Karadimos would know if

Welch were guilty. After all, it would've been his pilot, Ron Fischer, who flew him back to Southern California that day.

The waitress interrupted my thoughts. "Jimmy, you have a call. You can take it in the office."

"Thanks," I said.

I picked up the phone receiver resting on top of a small stack of invoices scattered across the desk. Sol said, "Jimmy, my boy, got a pencil?"

"Yeah."

"Here's the phone number for that *shiksa* you're so hot for." He gave me Bobbi Allen's home number. I wrote it on the back of one of my business cards.

Thanks, Sol, but–"

"Jimmy, gotta go. Having lunch with a *macher*. Tell you about it later."

"Wait. That's not why I asked you to call."

"You want more favors? You want I should call her for you?"

"No, this is about the case." I told Sol about the jet. How it had been flown the extra two hours without being logged. And I related my discussion with Tracy, the pilot's girlfriend.

"I think you're on to something. Something big," Sol said.

"We need to run a skip-trace on Fischer. I want to call him as a hostile witness."

"How do you know he flew the jet back here? He could've flown the plane anywhere. Isn't it rule number one, never put a witness on the stand and ask him a question that you don't know the answer he'll give?"

"It's too big of a coincidence, the exact flight time, and if it were an innocent flight Fischer would have logged it."

"He'd lie on the stand, wouldn't he?" Sol asked.

"Sure he'll lie. But when he does, I'll make him eat his words. Make him look like a lying bastard. When I'm finished with him, the jury will know the truth."

"Aren't we a mite self-assured, a little egotistical today?"

"Sol, you find the guy. I'll nail him."

"How long do we have?"

"Not long, today's Monday. The preliminary hearing is scheduled for Thursday morning.

"Not much time to find a guy who doesn't want to be found."

"I need to show a strong alternative to the DA's theory. They still won't drop Rodriguez as a suspect, but maybe they'll grant bail. I might be able to get him out on his own recognizance, no bail money. I gotta get Rodriguez out of jail." A horrible thought crossed my mind. "Sol, listen. If something happens to Rodriguez while he's in custody, if he somehow should happen to die, the DA would close the Gloria Graham murder case. It'd be all over. Welch and Karadimos would be off the hook."

"Yeah, a *mamzer* like Karadimos could have it carried out, jail or no jail. It's the easiest place on the planet to whack someone. A shiv in the back, it's over. The hit man's wife or girlfriend gets an unexpected deposit in her bank account. Yeah, I'd better get my guys looking for Fischer right away," Sol said.

"One more thing."

"Shoot."

"Can you get someone to sweep my office for bugs and check the phone as well?"

"I told you your place is bugged, but you wouldn't listen."

"Sol, please, just sent someone. Okay?"

"I'll send a sweeper right away, but it might be too late. The barn door and all that."

I left Foxy's and raced back to my office. Sol's electronics guy wasn't there yet and I didn't want to use the phone even to check my messages. I decided to make some coffee and wait.

When Rita went to the All American Home Center to get the rake, she also bought a new coffeepot. The old one had been smashed during the break-in. I didn't care; it was beat up and shabby. The one she bought looked sharp, kind of space age with a lot of dials and stuff. It was the newest automatic type that I'd seen on TV. But I didn't have the foggiest notion how to work the thing. I figured there must be an instruction book around here somewhere. After looking in a couple of desk drawers, I asked myself where I'd put the book if I were Rita. I went to the filing cabinet, opened the drawer, and sure enough, inside was only one file, labeled–*Pot, Coffee, Book*!

I fiddled around trying to hook up the high-tech gizmo, and was just about to give up when a small guy who looked about seventeen opened the door and walked in. I started to say hello, but he put a finger to his lips. "Shh. . ." he whispered.

"Sol sent you?" I whispered back.

He nodded his head.

Before the guy started searching the place, I asked in a low voice if he knew how to hook up a coffeepot. He glanced at it and shook his head. "Nah, I wouldn't waste my time on that piece of crap."

I'd stop for coffee later at Dolan's Donuts.

The kid wandered around carrying a device shaped like a large plastic wishbone. The arms were about ten inches long, and the handle was like a tennis racket but it had small lights and knobs on it. He walked around the place, holding the gadget in front of him, waving it up and down as if it were a divining rod and he had come looking for water. When he finished checking both offices and the restroom, he gestured for me to meet him outside.

"Yep, the place is hot. I haven't checked the phones yet, but they're probably hot too."

"Can you remove the bugs?" I asked.

"Sure, only take a few minutes."

We walked back into the office, where he took some tools out of his pocket, removed the plate covering the light switch, cut a wire, and pulled out a device about half the size of a pack of cigarettes.

"Wow," he said, his eyes bulging. "Look at this transmitter, isn't she sweet? See how small she is? This is the newest technology, very expensive. She'll broadcast on an FM frequency over five hundred yards. Can I keep her?"

"Yeah, why not." I wondered why he referred to a listening device using the female pronoun.

"Great! I'll check the phone connection box, outside. I'm sure they'll be another beauty like this one wired to the main line."

As soon as the sweeper left, I dialed my answering service. "Mabel, this is O'Brien. Any messages?"

"Yeah, the usual."

"Read them, okay?"

"My assistant took the messages while I was out. Left them around here someplace. Hang on." A few seconds later she came back on the line. "Okay, here's the first one. It says, 'Mr. O'Brien, please call me. Your car insurance is due. Signed, George Biddle.' Next: 'O'Brien, you're a dead man.' The third one is from a print shop. They've got a special this week–"

"What?"

"They got a special this week, you know, on printing... Wait a minute!" Mabel paused. "Oh, my God! The second one says, 'O'Brien, you're a dead man.' It's not signed. What the hell is this? You really must have pissed someone off."

"Must be a joke." I slowly hung up the phone. Karadimos had a special this week, too. Dead lawyers, a dime a dozen.

Chapter Twenty-Three

I didn't sleep well Monday night. I rolled around in tangled sheets and woke up about a dozen times. Finally giving up, I got out of bed at five, showered and shaved, and landed at Denny's Coffee Shop at 5:30. I ordered coffee and some eggs. Dawdling over the *Times*, I read it cover to cover. By seven I'd finished the paper, even the want ads, and set it aside. I couldn't get Welch out of my mind. It would do no good to phone his office again. I knew he wouldn't return my call, but what I really needed was a face-to-face meeting. I wanted to look him in the eyes when I asked him a few questions. I felt I'd know a lie when I heard one. But how would I get him to agree to a sit-down, when I couldn't even convince him to talk to me on the phone?

Finishing the last of my coffee–my fifth cup–I happened to glance out the large plate glass window at the front of the coffee shop overlooking the parking lot. I noticed a guy wearing a black leather overcoat walking toward my Corvette. He stood beside my car for a moment. Then with one swift motion, he pulled a baseball bat from under his coat and smashed the driver's side passenger window. He tossed something in through the opening then ran to a car that waited for him. The car, a dark blue Buick, sped away.

I shot outside, instinctively raced around the lot and ran halfway down the block. Of course, the guy was long gone.

I dragged myself back to the Vette. An envelope rested on the front seat among the dime-size chunks of glass.

I pulled it out and ripped it open. Inside was a handwritten note*: Quit the case NOW! Or I'll use this bat on your head instead of the window. We can get to you anytime. Don't think Sica's men are going to protect you. Big Jake won't always be there to cover your back.*

A moment later, Big Jake's Caddie rolled to a stop next to me. With a cigarette dangling from his mouth, he stuck his head out the car window and appraised the damage. "You see who done it?" he asked.

"Yeah, a big guy, six-one, six-two, lots of dark wavy hair, a scar on his face."

"Sounds like Angelo, one of Karadimos's best persuaders. He's only gonna send his primo guys from now on, now that they think I'm on the job."

"You know the guy?"

""Yeah, he's one of the ratfink *soldatos* that left Buscetta and joined up with that fat Greek."

"I thought you were going to cover my ass!"

"You told me to take a powder, not hang around. Anyway, you're in one piece, ain't ya? So, what's the problem?"

It wouldn't do me any good to get hot; the damage was done. Besides, I did more or less tell Jake to stay away, which might have been a little hasty. "Want some breakfast?" I asked, angling my head toward the coffee shop.

"Thought you didn't want to be seen with me, too low down for you."

"No...not really, Jake. What I meant–"

"What I heard 'bout you lawyers is true."

"Yeah, what?"

"Full of bullshit."

I sighed. "Yeah, guess so."

"Get in the car," he said.

I climbed into the passenger seat. "Maybe I made a mistake about you, Jake...ah... about not sticking close by."

Jake's massive hands gripped the steering wheel, squeezing and twisting the rim as he gazed out the front windshield. "I gotta keep outta sight. Joe wants it that way. You won't see me until I show up. No one will. Cops, Karadimos's torpedoes, nobody. I'll be invisible, but I'll be there."

It was hard to imagine a guy like Big Jake invisible. He'd be impossible to miss. He'd stand out like a dancing elephant among a bunch of scurrying field mice.

"Thanks Jake, I appreciate your help, and I don't dislike you, I–"

"O'Brien, let's get this straight. I don't give a shit what you *appreciate*, and I don't give a shit if you like me or not. Most people don't. I gotta job to do, that's all. Let's leave it at that."

I looked at Jake for a long moment, the ugly grimace on his face, and wondered about him. Did he have emotions–fears, highs and lows like the rest of us? Or was his life one deep, black pit of hostility? How did someone become so devoid of moral sensitivity? Was it a handicap to have a soul when one belonged to the mob? Or was it a benefit? He continued to stare out at the parking lot, at the people giving him dirty looks as they walked around his car blocking their path to the coffee shop."

"Jake, how is this supposed to work?" I asked.

Without turning his head toward me, he said, "Told ya before. You do your thing, I'll do mine. I'll be there when I'm needed."

"You think Karadimos and his gang would really use deadly force to stop me? Or are they just trying to scare me off?"

He wiggled his chunky fingers in a *gimme* manner. Jake had more muscles in his fingers that I had in my whole body. "Lemme see the note, the one you got from Angelo."

I pulled the paper out of my pocket and gave it to him. I had a newfound respect for Jake's erudition. He read it without moving his lips.

"Yep, they'll kill ya all right, if you don't stop messing with their shit." He spoke without a trace of emotion in his voice.

"Are you serious?"

"Dead serious. But, I'll stop 'em. I'm not sure why, but

136

Joe wants to keep you alive, for a while anyway."

"Suppose I can't bring Karadimos down. What's Sica going to do about him?"

Anger flashed from Jake like a spark from an electrical short. "Keep your trap shut. You got no lines. You ask no questions, goddammit!" He moved in closer. "I'll say it again, *don't ask questions*." His face looked like a big red balloon ready to burst.

"I'm not going ask any questions. Like you said, you do your thing, and I'll do mine."

"Okay, O'Brien, I gotta get outta here. Don't call the cops about the car. Don't want the bastards snooping around. They'd get in my way."

At eight-thirty I went back to my Corvette, cleaned up the glass, and set out for the office. Jake said he would follow me at a safe distance. He wanted to lay back and see if I was being shadowed by any of Karadimos's heavy artillery.

Although I couldn't kid myself about why Jake was trying to protect me, I knew it was a lot healthier having him around. But I also knew I was just a guy caught in the middle of the local Mafia and their new rivals. Things could change and I knew I was as useless and expendable as the Nehru jacket hanging in my closet.

Chapter Twenty-Four

When I arrived back at the office, Rita had the new coffeemaker assembled and plugged in. "Hey Boss, did you see the new coffeepot? It's the latest kind."

"Yeah, it's super," I said. "Do you think you can figure out how to make coffee with the thing?"

"Of course, a child could make a great cup with this pot," she said as she scooped Yuban into the machine.

"Oh."

"By the way, Joyce called. She said she has some more information about a company called Hartford something. She wants you to call her back. I'll get her on the line if you want."

"You work the coffeepot. I'll call her myself."

I remembered what Joyce told me about Hartford Commodities, the company that leased the Buick that had tailed me for a couple of days.

I picked up the phone and dialed. "Joyce, it's me, O'Brien. Rita said you have some information."

"It came this morning," Joyce said. "Hartford Commodities, remember? Controlled by Triple A Holdings, Incorporated?"

"Sure, I remember. Triple A is the offshore corporation. Have you found out who the real owners are?"

"No, but they use Mutual Trust as their correspondent bank. Mutual is headquartered in Los Angeles. But here's the important part: Thomas French, an attorney here in Downey, has fiduciary control over Triple A's accounts. He handles all the transactions, including signing checks," Joyce said. "There's more. French also sits on the board of the Bank. Do you know this guy?"

Yeah, I knew French: Welch's lawyer, the guy who gave

me the brush-off. "I don't know him personally, Joyce. But I know who he is." I paused and thought for a second. "What kind of business is Hartford, anyway? What do they do?"

"It's a produce company, started after the war by a guy named Sam Higgins. They import cantaloupes from Mexico. That sort of thing."

"From Mexico?"

"Yes, but Hartford was sold to Triple A shortly after Higgins died a few years back. The documents relating to the Higgins estate and the company's sale are missing. The secretary of state's office is in the process of logging all their files into a computer. The missing documents will eventually show up. And when they do, I'll call you."

"How long will that take?"

"A few months, at most."

"Oh."

"Jimmy, if it's important, Sol can assign an investigator to check out the company using the shoe leather approach."

"What's that?"

"You know, snoop around, go to the last known address, ask questions. Detective work, a real investigation. I just tapped into the records, had a friend in Sacramento pull the file."

"Better wait on that, Joyce. I'll talk to Sol first. By the way, did you find out anything yet about Fischer, the pilot?"

"No, sorry. It's still early, but Sol has a couple of our best men working full time on it. I'll call you soon as we get anything."

I hung up, leaned back in my chair and reflected on the news, trying to make sense out of it. The connections: Gloria Graham/Welch/Karadimos, and now French. The Saturday flight, not logged. Welch's pressure on Johnson—Karadimos's pressure on me. What about the bank? Cantaloupes from Mexico, Joyce said. What was I missing? I shook my head and tried to clear my mind; nothing came.

I remembered a guy from years back, a guy who might

know something. I put my feet on the floor and reached for the phone.

While a cop, I worked out of the Newton Street precinct of the LAPD, which covered the produce district located between Seventh Street and Olympic Avenue. I'd made friends with some of the brokers and dealers who did business there. I looked at my watch: 10:30 a.m., a little late in the day for these people to be working. They usually started at around two in the morning and quit when their delivery trucks returned before ten. But one old guy, Barney Corby, a melon broker, always stayed late. He was like the proverbial little old lady, knew all the gossip in the neighborhood and didn't mind spreading it around.

The information operator rattled off Barney's phone number and I dialed it. When he answered, I said, "Hi, Barn. Jimmy O'Brien. You're still working late, I see."

"Jimmy, great to hear from you. Yeah, but I don't come in so early anymore. Getting up there, you know. I'll be eighty-four next month."

We talked a bit about the old times and discussed getting together for lunch one of these days. But he didn't seem too excited about the idea after I told him I'd quit drinking.

"Maybe you can help me, Barney. I'm working on a case and the name Hartford Commodities came up, a produce outfit. You know the company?"

"Hartford, sure I know them. Used to have a packing shed down on Terminal Ave."

"You said, *used to*. They're not there anymore?" I asked.

"They closed up. Moved out. Still have their shipping rights and a telephone number, but no trucks, or customers. It's a dummy corporation."

"What do you mean?"

"Just a shell. Very strange. When I called the old phone number, it referred me to their new number. I called because I had a customer for them."

"What did they say?"

"Nothing, *nada*. They had one of those newfangled answer machines, some kind of a tape recorder. Left several messages. I think I did it right… But anyway, I never heard back."

"Maybe they were busy," I said.

"Maybe the trustees don't give a damn about new business."

"Trustees? Is the company in bankruptcy or something?"

"No, it's held in trust. Some kind of offshore corporation owns the company now."

"When was it sold?"

"It's been a few years. A real hush-hush deal. But I used to do a lot of business with Hartford before the old man died and left it to his stepson. He ran it into the ground, never worked the business. Fooled around with chippies, then got involved in politics."

"Politics?"

"Yeah, didn't I mention it? The old man who started the company was Senator Berry Welch's stepfather."

Chapter Twenty-Five

Shortly after I got off the phone with Barney, Rita came in with a steaming mug. "Hope it's okay," she said.

The last thing I needed at that moment was a caffeine kick. After what Barney had said my heart was beating a mile a minute, but I figured one sip wouldn't kill me. I put the cup to my lips and tasted the coffee. "Wow," I said. "This is the best cup of coffee you've ever made." I wasn't kidding, it was that good.

She beamed. "Thanks, Boss. It's the new pot. Hard to make a bad cup with it. Has a timer on the thing, goes on and off automatically. What will they think of next?"

Don't know, Rita."

"Maybe a computer to replace lawyers."

"Think so?"

She winked. "It won't have your blue eyes, though. I'll miss that."

"Aw, Rita..."

"Sorry about your car window."

Earlier I'd told her kids playing baseball broke the window. I didn't like telling her white lies, but didn't want her to worry. "I'm not one to mope."

"Can you give me a minute, Jimmy? There's something we should discuss."

I grabbed the phone, and started to dial. "Sure, Rita," I said. "But first I have to talk to Sol. The case is starting to heat up. I'll come out and talk after this call, okay?"

She turned and I watched the sway of her hips as she gracefully left the room. I finished dialing, and Sol came on the line.

"Hi, Jimmy. I'm just walking out the door."

"Sol, I just found out something important."

"Okay, meet me at Rio Hondo. I've got a tee off time in forty-five minutes. I'll be on the practice green. I have news, too. We can talk while I warm up."

"Why can't we talk on the phone?"

"See you in ten minutes." He hung up.

As I rushed past Rita's desk, she looked at me and started to say something, but I kept going. When I climbed in the driver's seat of my Corvette I remembered she wanted to talk to me about something. I made a mental note to call her from the clubhouse at the golf course.

As I drove, I let the facts of the case rattle around in my brain. I wondered about Welch's old company being sold to a trust controlled by an offshore corporation. Was Welch still involved? If so, what was he trying to hide? Maybe he didn't want the government to see the company books. Could this whole thing be some kind of elaborate tax dodge? A tax dodge wouldn't have henchmen in a Buick shadowing me, though. No, there was more to it than a simple accounting matter.

I turned into the Rio Hondo Country Club parking lot, killed the engine, and walked into the pro shop. The guy there said Sol was already on the practice green. I saw him through the window. He had on a yellow alpaca sweater, bright blue slacks with white shoes, and was crouched on his haunches holding a metal rod of some sort. One end of the three-foot-long rod rested on the grass, and he held the other end about two feet off the ground.

When I walked over to him, he was rolling golf balls down the groove in the inclined rod. "Hey Sol, what's that thing?"

He glanced up, didn't say anything, then looked down at the ball as it rolled to a stop about ten feet from the end of the rod.

"Sol, what the hell are you doing? Is that the way you putt, roll a ball down a piece of steel?"

"It's aluminum, a Stimpmeter. Had it made special. I use

143

it to check the speed of the greens. Someday all the golf courses will have one, but..." He took a tape measure out of his pocket and measured the distance the ball had traveled. "Hmm...nine feet, two inches, pretty fast."

Nothing Sol did surprised me anymore. "Does that help your game?"

"I'm playing your old friend, Judge Johnson today. I'll need all the help I can get. He's good and he cheats on his handicap."

"Yeah, he used to cheat a lot when we were on the job together. Mostly on his wife."

"I gotta put this thing away before he sees it." Sol said, indicating the aluminum rod. "Don't want him stealing my secrets. C'mon, we'll talk on the way to my car."

As we walked back to the parking lot, I told Sol about my conversation with Barney. "So the Buick that shadowed me is related to Welch's old company. That says a lot."

"Not necessarily evidence of murder."

"Yeah, but we know Welch and Karadimos are connected. Karadimos's plane was flown down the day of the murder, and Karadimos is threatening me. Now it looks like Welch is the guy who had me followed. That means they're both in on it together. I've got enough for reasonable doubt. It's looking good."

"Whoa, slow down, Jimmy. There's an old Jewish saying. Don't count your chickens–"

"I didn't know that was a Jewish saying."

"Yeah, we have sayings for everything. It means–"

"I know what it means, Sol."

"Let me finish. It means, *mach nit kain tsimmes fun dem*."

"Oh, that explains it."

"See, before you start counting chickens–"

"I'm not counting chickens–"

"Forget about chickens. You have to think about what Welch and Karadimos are up to," Sol said. "Think about this:

144

Karadimos is a crook and we figure he's working with Welch. Maybe Gloria found out something that she shouldn't have."

"I've been thinking about those calls Gloria had made that day."

Gloria placed two long-distance phone calls on the day she died, the first one at around three in the afternoon to a Kansas number. The police didn't investigate that call other than to report that it had been made to a friend. The second one about an hour later had been routed to the Sacramento Inn. It turned out to be a dead end. The hotel had no way to trace the call to any particular room.

"Didn't we figure her Sacramento call was to Welch?" Sol said as he opened the trunk of his Lincoln Continental Mark IV. He tossed in the rod and pulled out his golf bag. Leaning against the side of his car, he said, "It'd be good to know what they talked about on that last phone call."

"What about the earlier call to her high school friend in Kansas? Wasn't she the girl who told you Gloria and Welch were having an affair?"

"Yeah, Bonnie Munson. Lives in Manhattan, Kansas. She went to high school with Graham. That's how we found her. We called the school and talked to a teacher. The teacher remembered Gloria, told us Bonnie had been her best friend."

"Do you think Bonnie would talk to me if I called her?" I asked.

"No, I don't think so. My investigators called her several times. She clammed up when they tried to get her to talk in depth about Gloria's relationship with Welch. I felt there was more troubling Bonnie about Gloria than just the affair, but that's just my thinking. I even called her myself, but could get nothing more out of her. She hung up on me." Sol shook his head. "Nah, she won't talk to you, Jimmy."

"I think you're right. She knows more than she's telling. Might not even know it's related to the murder." I glanced off into the distance. Was that Big Jake's Caddie about a quarter mile away, moving slowly along Old River School Road? I blinked, and didn't see it again.

"Jimmy, I know what you're thinking. You're going to Kansas to see her, aren't you?"

I turned back to Sol. "Yeah, I've gotta leave right away. Today is Tuesday. It'll be an overnight flight. I have to be back for the preliminary hearing Thursday morning."

"Hold on buddy boy. Even if she knows something, I doubt that she'll see you, and if she does, she won't talk. Sounds like a long shot."

"Sol, it's the only shot I've got."

"Maybe not the only shot."

"You got something else?"

"You wanna talk to Welch, don't you?"

"Hell, yes!"

"I've arranged for a sit-down, one on one. You'll get ten minutes with Welch. Next Friday night at his fundraiser. It's going to be held at Chasen's restaurant in Beverly Hills."

"Jesus, how'd you arrange that?"

"Remember I told you I was having lunch with a heavyweight when you called yesterday? By the way, did you call her yet?"

"Bobbi?"

"No, the Queen of Sheba, you schmuck."

"She doesn't want me to call. We're on opposite sides–but anyway, who were you having lunch with?"

"Chuck Manatt."

"The political guy."

"Yeah, I complained about the way Rhodes took off after we went to all the trouble to show him a good time at Del Mar."

"I treated him nice. I smiled when I called his client a crook."

Sol laughed. "Anyway, I told Manatt the only way to square it would be to set up a face-to-face meeting between Welch and you."

"What did Manatt say?" I asked.

146

"Done. It's arranged."

"He did? That's what he said, just like that?"

"Well, just about. I had to buy ten tickets to the dinner."

"How much?"

"Five hundred."

"Christ Almighty, you gave that asshole, Welch five hundred bucks?"

"Each."

"Whaddya mean–each?"

"Ten minutes, ten tickets, five thousand."

"Holy Christ–" I gasped. "Sol that's a lot of money. Are you sure–"

"Jimmy, you'll get food. Chasen's makes great chili. And don't forget, you get to have your picture taken with the Senator."

"Yeah, I'll hang it on the wall."

"Look good if he's the governor someday," Sol said.

"Look better if he's in jail," I said.

Chapter Twenty-Six

From Los Angeles I'd flown to the Kansas City Airport, stayed overnight at a Howard Johnson's and caught the early morning air taxi to Manhattan.

The six-passenger Beechcraft King Air made a sweeping turn and lined up for a straight-in approach to the Manhattan Regional Airport. This part of Kansas was wheat country, the breadbasket of the world. When I looked out the airplane window I expected to see "amber waves of grain." I didn't. It was August and the farmers cut the wheat in June. From the airplane I saw a sea of dirt and stubble that stretched to the horizon under a beautiful, spacious sky.

I'd stopped at the jail the day before on my way to LAX and explained to Rodriguez the purpose of Thursday's hearing. His spirits seemed to be holding up, and I was relieved to find out he'd been removed from the psychopath section and placed in a normal cell, but at the same time I was nervous that he was now in the general population where someone could get to him. I told him to be careful and watch his back. I didn't tell him what I'd discovered about Welch and Karadimos, though. I didn't want to get his hopes up. I'd wait until after my meeting on Friday with the Senator.

At ten thirty-five Wednesday morning the King Air finally touched down. Walking into the single airline passenger terminal, I noticed a sign welcoming visitors to the "Little Apple." It said that Manhattan, Kansas was the birthplace of the writer Damon Runyon. I remembered a line immortalized by one of Runyon's outrageous characters that roamed Broadway in the big Manhattan. *"I long ago came to the conclusion that all of life is six to five against."*

At this point, I would be happy with those odds.

After I signed the forms and got the keys to the Ford

Falcon that Rita had reserved for me, I found a pay phone. With the time difference, it was early in L.A. I hoped I might be able to catch Bobbi in her office before she went to court. I charged the call to my home phone. The switchboard put me through.

"Allen speaking," she said in a soft and pleasant voice.

"Hi, this is O'Brien. I'm calling from Manhattan."

"Jimmy, what are you doing in New York?"

"Manhattan, Kansas. It's just like New York only smaller," I said.

"Great shows and all that?"

"Yeah, they're terrific, the Quilting Bee was sold out, but I got a ticket to Maude Pricket's recital on the pleasures of pea picking. Wish you were here."

After a brief moment of silence, she said, "Me too."

I became more serious. "You'd like to be in Kansas with me?"

"Well, perhaps not Kansas on our first date, but maybe dinner and a movie somewhere." Her voice sounded light and slightly flirtatious.

"You'd go out with me? Dinner and a movie?" The thought of being on a date with Bobbi had my mind reeling.

"I think you're a nice guy. I'd enjoy going out with you occasionally–provided we could separate our professional lives from our personal. Erect a Chinese wall, so to speak."

"We could do that."

"It might not be that easy. I've been promoted. I'm now a member of the Serious Crimes Sector. The SCS handles capital murders and other major crimes. That means I'll be the lead prosecutor on the Rodriguez case. We'd have to wait until the case is closed, of course."

"Congratulations on the promotion. You deserve it…but the case could go on for a long time, months, maybe."

"Let me explain something. You have time?"

"Sure."

"Being a woman and having a career in what some

asinine people believe is solely a man's profession, has had its difficulties. My new supervisor is also a woman and by promoting me she's going out on a limb."

"I can imagine that it hasn't been easy, and I think your boss has made an intelligent decision." I didn't want to be the cause of any setbacks in Bobbi's career, but I wanted to see more of her. "We could build that Chinese wall, as you call it. We could keep work out of our social life."

"Jimmy, it goes without saying that I trust you. If I didn't we wouldn't be having this conversation, but it's just the *appearance* that could cause trouble," she said. "Not to mention, I'm working very hard to put your client away."

"I'm working hard too, but I know we'll be fair and honest with each other. You're the only prosecutor that I know of who isn't in it just to rack up convictions."

"If we could keep our professional lives separate I think we could work in a date or two after the trial without compromising our careers. That is, if you still want to take me out after I mangle you in court."

"I'd love to go out with you," I said with sincerity. I couldn't think of a snappy comeback for the *mangle* comment, but perhaps this wasn't the time for it anyway.

"Bye, Jimmy. Call me when you're back in L.A." She started to hang up.

"Wait! I have to talk some business with you. That's why I called. Bobbi, are you there?"

There was a strained silence on the line, just the crackling static of the long distance wires. She answered at last: "You mean you didn't call just to ask me out?" I could almost hear the smile on her face.

"Of course that's why I called you from a hot, sweaty pay phone in the middle of Kansas, but seeing as how you're on the line, we may as well discuss the case. Then these outrageous toll charges will be tax deductible. Clever, huh?"

"And I just got through saying such nice things about your ethics. Go ahead; I'll be your tax dodge."

"Remember when you said if I could show that Welch was in town at the time of the murder, you'd reopen the case?"

"Yes, I remember. . ." she said with more than a little skepticism in her voice.

I told her about the extra flight time on the jet, exactly the number of hours needed for a round trip to Sacramento, the hidden Hobbs Meter, the failure to log the time, and the missing pilot. "So, Bobbi, someone came back Saturday and whoever it was tried to cover up the flight. What do you think?"

"Now that is something significant. Hold on a minute."

While waiting for Bobbi to return, I glanced through the terminal plate-glass window overlooking the runway. A small twin-engine airplane had landed and two middle-aged guys dressed as cowboys got out and strode through the terminal, headed for the café.

I'd missed breakfast and the thought of eggs and bacon sizzling in a pan made me hungrier than I already was. The only thing they'd served on the plane had been a small bag of stale peanuts. In first class they probably had a suckling pig roasting on a spit with dancing girls slicing off morsels and popping them in the passengers' mouths between sips of their Dom Pérignon champagne.

"I'm sorry for the delay, Jimmy. I had to make a call on the other line."

"Did you think over what I said?"

"It's not enough to re-open the case, but I'll tell you what I'm willing to do. I've just talked to Detective Hodges, South Gate PD. I've asked him to follow up on the Hobbs Meter thing. If it pans out, we'll make further inquiries. We'll look for the pilot."

I didn't like getting the cops involved, especially after what Big Jake had said. Plus, I didn't like the idea of tipping my hand to the other side. But I had to trust her. It was the only hope Rodriguez had. "Fischer is the key, Bobbi. He knows who murdered Graham."

"We'll see. Do you have anything else?"

Although I trusted her, I'd already told her enough. I didn't tell her my office was tossed, and that the only thing stolen was the Rodriguez file, or about the threats. "That's about it," I said.

"You're in Kansas. Are you going to be back in time for the hearing tomorrow?"

"Sure, I'm flying home tonight."

"The hearing starts at ten-thirty. Let's meet in the courtroom at nine-thirty. We can go over everything then. I won't promise you anything, but if what you told me checks out, I'll recommend bail and ask for a continuance on the hearing, and we'll investigate further. Does that sound fair?"

I tried not to show my excitement. "Yeah, that's fair. I'll see you in the morning."

"Okay. And, Jimmy..."

"Yes?"

"Don't forget, the Chinese wall."

"Yeah, I understand."

We said goodbye again. I hung up, and walked on clouds to the airport café.

While eating, I unfolded the map from Avis. Bonnie Munson lived on a farm somewhere twelve miles northeast of Manhattan.

I tried to plot my route but couldn't figure it out, so I asked the waitress for help. She said something like: Take Highway 113 through town. Then turn off on a dirt road somewhere, go past a red manure spreader, and after a while look for a mailbox with the Munson name painted on it.

What did a manure spreader look like? I wondered.

Chapter Twenty-Seven

I had second thoughts. Maybe it was actually being here in Kansas, the land of good manners and courtesy, that changed my mind. I decided I wouldn't just barge in on Bonnie Munson. I'd call her first to let her know I was on my way to see her. If she said no, stay away, *then* I'd barge in on her.

I went back to the same pay phone and dialed her number. When she answered, I told her who I was. At first she said that she wouldn't talk to me about Gloria. I explained that I wouldn't take much of her time. I just wanted to go over a few details concerning the comments she'd made to Sol and his men. When she heard that I'd flown all the way from California just to meet with her, Bonnie's Midwest hospitality kicked in. With a slight hesitation in her voice, she agreed to see me.

After missing a few turns and backtracking a bit, I spotted the remains of derelict piece of farm equipment leaning on the side of Highway 113.

"Is that a manure spreader?" I asked the farmer standing near the rusty hulk.

He peered at me sideways through a squinted eye. "Nah, it's an old combine. Why?"

"I need some help," I said glancing at the note in my hand with the waitress's directions scribbled on it. "I need to find a manure spreader. You see, I'm a lawyer–"

"That so? Well, then I can see why you'd need one."

Kansas humor, no doubt. "Uh, do you know how to get to the Munson farm?"

The old guy pointed to a farmhouse about a hundred yards down the road.

The house, a small, well-maintained white wooden

153

structure with a cupola on top, stood far back from the road, nestled among some tall trees. A wood-rail fence enclosed the green lawn and flowerbeds that surrounded the home. Vegetables flourished off to the side in a small garden.

After parking the Falcon next to an olive green John Deere tractor, I climbed out of the car. Two Labrador retrievers bounded over and loped around me, their tails going a mile a minute. They threw a few barks my way. I jumped back, "*Jesus*," I exclaimed.

"Johann. Sebastian. Leave the man alone. You know better, now go away."

I shifted my attention from the dogs to the woman standing in the doorway of the house. She had on a sleeveless blouse and tight fitting jeans that flattered her impressive figure. By Los Angeles standards she'd probably be considered overweight, but by Kansas standards I imagined that she was just about perfect. If it were a contest, I'd vote for the Kansas standards.

"Don't worry, their Bach is worse than their bite." More Kansas humor. She walked over and stuck out her hand.

"You must be Bonnie Munson," I said.

"Yes, and you must be Mr. O'Brien."

She invited me into the house, where the yeasty aroma of fresh-baked bread enveloped me like a warm blanket. The cozy smell was in keeping with the unpretentious décor of the home. Being there gave me a sense of security and peacefulness that I never felt in the city. I followed Bonnie into the kitchen. The table was set for three.

"My husband, Jack, will be here shortly. I phoned him at work and told him you were coming. He suggested inviting you to have dinner with us."

I glanced at my watch: twelve-thirty. "I'd love to, Bonnie, but I have to be back at the airport by five."

Her smile flickered for a moment. "Oh, dinner is our mid-day meal. We have supper in the evening."

"Of course," I said. "I'd be delighted to have dinner with

you."

"I'll finish setting the table." She pointed to a door. "You can wash up in there."

I finished washing my face and hands and returned to the kitchen. Jack had just arrived. He stood six feet tall, had a sturdy build, a ruddy complexion, and red, thick hair. We shook hands. His grip was strong, his hands were callused like a man who spent his life doing physical labor.

As anxious as I was to find out what Jack and Bonnie knew that might help my client, I felt I'd have to go slow. Jack said we would talk after dinner and I didn't push it.

We sat at the table. Bonnie and Jack rested their folded hands on the edge. I waited. They looked at each other and nodded. Bonnie bowed her head and Jack glanced at me. "Mr. O'Brien, we say grace before meals. Do you mind?"

"Not at all." I followed suit.

"Heavenly Father, we thank thee for the food we are about to receive and we beseech you to bless our home, our family, and the visitor from California who is with us today. We beg thee to protect us from the evil that befell your servant, Gloria. And please grant courage and hope to the man who is wrongly accused of her murder. Amen."

I snapped my head up. Jack nodded. "Yes, Mr. O'Brien, we know he's innocent. Your client didn't murder Gloria."

Chapter Twenty-Eight

After we finished the meal I offered to help with the dishes, but Jack said the dishes could wait. We all moved into the living room. Bonnie sat in a straight-backed antique chair next to an upright piano. Jack eased into an old overstuffed armchair, then reached for his pipe resting on an end table. He filled the bowl with tobacco, tamped it down, and lit it with a lighter he held at an angle. Bonnie coughed and waved her hands slightly. Jack pretended not to notice. I sat on one end of a blue davenport. As I sank into it, I wondered if I would ever be able to get up again.

"Do you want to ask questions or shall we just tell you what we know about Gloria?" Jack asked.

"I'll ask questions later, if that's all right."

"Bonnie, go ahead and tell him. And honey, tell Mr. O'Brien *everything*."

"Everything?" Bonnie asked, a concerned look on her face.

"Yes, just as we discussed on the phone. Bonnie, we knew someday it'd have to come out. We can't keep the truth locked up when a man is in prison. It's time to clear our conscience."

Bonnie took a deep breath, exhaled, and turned to me. "Gloria and I were very close, best friends all the way through school." She stood and went to a framed photograph resting on the piano. "Come here please, Mr. O'Brien."

She handed me the picture. I stared at a teenaged girl dressed in a cheerleader outfit, a pretty girl. Her eyes were alive and sparkling, not at all like the eyes that stared back at me from the crime scene photos.

"Gloria and I were cheerleaders," Bonnie said. "That's how Jack and I got together. Jack was the Tigers quarterback, the team captain. He–"

"Bonnie," Jack said, "just talk about Gloria, not me."

"Yes dear, of course." She replaced the photograph and moved back to her chair. "Gloria was not only pretty, but smart." Bonnie paused, struggling to keep her emotions under control. "She loved history and politics, wanted a career in that field, thought she could make a difference. She graduated and won a full scholarship to UCLA."

"Yes, I know this part, poly-sci, had a boyfriend at UCLA." I wanted to speed this along. "Did she talk about him?"

"Yes, but she wasn't very serious about the guy. She set her sights higher. Wanted someone who was going places. That's what she said. But then when the guy dumped her, she became terribly upset. I saw a new side of her, a darker side."

"How do you mean?" I asked.

"She said, 'he'll never get away with it. I'll get even,' that sort of thing. I just thought it was the pressure of living in L.A. But finally she put the guy behind her. Then later, she somehow got involved with a married man. She was working for Senator Welch by that time, and her new boyfriend supposedly had a promising career. The only trouble was he had a wife. She didn't tell me it was Welch; she promised him she'd keep it a secret. But friends know."

"Did he make promises to her, leave his wife–you know what I mean?"

"He's running for re-election, told her after the election he'd get a divorce and marry her. She helped him with his campaign." Bonnie glanced at Jack. He nodded. "Gloria was naïve. She actually thought he'd leave his wife, and to make it worse, she fell deeply in love with him."

"We tried to talk her out of it," Jack added. "I spoke with her a few times myself, gave her the man's point of view."

"Gloria wanted a touch of the high life. That was the expression she'd used." Bonnie looked at Jack. He just shook his head slowly.

"A touch of the high life," Bonnie repeated, looking at the rug.

She twisted her wedding ring as she spoke. "Gloria could've been a big success. If she stayed, Mr. Ferguson would've hired her at the bank. But she had that scholarship."

"Bonnie," Jack said. "Gloria was on a collision course with ruin from the moment she left Manhattan. Her life was out of control in L.A."

"Not in the beginning. It was Welch who got her on that track—the lies, the deceit, and all that money."

"What money?" I asked. "The police report said she had less than $300 in the bank when she died."

"About six months ago, she started sending us money," Jack said. "We were supposed to hide it for her. Said if anything happened to her we should just keep it. I told her not to talk nonsense." He set his pipe down and left the room.

Bonnie kept talking. "She told us that she had some kind of problem with the IRS, and until she could solve it, she needed to hide her savings. She was my best friend. What could I do? It started small, but then the amounts got bigger. Once or twice, I asked her about it. She was reluctant to discuss the matter. I didn't want to pry, but we had to know what was going on."

Oh, my God! I realized what Bonnie was telling me. Gloria had stolen money from Welch and Karadimos and because of that she'd been murdered. I leaned forward and sat on the edge of the davenport. "What did she say after you confronted her?"

"She always had some tall tale. Finally, I got upset and told her not to insult my intelligence any longer. Then the truth started to come out. She learned that her boyfriend was not only unfaithful to his wife, but he also cheated on *her*."

"That's not all she found out." Jack returned with an aluminum briefcase.

"I was getting to that, Jack," Bonnie said. "Anyway, she must've found out Welch was a crook and involved with some very vile people. She seemed frightened."

Jack put the case on the coffee table. "She was scared because she was stealing his money." He shook his head. "Stupid, stupid, stupid."

Bonnie's face grew stormy. "We don't know she stole it. Here's what she'd said: 'The bastard owes me.' Please excuse my language, but that's what she'd said."

"Either she stole it or this was her share of the loot." Jack opened the case and stepped aside.

I took a deep breath. It was full of currency. I stared at the hard cash arranged neatly in rows. "Did you count it?"

"Sixty-seven thousand and change," Jack said.

Bonnie stood and paced the room. She stopped and looked at me, her eyes pleading. "You're a lawyer, Mr. O'Brien. Are we in trouble? Are we going to jail? What should we do?"

"Oh, Christ," I blurted out. Then I realized that in this household, taking the Lord's name in vain was not acceptable. "I'm sorry. Well anyway, I'm not licensed in Kansas. I can't give you legal advice."

"We're not asking you as an attorney, just as a person. We don't normally trust lawyers, but we trust you, defending that poor guy," Jack said. "We don't know what to do, or who to turn to. Please, Mr. O'Brien."

"I have to know more. What else can you tell me?"

"There's not much else to tell," Bonnie said.

"You said Gloria told you Welch was involved with some bad people. Did she mention any names?"

Bonnie's eyes started to fill. "No, I don't know if she even knew–"

Jack jumped in. "I think she knew and I think she was in cahoots with them."

Bonnie sat down and covered her face with her hands, shaking her head. "I don't want to hear this, Jack. I'll admit, Gloria wasn't an angel, but she wasn't an evil person."

"Oh, Bonnie." Jack put his arm softly around her

shoulders. He looked up at me. His face reflected his wife's deep sadness. "That's all we know, Mr. O'Brien."

"The day she died, that afternoon, she made a long distance call to Kansas," I said.

Bonnie slowly raised her head. She remained silent for a few seconds. Then her eyes opened wide. "Yes, of course. I remember now. It was suppertime. I was setting the table, had the phone in one hand and the dishes in the other. I wasn't paying close attention."

"What did she say?"

"She was angry, ranting about her married boyfriend. He went out of town to some big to-do with his wife. He'd sent her a Dear John letter, dumped her. She'd gotten it in the mail just before she phoned here. Gloria had said she was going to call him and have it out. She was going to put the screws to him. That's how she phrased it, *put the screws to him*." She pulled a Kleenex from the box on the end table and wiped her eyes. "I'd heard all about her troubles with her boyfriends before. I wasn't really listening too closely. Wait a minute. She seemed worried about something else. I don't remember exactly what she said; something like she thought the Greek might be on to her."

The Greek! It had to be Karadimos.

"Does that mean something, this Greek guy?"Jack asked. "Do you know who or what she was talking about?"

"God almighty, this could break the case wide open." I thought for a second. It might be a problem getting Bonnie's statement admitted–hearsay–but now was not the time to think about the evidence code. "Is there anything in writing? Letters, a note about the money, anything like that?"

They both shook their heads.

"Do you think we should talk to the authorities?" Jack asked.

I grabbed him by his shoulders. "Please, by all means, don't talk about this to a soul. And I mean not anyone! We have to keep this top secret for a while. You could be charged with receiving stolen money. And listen, Jack: Gloria had been involved with some very bad people. If they knew about this, it could be bad for *you*. I won't get into that, but please keep quiet about this."

"I understand. We'll keep our traps shut. Won't we, Bonnie?

"What are we going to do?" Bonnie asked.

"I won't lie to you. This whole thing, the money, all of it, may come out. This is a murder case, after all. Let me think a moment."

I now believed that Gloria had been involved in criminal activity, and Bonnie and Jack had accepted money from her. That meant they would most likely be charged as co-conspirators. I strongly felt that they were innocent, decent people just doing a favor for a wayward friend. But the law wouldn't make that distinction. And what about Karadimos? He'd have them whacked as soon as he realized they knew about Gloria, the money, and the fact that the Greek was on to her. But I also knew they would be of no help at the Rodriguez trial. Whatever they told me would not be allowed. It was all hearsay and no court in the land would allow their testimony to be admitted.

My eyes scanned the room and settled on the couple, on the sadness and guilt written on their faces as they huddled close to each other. I felt compassion for them, felt it in the depths of my soul. "Look, Bonnie, you won't have to come to California to testify. But with what you told me, there's a good chance I'll be able to prove my client's innocence without even going to trial."

"What about the money?" Jack asked.

"Hide it. Don't put it in the bank. Don't let anyone know you have it. It's probably untraceable, anyway. Bury it for a few years. Then after this is over, spend it a little at a time." I stopped and looked at their worried faces. "Listen, I'm not telling you this as a lawyer, you understand. But by admitting you took the money, you could be in serious trouble. Don't tip your hand. Please, *please*, listen to me."

Bonnie made a tent with her hands and placed them in front of her mouth, then shook her head. "We don't want the money. It's corrupt. Gloria probably died because of it. I'll burn it. I'll burn it all up." She wept openly; tears ran down her face. The hurt came from deep within. "The Bible says money is the root of all evil."

"Bonnie," I said in a calm voice. "Money is not evil. It is not corrupt. It has no soul. It's just money. The correct quote is, 'The *love* of money is the root of all evil'. You and Jack don't love money. You love each other. Money won't change that."

I walked around the room and tried to persuade her as I would a jury. "Perhaps you guys could do something virtuous with the money. If nothing else, it will give some meaning to Gloria's life. Please think this over. I know you're upset, but don't do anything foolish, okay?"

Jack came over, grabbed my hand and shook it. Bonnie looked up at me and dried her eyes with the palms of her hands. It looked like a tiny smile was beginning to surface.

"Thank you, friend. Thank you very much," Jack said.

"Don't thank me. I want to thank you." I glanced at my watch; it was time to leave. "Bonnie, you are without a doubt the best cook on the planet. If you ever decide to move to L.A. you could make a fortune in the restaurant business."

She laughed at the absurdity of the remark. "As they say in L.A., no way, daddy-o."

I didn't have the heart to tell her that no one in Los Angeles has said *daddy-o* for over fifteen years.

I caught the shuttle flight at Riley County Airport and forty-five minutes later arrived at Kansas City. Transferring terminals, I boarded the Hughes Air flight to LAX. Soon we were airborne, soaring through the twilight at five hundred miles per hour. I loosened my seatbelt and leaned back. The constant hum and gentle vibration of the engines was sedating and I relaxed for the first time in a week. Closing my eyes, Bobbi's face floated into my mind. *"You're up in an airplane, you're dining at Sardi's...this could be the start of something big..."*

Sol had given me her home number. I'd tucked it in my wallet. When I pulled it out and gazed at it, I felt a soft warmth flourish within me, a feeling that I hadn't felt in years. It was Bobbi's number, something personal, a slight connection to her. I thought of a new movie playing in theaters, *The Godfather*, about gangsters. It was getting rave reviews.

I wanted to call her the minute we landed at LAX and ask her out. Convince her we didn't have to wait for the trial to end. Anyway, with the new evidence there would be no trial. Maybe I'd set our date up for Saturday. We could take in the movie and have a late supper at the Regency. I hadn't thought about my loneliness a great deal since I'd been working on the Rodriguez case, but thinking about Bobbi reminded me how disconnected I'd really been. It didn't seem possible for someone to live among so many people and still be so alone. It seemed as if I were living in a bubble. I could interact with women but never really get close. I guess I wanted to break out and start a life again.

We bucked headwinds most of the way and landed at LAX a little behind schedule. I exited the plane and rushed to the bank of pay phones lining the wall across from the check in gate. My stomach tightened with excitement as I dialed Bobbi's number.

"Hello." Bobbi's warm voice came on the line.

"Hi there," I said.

All I heard was unnerving silence.

I waited for what seemed like an eternity. "Hey Bobbi, it's me, Jimmy. Are you there?"

Silence. I was about to say something else, when the line came alive.

"How'd you get this number?" Her voice sounded

callous.

"I just got it. Is that a problem?"

"Listen, Buster, you'd better just lose it. Don't call me again. Ever!"

"Bobbi, what's the matter–"

The line went dead. She'd slammed the phone down, hard.

Chapter Twenty-Nine

Reeling from the phone call to Bobbie, I headed to the luggage area in a daze. I was halfway down the long corridor when I spotted Sol and his driver rushing toward me, weaving through the horde of deplaned passengers. When he got closer I could see the expression on his face. It wasn't pretty. He grabbed my arm and hustled me aside.

"Jesus Christ, Sol. What's going on? Did someone die?"

"Yeah, your case. C'mon, let's go in here where we can talk."

We darted into a small, dimly lit cocktail lounge just off the corridor. A curved bar ran along one side. The bartender looked bored as he wiped glasses while watching the local news on a TV mounted high in the corner. A dozen round cocktail tables were scattered inside, only a few occupied, mostly by tired looking businessmen. Sol and I sat at one. At his urging, I handed my claim check to his driver. He left to fetch my luggage.

"I called you yesterday. You didn't return my call," Sol said.

"I was in Kansas."

"In Kansas, they don't have phones?"

"Goddammit, Sol, what's up? You got me nervous, coming out here like this and telling me my case is dead."

"You've been submarined, my boy."

"What are you talking about?"

"Your client's confessed."

"Whoa–*confessed*? What do you mean, confessed?"

"He told his cellmate."

"Told him what?"

"That he murdered the girl."

I tilted my head back and stared at the ceiling. "That's

bullshit."

"The DA has the cellmate's statement."

I couldn't believe what Sol was telling me. How could Rodriguez confess? After what the Munsons had told me, there was no doubt about his innocence. "When did this so-called confession take place?"

"I got the call yesterday afternoon from one of my spies. The DA's office is keeping the confession and the witness under wraps, gonna spring it on you at the hearing tomorrow. I know it's a setup. I'm trying to find out what kind of deal your pretty little DA friend cut with the cellmate. You need to find out who the guy is and what he'd been arrested for."

"I'll find out when they parade him before the judge at the hearing in the morning."

A waitress strayed over to our table. Sol ordered his usual: Beefeater rocks. I didn't want anything.

I glanced at the full-length window lining the far wall, peering out into the darkness. "Is Bobbi Allen in on this?"

Sol didn't answer directly. "Do you think the judge will buy the guy's testimony?"

"Doesn't matter, the purpose of this hearing is for the DA to present just enough evidence to show that a crime had been committed and that they have grounds to bind Rodriguez for trial. The rules are stacked in the DA's favor. Doesn't look good."

The waitress returned with Sol's drink. He took a sip, set the glass down hard. "Jimmy, it smells. You told me Bobbi Allen is a straight arrow, plays by the rules."

"Maybe she believes the cellmate. Maybe he just made it all up."

"Yeah, sure he did." Sol groaned. "They planted the guy. You told me yourself that they just recently took Rodriguez off psych watch and gave him a cellmate. Then, bingo, he up and confesses. Nah, she set it up. Hey, wait a minute. I gave you her number. You didn't call her and tip your hand, did you?"

I hesitated. "Yeah, I called her twice. First time she was all friendly. Then when I called her back just a few minutes ago, she wouldn't even speak to me. Something turned her. I don't know what. It couldn't just be the cellmate's statement. She wouldn't hold that against me personally. It has to be something worse, something bad, real bad."

"Jimmy, wise up. She's using you to advance her career." He nodded. "Yeah, murder conviction, first time. It'd look good to the big guys."

"I don't believe that," I said.

"Don't let your feelings for her cloud your thinking." He paused. "I suppose it's my fault. I gave you the goddamn number. She had me fooled, too."

Sol waved at the waitress. He wanted a fresh drink.

"Thanks for the heads up, Sol. I'll have a couple of minutes to talk to Rodriguez before the hearing. I'll be somewhat prepared."

"That's why I figured you'd better know about the alleged confession before you walk into the courtroom tomorrow. Maybe you can defuse the situation somehow."

"Yeah," I said, wondering what I could do.

"Tell me about your Kansas trip."

While Sol polished off his second drink, I brought him up to speed on my meeting with the Munsons. I explained about the money Gloria had been embezzling, and my thoughts that the money came from Karadimos and Welch's criminal activity.

"Maybe they found out she stole from them and had her hit. One of Karadimos's henchmen could've done it. Maybe it had nothing to do with the affair, after all," Sol said. "Maybe we're barking up the wrong tree."

"You saw the crime scene photos. It had to be a crime of passion. A hit man would have put a bullet in her head, over and done with." I paused, collected my thoughts. "Sol, here's what I think happened. The money is just a red herring. Oh, she stole it from them, all right, but I have the feeling they

167

didn't catch her at it."

"You don't think it was the money?"

"I thought about it on the plane. I figure Welch dumped her. Gloria was becoming a political liability. Then after she got the Dear John, she called him at the hotel and probably threatened to expose him. He flew down to confront her. It got out of hand and he killed her. We know the jet was flown down here that Saturday," I said. "The pilot is the key. He'll tell us who was on the plane that day. Any leads on finding Fischer?"

"I'm working on it. But when we find him, I don't think he'll tell us Welch was on board. We've been secretly interviewing people who were at the fundraiser. They all say Welch was there the whole time."

"Lots of drinking going on. Maybe they're just assuming he was there."

"Will Bonnie Munson be willing to testify at Rodriguez's trial?"

"Her testimony would be no good. It's all hearsay. Wouldn't be admissible."

"I guess the pilot is your only hope. Don't worry, we'll find the guy."

"Are you staying in town today?"

"Canceled my table at Del Mar, thought you might need me."

"I'll call you after the hearing," I said.

I woke up the next morning, stumbled around getting ready to leave. I had to be in the courtroom at nine-thirty. Bobbi had said she'd meet me there before the hearing. Maybe I was delusional, but there was an off chance she'd still show up and tell me what this was all about. I knew I was hoping against hope, but it wouldn't hurt to be there.

On my way to the court, I stopped at Paramount Chevrolet and while waiting for them to fixed my car window, I made notes about the case. But no ideas came. I just thought about Bobbi.

I entered Division 5, Judge Koito's courtroom, on the third floor of the Norwalk Superior Court at nine-thirty on the dot. I looked around the empty room, my stomach tied in knots.

I had to get a hold of myself and quit thinking about Bobbi. I wondered again why she'd been so hostile on the phone. Rodriguez's alleged confession wouldn't have caused that kind of reaction. Her hostility was personal, and directed at me.

Twenty minutes had passed when I heard the courtroom door open. I turned to look. Sergeant Hodges swaggered over to me with his partner in tow.

"O'Brien," Hodges said. "Deputy DA Allen asked me to meet you here. It seems you've been a naughty boy."

Here it comes. I knew there had to be more. "What's that supposed to mean?"

"Did you think you could manufacture evidence and get away with it? I figured you were smarter than that, being an ex-cop."

"Maybe that's why he's an *ex-cop*," the partner said.

"Is that what happened, O'Brien? Got a little clever with the LAPD, too? That's why you're an ex-cop? You don't have to answer that. It'll come out in the investigation."

I jumped to my feet. "What investigation? What evidence? What the hell are you guys talking about?"

"I think you know, but I'll tell you anyway. Allen bought your story about a hidden meter on Karadimos's jet. I told her it was a line of crap. I'd already checked out the plane. She wanted me to check it again. No problem, I said. What the hell, I'll go on the goose chase."

"You checked the Hobbs meter?"

"Yeah, and guess what we found, O'Brien? But you already know what we found."

"Tell him, Phil," the partner said.

I stood there in shock, taking slow deep breaths.

"You guessed it, O'Brien. We found the mechanic." Without taking his eyes off me, he snapped his fingers in the direction of his partner. "What's the mechanic's name?"

The partner took a notebook out of his pocket and flipped it open. "Fred Vogel."

"Yeah, good old Freddie boy decided to come clean, told us the whole story. How you pressured him to lose the logbook. How you made up a story about some hidden meter, and how you bribed him to go along." Hodges snapped his fingers again. "How much money did O'Brien give Vogel?"

"Forty bucks, cash."

At least they got the amount right. "This whole thing's absurd, he—"

"There's more," Hodges said.

"More? More what?"

"Tell him about the mob, Phil."

Hodges turned to his partner. "Shut up, Johnny," he said and turned back to me. "We know you've been hanging with the Mafia."

"I don't believe this—"

"You better believe it, my friend. FBI says you're a known associate, going to their bust-outs. They say you like to party with the Wise Guys?"

I didn't say anything. Hodges turned to his partner and made a gesture with his head in the direction of the door. The partner snapped his book closed and stuffed it into his pocket. As they drifted toward the exit, Hodges stopped and turned back. "If you pulled that evidence trick in my jurisdiction, I'd slap the irons on you right now. But we turned it over to the Long Beach PD. They're conducting the investigation."

I glanced around. No one else was in the room. Nobody came in and told me the whole thing was a joke. Allen Funt wasn't lurking anywhere, no hidden cameras.

"By the way, the pretty DA lady filed a complaint with the State Bar. Gonna pull your law ticket. And, my friend, she's filing a motion with the court to have you removed from the Rodriguez case. Won't be a lawyer long enough to see it through."

"Rodriguez is guilty," the jerk partner said. "He's confessed, doesn't matter who his lawyer is. He's toast."

"Yeah, I heard," Hodges said. "See ya later, O'Brien."

They started to leave again. Hodges stopped, looked at me with a smirk plastered across his face. "Hey, O'Brien."

"What?"

"Have a nice day," he said. They left the room.

Chapter Thirty

I watched the courtroom door slowly close. Minutes passed with me still staring at the door. Hodges's smirking face lingered in my mind.

I thought of my phone call to Bobbi and what she had said: *"Don't call me. Don't call me ever."* Why was this happening to me? What had I done? Had I overreached, taken on a case beyond my ability? Had I been too trusting? Outsmarted? I'd told Bobbi about the hour meter on the jet, but by the time Hodges checked it out, Karadimos had already gotten to Vogel. The second meter was gone, and with it my hope that the police would reopen the case.

I sank into a seat and faced forward. The room was quiet, nothing stirring. I covered my ears with my hands, elbows on the table, as if to block out the deafening silence.

Karadimos's frame-up was thorough and complete. My most concrete lead had crumbled to dust and vanished like powder in a breeze.

Ten minutes later the bailiff and a guard shuffled Rodriguez to my table and forced him in the chair next to me. I glanced up at the guard.

"Don't ask," he said. "We're not removing the restraints." He stepped around and stood behind Rodriguez.

Bobbi and her assistant, a thin man about forty, marched into the courtroom, and without acknowledging my presence, sat at the prosecutor's table. They placed their briefcases on the table and faced forward, all prim and proper. I felt like shouting at her that I'd been framed. But then I thought, maybe I *had* let my feelings for her get in the way of defending Rodriguez. Maybe she's in on it. Sol thinks so. I didn't know what to think. I knew I'd get over Bobbi. But if my client went to prison because I trusted her, I'd never forget that.

The hearing would start any minute and I had nothing to present today that would convince the judge to drop the charges. Even if by some miracle I could've arranged to have Bonnie Munson testify, her statements would be ruled inadmissible. It was all conjecture, with nothing to sustain her allegations.

The immediate problem at hand had to do with the alleged jailhouse witness. I leaned into Rodriguez. "*Amigo*," I whispered, "we've got problems." His eyes asked the question, and I answered: "Your cellmate told the DA that you admitted killing the girl."

There was no shock or surprise on his face, no rage, or outbursts of anger, just his same stoic expression. He must've felt there was no hope. Felt the system was stacked against guys like him. After a while the mind becomes numb to the abuse and the body becomes a formless lump of flesh and bone.

"I know you didn't tell him that, but I have to know everything you said to him." I paused for a moment. "Did you say anything to him?"

"No."

"Must have said something."

"*Nada*."

"Tell him your name, anything at all?"

He looked at me. "I told you, I said nothing."

"How long was the guy in your cell?"

"One day. They took him away in the morning, yesterday."

It wasn't hard to believe that he didn't talk to his cellmate. I was his lawyer trying to save his life, and he would hardly talk to me. "I believe you, Ernesto, but I'll have to convince a jury when we go to trial."

He slowly turned his head and looked into my eyes. "Sounds like they're playing tricks on you."

"Yeah, they're playing tricks."

"*Iay*! They can't fool you. You're a smart guy."

Yeah, I'm a smart guy, all right. Smart enough to give the DA advance notice about my defense of this poor man sitting next to me. "One more thing," I said. "The cops and the DA have filed charges against me. It just means they're worried, that's all. I'll beat the rap."

"The judge is after you too?" His expression changed to one of concern.

"They say I made up some false evidence."

"I know you do nothing wrong. *Esta muy malo*; you are in trouble 'cause of me."

"Don't worry about me. They don't have squat."

"Squat? *Que*? What is squat?"

"Well, it means they can't pin anything on me. Anyway we're going to play our hand close to the vest from now on."

"Close hands, *vest*, I do not understand. Is that lawyer talk?"

"It means we are going to kick their asses." I started to get hot, thinking how Bobbi had betrayed me after I made a fool of myself, asking–no, almost begging–to take her out. And all that bullshit about the Chinese wall.

"Ah...I understand. You kick their asses for me too, huh, Jimmy?"

"You got it, Ernesto. I'll kick her ass, goddammit." I patted him on his back. "But not today. We'll win at the trial. You wait and see."

The hearing started. Bobbi managed to get through the first half-hour without looking my way. I watched as she presented a few witnesses: the cop who had arrived first at crime scene testified as to what he'd discovered. The medical examiner told the cause of death, which was consistent with a murder, and the arresting police officer explained how and why they had arrested Rodriguez. There was nothing new, nothing that wasn't in the police report. I couldn't object to the evidence or the manner in which Bobbi presented it. I just sat there and waited for the People to call their new witness: Rodriguez's cellmate.

"Your Honor, we had a witness that we planned to call, but in light of recent developments we decided to save him for the trial." Bobbi shot a glance at me that could have frozen Dante's Inferno. "At this time, the People would like to make a motion."

"Go ahead," the judge said.

"The People move to have Mr. O'Brien removed as counsel for the defense, for cause. It's obvious that he is incompetent and–"

I bolted out of my seat. "Your honor, Miss Allen knows nothing about my competence. I passed the bar–"

The judge waved his hands in front of him. "Let her finish. You'll get your turn."

"He's not only incompetent, but he tried to bribe a witness. Falsify evidence–"

"That's absurd and you know it," I shouted at Bobbi.

"O'Brien, I told you let her finish," the judge said in a stern manner.

"I've filed a complaint with the State Bar and turned over the facts to the Long Beach Police Department. They're doing a full-scale investigation."

Through clenched teeth, I said, "You did that behind my back. Didn't wait to hear my side."

Bobbi turned my way and hissed her reply. "You lied to me. You've been seen with your friends in the Mafia."

The judge stood. "Counselors, direct your arguments to the bench."

Bobbi faced the judge. "Your honor, he's been seen with gangsters."

"I'm a criminal lawyer, for chrissakes, who do you expect me to be seen with?"

She whipped around. "You go to their *disgusting* bust-out parties, prostitutes, hoodlums."

"They aren't that disgusting. The food is great, and I

didn't see any prostitutes. But I only went once, to see my client."

"Joseph Sica? Your client?" She smirked. "The kingpin of the Mafia? *Ha*, bet me. He'd hire an idiot like you?"

Judge Koito stood and pounded his gavel. "Allen, O'Brien, approach the bench."

"I'm an idiot? If I'm an idiot why did you ask me out?"

"That's a lie! You called *me* in the middle of the night!"

"It was eight-thirty."

The gravel banged again. "One more word out of you two and I'll–"

"You deceived me! Told me all those lies."

"That's it," the judge said, "you're in contempt, Miss Allen."

Bobbi shifted her attention to the judge. "I want a restraining order. I want to file it right now."

"Approach. Both of you. Now!"

Bobbi darted around the table and started for the bench. I yelled at her back, "You don't need an order. I wouldn't get near you for all the tea–"

"Enough. That's enough! O'Brien you're in contempt too. I want to see both of you in my chambers." The judge flew down from the bench and rushed to the door. He stopped and pointed his gavel at the bailiff. "Ed, escort these people to my chambers. If they give you any trouble, arrest 'em."

We went peaceably; no one was cuffed. They took Rodriguez back to the holding cell and we were escorted to the judge's chambers. Bobbi sat in a maroon leather armchair that faced the desk. I could almost feel the heat of her slow burn as she sat with her hands folded primly in her lap, her mouth clamped shut. I paced behind Bobbi and waited for Judge Koito to enter the room. Ed the bailiff guarded the door.

The judge's absence had to be a ploy. He was giving us a cooling-off period, time to calm down and reflect on why we were here. The hearing was not about us. It was obviously much more important than Bobbi and me. We were just a couple of idiots who were acting like teenagers. I felt like a schoolboy who'd been sent trembling to the principal's office to wait for his parents to pick him up and administer punishment. No television for a week. It didn't matter to me. My TV was on the fritz.

Standing behind her, I leaned in close to Bobbi's ear and whispered, "You didn't even wait to hear my side of the story."

Her body quivered slightly, but she didn't turn around. "You're just like all the rest, just using me," she whispered back.

"I trusted you, and you set me up." I walked away from her.

The door opened, and Ed snapped to attention. "All rise," he shouted.

Judge Koito entered and gave Ed a dismissive wave. "That's not necessary, Ed, we're not in court. Everyone sit down."

I sat next to Bobbi in the only other chair in the room, close enough to smell her perfume, a light and sunny fragrance. She squirmed a little and leaned as far away from me as she possibly could without leaving her seat. The judge sat behind his desk.

"Before we begin, I want to warn both of you, if you speak out of turn or to one another without directing your remarks to me, you'll spend the night in jail. Is that clear?"

I nodded. Bobbi raised her hand, the school kid routine. Hey, maybe she brought an apple.

"Yes, Miss Allen?"

"Your Honor, I'd like to apologize for my behavior in your courtroom this morning."

"Accepted, but you're still in contempt. Before I establish the fine, we'll see how it goes here and now. Do you have anything to say, Mr. O'Brien?"

177

"Nope."

"Okay, now let's get started. The remainder of the hearing will be held in here and the record will reflect only the outcome. Do you both agree to that?"

After Bobbi's apology, it would've been hard for her to disagree with Judge Koito. As for me, if I were going to be excoriated, no way would I object to it happening in his chambers, instead of open court. Would've been okay with me to hold the thing in the toilet. We both agreed, and nodded.

"Fine. Now, I'll ask the questions and the appropriate party will respond."

Bobbi raised her hand again.

"Yes?" Koito said.

"May I bring my assistant in here? He has my files."

"No." he answered and turned to the bailiff. "Ed, go tell Miss Allen's assistant that he's dismissed. We won't need him."

Ed left the room. I noticed that Bobbi sat a little straighter and tried, without success, to hide her anger. She folded her arms tightly across her chest and rocked almost imperceptibly back and forth.

Judge Koito pulled his chair closer to his desk. "Miss Allen, I have a few questions for you. Mr. O'Brien, you will keep your mouth shut until I'm through and then I'll ask you to respond."

"Agreed," I said.

"Regarding the motion to remove Mr. O'Brien, have criminal charges been filed by your office pursuant to this matter, Miss Allen? Just answer yes or no."

"No, Your Honor."

"Has the State Bar reviewed the case and recommended any disciplinary action?"

"Not yet, but they will."

Judge Koito pounded his hand on his desk. "Yes or no."

"No."

"The motion is denied."

Bobbi started to raise her hand, pulled it down, and jumped up instead. "Your Honor, I have grounds."

"Sit down," the judge said. "Mr. O'Brien is an attorney, licensed by the state to practice law, and until that fact changes he shall remain on the case. Miss Allen, when we go back into the courtroom, I strongly recommend that you withdraw your motion."

Bobbie sat down and kept quiet.

"Mr. O'Brien, I don't know what you may or may not have done, but that's not why we're here today. Do you have anything else to add pertaining to the case at hand?"

"Yes." I pointed at Bobbi. "Miss Allen, I'm told, has an alleged jailhouse witness. She cut a deal with him to falsely testify that my client has confessed to the crime."

Bobbi shot out of her chair again. "Judge, I won't sit here and be accused of suborning perjury. Mr. O'Brien knows full well that I–unlike him–would not pull that kind of stunt."

"I know nothing of the kind. I want the witness's name, and I want to know what you offered him in return for his outrageous and mendacious statement," I said.

"That's enough, both of you. Mr. O'Brien, if you want any information from the prosecution, I suggest that you serve the proper discovery requests. Miss Allen, you will turn over to the defense any and all evidence required by law, including all witness statements. Is that understood?"

"Yes, Your Honor," we both said in unison.

The judge glanced at Bobbi and then at me. "Anything else?"

"Bail," I said.

"Denied," he said.

We paraded back into the courtroom. Bobbi withdrew her motion on the record and Koito officially denied the bail request. The trial date was set for Monday, October 2. Judge Koito fined us both fifty dollars for the contempt citation, and admonished Bobbi, telling her the fine was personal. It was not to be paid by the district attorney's office. He didn't need to give me the same lecture. He knew I had to pay my own bills. Nothing more was said about Bobbi's restraining order.

I loitered in the courtroom, scribbling on a yellow pad. I wanted to avoid getting into the elevator with Bobbi when she left the building. I didn't think I could've handled that; might have said something I would regret. After she left, I went to the bank of pay phones on the first floor.

Chapter Thirty-One

"Rita, I'm just checking in."

"How'd the hearing go?" she asked. "Like we expected?"

It was noisy in the hallway. I put the phone between my jaw and shoulder and tried to close the booth door, but the handle snapped. A bailiff, hands on his hips, glared at me. I shrugged.

"Yeah, guess so."

"I'm sorry, Boss, but hang in there, you'll win at the trial." I heard her sigh.

"Thanks Rita. Any calls?"

"Yeah, a cop from Long Beach. Said his name's Detective Farrell. What's this all about, Jimmy?"

I knew what it was all about, but I wanted to talk to the guy before I discussed it with Rita. "I'll call him later and find out," I said.

My next call was to Sol. I told him about the hearing, about the meeting with Hodges, and the call from Detective Farrell.

"Don't worry. It's a scam. You can beat these charges."

"It's basically my word against Vogel's, but I did give him some money."

"You gonna tell them that?"

"If I'm under oath I'll have to, but Ron Fischer is the most important thing to worry about. We have to find the pilot fast. I desperately need his testimony."

"I'm working on that right now. We have a lead and I'm waiting for a call back. It's lunchtime. Let's meet at Rocco's. If the call comes in, I'll have them transfer it to my table. We'll go over everything there."

"I'll head over right now."

"One more thing."

"Yeah?"

"I had your apartment swept for bugs, too. Your phone was tapped."

I racked my brain trying to remember what calls I'd made from my home phone. It depressed me to realize I hadn't talked to anyone in the last couple of weeks.

Shortly after one o'clock I entered Rocco's. Lively music came from the bar. The piano player, a short cocoa-skinned man wearing an Afro, had a voice like steel wheels rolling on a gravel road, but he was spunky and the crowd loved him.

An unruly queue had formed in front of André, customers vying for tables. As I approached the dining room, he noticed me and gestured with his hand to follow him to Sol's booth.

"Mr. Silverman hasn't arrived yet," André said. "His secretary called and said he would be here soon."

I slid into Sol's booth. Janine appeared, whisked away the reserved placard, and asked if she could bring me anything.

"Yes, thanks. A Coke, and a telephone," I said.

Janine returned in a few moments with the phone. She plugged it in and a busboy rushed over with my Coke. I dialed the Long Beach Police Department. "This is O'Brien. I'm returning Detective Farrell's call."

"I'll have to patch you through. It may take a few minutes."

While waiting, I listened to the piano music that drifted into the dining room from the bar. The guy was righteous on the piano, but I wasn't sure about the rest of his shtick. He had a way of taking popular songs, jazzing up the music, and altering the lyrics. He massacred "Alone Again, Naturally." He sang with style, but he changed the words to "Alone Again, *Ralph*." I didn't know why everyone laughed.

"This is Farrell," a monotoned voice said.

"Detective, I'm O'Brien. You wanted to talk to me."

"Yeah, need to get your side of the story on the

tampering complaint. The DA's hot on this. I already talked to Vogel, said you tried to bribe him."

I hesitated. I wanted time to think this through. I actually did bribe the guy, but only to get off his ass and look at the hidden meter, not to falsify evidence. But I had to figure exactly how to approach the problem. I took a sip of my Coke. The gang in the bar was getting boisterous, the music louder. The piano player sang, "I'm in the *nude* for love"–riotous laughter followed.

"You there, O'Brien?"

"Detective Farrell," I said, "I think you should drop the case."

"Drop the case? I told you the DA's all over me about this. What are you, some kind of nut?"

"Yeah, I'm a lawyer."

"Hey, if you don't want to talk to me, I'll just file the report."

"I'll talk and tell you why you should drop this thing, now."

"All right," he sighed. "I'm listening."

"First of all, it's my word against Vogel's."

"You're saying you didn't give him any money?"

"That's the point–I gave him forty dollars in cash, a service charge for the labor. I wanted him to unfasten a panel on the plane, check for an additional hour meter, then return the aircraft to its original condition."

"A service charge?"

"Yeah, it looks like Vogel decided to pocket the cash, not turn it over to his employer. He's trying to cover up a petty embezzlement. I paid Vogel to examine the plane for variations in the time flown and the time logged. That's all–information useful for research purposes."

"You get a receipt?"

"Embezzlers rarely give receipts."

"Let me get this straight," Farrell said. "You're saying you just paid Vogel a labor charge. Is that correct?"

"That's it."

"And Vogel pocketed the money."

"He sure did, Detective. There was no intent on my part to falsify evidence. There was no motive to do that. Alone, the fact that the plane had been flown extra hours wouldn't do me any good with the jury. I needed that information myself, background. I wanted the truth. If the plane was flown those extra hours, then I would look for the person who was on the plane that night."

"So you're saying you had no motive. No evidence could come from the plane itself."

"That's right. I had no motive to falsify anything, but Vogel had a motive."

"He did?"

"Yeah, he put the money in his pocket, and your case rests on my word against his."

"I see your point, but why would the deputy DA ask me to investigate if it was that simple?"

"I'll let you in on something, but don't put it in the report."

"What?"

"It's a personal matter between Miss Allen, the deputy DA, and me."

"Personal matter?"

I paused. Watch out, I told myself. I had second thoughts about bringing up my feelings toward Bobbi. I felt guilty about my outburst in court, saying that she asked me out. I really didn't want to hurt her.

"Nah, not really personal, this is her first murder case and she wants to do a thorough job, I can't blame her."

"Okay, I'll file my report," the detective said.

"What's it going to say?"

"You know I can't answer that." He stopped talking but didn't hang up. I remained silent. Finally he said, "Look, O'Brien, I'm not supposed to tell you this but you're an ex-cop and you know the score. I'm going to recommend that we drop this thing. It's a pissing contest between you and the Deputy DA and I have real crimes I should be working on. There's a four-inch stack of complaints on my desk right now, including a few murders, and more coming every day."

"Thanks," I said.

"You didn't hear it from me, but this thing is over. I don't see where any crime had been committed. You hadn't called the guy to the stand and paid him to lie. Maybe you would've, but the point is you hadn't. "

I hung up. Sol still hadn't arrived, so I had time to think a bit. I figured the State Bar charge would also disappear when the criminal complaint was dropped.

Did I feel better? No not really, Bobbi still thought I was guilty. That's what mattered, and that hadn't changed.

When Sol arrived, he had a drink in his hand and a file under his arm. He set the file on the table and slid into the booth across from me.

"You were on the phone so I had a drink at the bar. That new piano player is hilarious," Sol said.

"I heard him."

"Guy's terrific, huh?"

"Sol, the guy sucks." I'd told enough lies for one day.

"Well, *excuuuuuse* me," he said. "Not everyone can be Louie Armstrong."

"True," I said.

Sol glanced around the room, then leaned forward. "I got the call I'd been waiting for, you know, the lead on the pilot, Ron Fischer."

I straightened up. "What did you find out?"

"First we eat," he said, looking around. "Hey, did they bring the menus?"

My stomach did somersaults. "What?"

"The menu. What's the catch of the day? Feel like a nice sautéed sole or–"

"Goddammit, Sol, you do this every time."

"I think you should eat before I tell you the news."

"Why? Will the news kill my appetite?"

"Fischer is dead."

"Oh my God! What are you telling me?"

Sol just looked at me.

I reached across the table and grabbed his arm. "Tell me you were kidding about Fischer. I need his statement. He's gotta tell me who was on the plane that night. *Christ*, he can't be dead."

"Jimmy, Ron Fischer's been dead for over a year."

Chapter Thirty-Two

Sol insisted we eat first, then we'd talk about Fischer. I knew from experience that it'd do no good to try to change his mind; food and wine always came first. I also knew there was more to the story about Fischer being dead than what he just told me. There had to be a postscript, an explanation of some sort. Sol and his games...

He ordered lunch for both of us: salmon almandine. He'd Mondavi Chardonnay with his. I'd have coffee.

André brought Sol's wine draped in a linen towel. After uncorking the bottle with reverence, he poured an ounce or so into a glass that seemed to appear magically from his free hand. Sol sipped and nodded and told him some crap about the fruity aroma having the essence of a romantic melody.

I remained patient during the wine pouring ceremony, but I couldn't keep quiet any longer. "Sol, for crying out loud. Tell me about Fischer."

"Sure, my boy, but first sit back and relax; everything's going to be okay. I have it worked out—"

"Goddammit, Sol! What about Fischer?"

"As far as I know, Karadimos's pilot is still alive, but he's an imposter. He's not Ron Fischer."

"Thank God, he's not dead. But why do you always play games? You had me crazy."

"Ah, Jimmy, my boy, a little suspense in you life is like pepper in your soup."

The food thing again. Suspense, he says. Bad guys following me around, cops on my ass, and a woman who dumped me before we even got started because she thinks I'm a crook. That's right; a little suspense is what I needed. Still, a wave of relief flowed over me knowing the pilot was not dead. "Yeah, pepper in my soup. I hate soup," I said. "But anyway, who are we looking for now?"

Sol opened his file and read from it. "The real Ron Fischer died in a car crash last year in San Diego. The guy was a Navy fighter pilot, flew off aircraft carriers at night–very dangerous." He looked up. "The guy had nerve."

"And he died in a car crash," I said.

"Yeah, ironic, isn't it?"

Janine appeared with our food. The appetizing aroma triggered within me a hunger that I did not think existed. Sol and I tucked into the salmon, and after several mouthfuls I asked him, "You said you have it worked out?"

He swallowed. "You bet. We have to find the guy, correct?"

"Of course."

"And we don't know who he is, also correct?"

"Yep."

"Be easier to find him if we know who he is."

"Sol, please. I think you know who he is. Just tell me what's going on. Okay?"

"No. First we've got to figure out how we're going to fight those phony charges against you."

"Don't worry about it. I'm off the hook."

"You're off the hook? You didn't tell me."

"How could I? You were going on about the fish, and jiving André about the wine like some kind of connoisseur."

"Hey buddy, I drink enough of the stuff to be an expert."

"No argument about that."

"Now, tell me how you got the charges dropped."

In between bites of fish, I told him about my telephone call to Detective Farrell.

"I knew you could beat those *farmisht* charges."

I set my fork down. "Lot of smooth talking."

"I've been using my *yiddisher kop*, been busy." Sol drained his wine glass.

"Busy doing what?" I asked Sol.

"We found out last Monday that Fischer was dead."

"Why didn't you tell me then?"

"I didn't want to tell you until I had things worked out."

"So I gather."

"Now I'm going to explain how the world's foremost detective operates."

"That would be you," I said.

Sol gave me a look that said, *isn't it obvious*. "I've had his girlfriend's apartment staked out for a while, but pulled my men off when we found out the guy's a fugitive. He ain't coming back."

"The guy's a fugitive, running from the law? What's his name?"

"Let me finish," Sol continued. "As soon as I found out the real Fischer was dead. I got in touch with a friend in the FBI. I asked him to get me the Federal Aviation Agency's list of all the pilots that are Cessna Citation rated. Remember, Karadimos's jet is a Citation."

"I know."

"To be able to fly the plane, unless you're military trained in jets, you'd have to take a course at the Cessna factory. It's a very sophisticated airplane; regular private pilots wouldn't be able to fly it."

Sol stopped talking and angled his head close to the table. He jabbed at something on his plate with his fork, then held it up and inspected the tidbit impaled there. "Hey," he said. "This doesn't look like an almond. Where's André? This is a goddamned walnut."

"Sol, forget the walnut. Tell me about the pilot."

"Okay, hold on." He popped the walnut into his mouth. "Not bad," he said. "Now, where were we? Oh yeah, when you pass the Cessna course, you get a type rating. The factory notifies the FAA and they send you a new license."

"Must've been hundreds of pilots."

"No, very few. The Citation jet just came out this year. Karadimos' plane is one of the first. Anyway, we ran a check on the pilots to see if any of them had a record. Remember, his girlfriend said he had some trouble with the law."

"I see where you're going with this, but how did you know the imposter would use his real name to get the rating?"

"To take the course, you need a multi-engine pilot's license. Couldn't use Fischer's ticket, he was dead before the Cessna Citation was introduced to the public. Also, you need to pass a medical exam to get the license."

I laughed. "I doubt that a medical examiner would certify a dead guy; might look bad."

"Wouldn't look good." Sol chuckled.

"How many names fit the profile?"

"Only eight."

"That's all? Just eight people?"

"Yep, that's all. And only one guy's a fugitive," Sol said.

"He'd be our guy."

"Yes, indeed. We have his name and a mug shot."

"What's his name?" I asked again.

"Kruger. Danny Kruger. Now all's we've got to do is find him."

"How long will that take?"

"We'll find him in time for the trial, that's for sure."

"I know you will. I'm counting on you, Sol."

He paused for a moment, pulled a cigar from the vest pocket of his jacket, and set it on fire with a solid gold blowtorch. "I've been thinking about your theory of the murder," he said as smoke from his cigar swirled to the ceiling. "I have some ideas. You wanna hear them?"

"Absolutely."

"Remember what Gloria said to Bonnie: 'The Greek might be on to me.' She was talking about the money, right?"

"Yeah, the money."

"Here's the way I figure it. We have two suspects and two possible motives. Each separate from the other. The first motive and suspect is the one we've been working on–Welch. He was having an affair with Gloria. He sent her the letter dumping her, didn't need the baggage now that he's running for re-election. Gloria got it Saturday. She called and threatened him. He flew down and killed her, and immediately flew back to Sacramento. But Welch has an airtight alibi."

"Yeah, the alibi is a big problem," I said.

Sol looked at me, nodded, and puffed on his cigar. "Now here's a second theory."

"Go ahead."

"Gloria was involved with Karadimos in his money laundering scheme, and she skimmed some off the top. Karadimos found out. He was on to her–Bonnie said so–and he flew down and killed her."

"Then he stashed the murder weapon in Rodriguez's truck, and made the anonymous call," I said, finishing his theory. "But if that were the case, wouldn't he just have one of his henchmen take care of the problem?"

"I dunno. Maybe he wanted to get his revenge personally. But when I find the pilot, he'll tell us who he flew down, Karadimos or Welch, and we'll have the murderer," Sol said.

"But we still have to tie the motive in with the flight. The passenger could come up with some other reason for sneaking back into town."

"We'll have to blow the lid off Karadimos and Welch's secret enterprise. That would show motive."

"Motive, means, and opportunity, it all fits–and we know Welch and Karadimos are working together," I said. "That's probably why the pilot took it on the lam. Must've figured he was hot, and Karadimos would get rid of him because he knew too much."

"I'll have to find the guy before Karadimos does, or he'll be a goner."

"I'll head over to Gloria Graham's house and snoop around. Even though the police have combed the place, and would have bagged any evidence by now, maybe I'll spot something."

"Can't hurt, and you'll be talking to Welch at Chasen's, at the fund raiser."

"Yeah, who knows, maybe he'll say something." After a pause, I added, "So how do you intend to find the pilot?"

"People can change identities, but they rarely change their old habits, hobbies, and skills. If he's hiding out, he still has to eat, still needs a job. I have ways of finding guys." Sol pulled the mug shots of the pilot out of the file and handed it to me. "Danny Kruger had a lot of odd jobs other than flying, but mainly bartending."

I gazed at the photos, both the front and side views. The sign around his neck said, *Houston Police Department, Danny Kruger, arrested 4/17/71.* There was a booking number under his name.

Kruger looked like a million other guys who grew up in the mid-fifties listening to the King's immortal classics– "Heartbreak Hotel," "Don't Be Cruel," "You Ain't Nothing But a Hound Dog." He had a full pompadour, well oiled, and cut long, Elvis style. He didn't look like the Presley impersonators who worked for Karadimos. Kruger looked more like the young Elvis, when the singer was first starting out. I figured that if you wanted to get a job with Karadimos, all you had to do was grow sideburns and dress up like the King.

"What was he arrested for?" I asked.

"The *shmuck* got caught trying to fly drugs across the border. First offense, his folks posted bail, he assumed Fischer's ID, and then split. Pop and Mom lost the house. Nice guy, huh?" Sol said.

"Probably likes pepper in his soup," I said.

Chapter Thirty-Three

We finished lunch at two o'clock, but before we left Rocco's I stopped at the phone booth, called the district attorney's office and asked to speak with Bobbi Allen. After the encounter in the courtroom, she was the last person I wanted to talk to, but I had no choice.

I had filed a motion asking the court to grant me access to the Graham house. The motion had been approved, which meant I had a legal right to visit the crime scene. But in order to cross the police line legally, someone from the DA's office would have to accompany me.

"What do you want, O'Brien?" Bobbi's voice had the same harsh tone I'd heard in the judge's chambers.

"I'm going to the Graham house. I'll be there in twenty minutes."

"It's still a crime scene."

"I want an escort."

"I'm too busy."

"Send someone."

"I can't spare anyone. Try back in a few weeks."

"I'll be at the house in twenty minutes."

"Better not cross the police line."

"I'm going in, with or without someone to escort me."

"You cross the line without an escort and I'll—"

"You'll what?"

"I'll see if I can send someone," she said before slamming the phone down.

She knew I would file a complaint with Judge Koito. It would make her look bad. But she wasn't going to make anything easy for me.

It took me twenty-two minutes to drive to Gloria Graham's house on Rosewood Avenue. I parked at the curb but didn't see a cop or anyone from the DA's office. I decided to wait, but I wasn't going to wait forever.

From the inside of my car, I surveyed the neighborhood. Rosewood was a pleasant enough street. Mature elm trees shaded the sidewalk in front of well-maintained tract homes. A late model black Ford pick-up truck, polished to a mirror shine, was parked in a driveway a few doors away. A man wearing a sleeveless undershirt and khaki chinos stood in his front yard sprinkling his lawn and smoking a cigar. A woman in the doorway of the house shouted something to him, but I was too far away to hear what she said. I sat in the car for fifteen minutes, waiting. *To hell with Bobbi, I'm going in.* Let her file the complaint. I'll get a slap on the wrist, so what.

Gloria's property was bound up, trussed, with yellow police tape. The tape wound around the perimeter of her yard, driveway, and house. Printed on it repeatedly were the words, POLICE LINE DO NOT CROSS. The tape fluttered and twisted in the breeze and offered no resistance to my intrusion as I slipped under it and entered the crime scene. Doing a slow shuffle up the driveway with my eyes on the ground, I kicked a dirt clod that rested on the concrete. It disintegrated into a spray of dust.

The police investigators would have picked the scene over and bagged, tagged or photographed any piece of evidence that would help their case against Rodriguez. I too had the right to have any article I found at the scene tagged and placed in the evidence locker. I doubted that I'd find anything, but still, I wanted to get a feel of the place.

Walking around the corner of the house to the backyard, I sidestepped the faded white spray-painted outline of her fallen body where the police had marked it. I thought of the pretty girl in the cheerleader's outfit. The girl in the photograph at the Munsons' home. The girl, young and full of life, the girl with dreams of a future filled with happiness. Her future wasn't much, just a ghostly image sprayed on the uncut grass with two cents worth of white paint.

The trees that Rodriguez had planted–just sticks really–were flourishing. On one of the trees a few baby green leaves, still tightly curled, sprouted from tiny buds on the web-like branches. Glancing around the yard, I noticed Rodriguez's shovel lying on the grass. A lemon-colored hose snaked from a bib at the side of the house, its nozzle resting on a circle of dirt. There were two other dirt patches next to it, each about two feet in diameter. I figured this must have been where Rodriguez had originally planted the tress.

My feet left deep impressions in the grass as I walked across the lawn to the house. It needed mowing. Who would do that now? I wondered as I mounted the porch steps that led to the house.

The screen door hung by a single hinge. I pushed it out of the way and tried the knob of the back door, the one that opened into the kitchen. Locked. I descended the steps and heard the sound of someone approaching.

"Hold it right there." A police officer in uniform stood a few feet in front of me, his legs spread, his right hand resting on his holstered gun. He stared at me with a severe expression on his face.

"Bobbi Allen send you?" I asked.

"You're in the middle of a crime scene."

"I'm the defense lawyer on this case. I have a right to be here."

He waved his fingers at me in a come-on manner. "Let's see some I.D. Slowly remove your wallet and hand it to me."

"I called the DA's office and told Miss Allen I was going to be here."

"You should've waited until someone got here before you busted in and contaminated the place."

I passed my driver's license and bar card to the cop. "I didn't contaminate anything."

He handed back my ID. "Lotta talk about you at the station, O'Brien. Now, did you mess with anything here?"

"I'm an officer of the court, for chrissakes. What do you

think? I'd plant some false evidence? Especially after the forensic team has swept this place clean?"

"From what I heard, it wouldn't have been the first time you tried something like that."

"What's your name anyway?"

"Officer Kemp, Leon Kemp."

"You're out of line, Kemp. Those charges were dismissed."

"Yeah sure, just don't try it here. You won't get away with that sort of thing while I'm on the job."

I shook my head and sighed.

Kemp unlocked the kitchen door and moved aside. I opened it and the thick and strong, sour stench of mold and rot engulfed me. I moved slowly into the dark kitchen. The shades were drawn. I exhaled slowly as I flipped on the light switch. The room was a mess. Patches of black powdered graphite covered the cupboards, tabletop, and drawers, places where Rodriguez's fingerprints might have been found.

Nothing in the room seemed to have been changed or altered since the night of Gloria's murder, except for the disturbance caused by the police investigation. Dirty dishes from her final meal were still in the sink. A full trashcan sat by the door. A broom leaned against the table. I stood in the center of the kitchen and glanced around. But I knew right off that several little things didn't seem right. The cabinet doors were partially opened, some drawers were pulled out about an inch, and four ice cube trays were on the countertop.

Walking into the living room, I had the same feeling as I did in the kitchen. I darted into the bedroom and looked around. The closet door was open, her clothes were in a heap on the floor, and her dresser drawers were pulled out an inch or so. Then I remembered the police report. It said that the house had been searched. I knew what was troubling me. After murdering Gloria, why would the killer toss her house? What did he hope to find? And, I wondered, did he find what he was looking for?

My eyes swept the small bedroom. A dresser rested against the wall, close to her bed. A mirror mounted over the dresser had photos and other memorabilia tucked into the edges. Her pretty face smiled at me from the pictures: at the beach, the mountains around a campfire with friends. She looked young and carefree, a girl full of life, not like someone who had been embezzling from a criminal enterprise.

Ticket stubs to a concert–the Grateful Dead at the Hollywood Bowl–a few cards, a scattering of dried flowers rested on the dresser.

When I picked up one of the pictures to take a closer look, a small card in an envelope, the kind used when sending flowers, fell out from behind it. I picked it up by its edges. The card inside wasn't signed, but there was a quote written on it: "*Not till the waters refuse to glisten for you and the leaves to rustle for you, do my words refuse to glisten and rustle for you.*" The quote sounded vaguely familiar, but I couldn't place it. I wondered if Welch had sent the card. The DA's office obviously knew the card couldn't be used in their case against Rodriguez, or it would have been tagged and bagged. But, I made a mental note to petition the court to have it marked as evidence for the defense, if needed.

I walked over to the desk on the other side of the room. Papers littered the top; open bills were tossed about. The wastebasket next to the desk was turned over, the trash spilled out onto the floor. I bent down but didn't see anything incriminating. I righted the wastebasket and saw an empty letter-sized envelope that must have been under it. I picked it up and flipped it over. It was addressed to Gloria, handwritten, and postmarked Friday from Sacramento, the day before she died. The envelope didn't have a return address, but the handwriting on it matched the writing on the little card with the quote–tall and spidery, with exaggerated loops. It looked like the scrawl of an egomaniac, but maybe it was just my mood. I would want the envelope tagged and dusted for prints.

Kemp tapped me on my shoulder. "You through? My shift's about done."

I tossed the envelope on the desk. "Yeah, let's go."

Hodges's theory about the case stated that Rodriguez killed Gloria in a rage because she resisted his sexual advances. But how'd he explain to the DA that Rodriguez searched the house after he supposedly killed her? He didn't kill her in a fit of passion and then decide to burglarize the home. Gloria's TV and her stereo had been untouched—and what kind of burglar leaves behind a box full of jewelry? Was Rodriguez looking for his lawnmower? I didn't think so.

I left the house and walked back to the Corvette. When I reached my car, I sat behind the wheel and let my gaze drift down the street. The guy in the undershirt was gone, but his hose, lying on the grass, continued to gush.

I had to think. I had a feeling I was on to something. What about the envelope I found: could it have held the letter that ended the relationship? Maybe it was nothing. The cops knew the envelope had nothing to do with Rodriguez or it would be in the evidence locker. I knew they'd only take evidence that would help their case against my client.

But what about the house being searched? What was the murderer looking for? Incriminating love letters, perhaps?

My mind reeled; questions kept coming. Perhaps the killer was looking for the money Gloria had embezzled. Who knew about the money? Bonnie Munson said that Gloria had been worried about the Greek. Would Karadimos suddenly fly down from Sacramento and kill her, as Sol had figured, then search the house in the middle of the night for cash that wasn't even there? No way, he's smarter than that. If Karadimos tossed the house, it had to be something more important than money to lure him here. It had to be an immediate problem.

Gloria had called Sacramento on the day she died. Did she call Welch and make demands? Maybe hit him with a threat, a little jab to the solar plexus? Tell him she'd ruin him?

Maybe Gloria had something other than her words to back up the threats. Maybe she had something in writing, something more than the Dear John letter. Maybe she had documents, ledgers, or journals that tied the senator to Karadimos.

Welch could have told Karadimos about the call, told the Greek to have her taken care of. That would have gotten the Greek's fat ass into the plane that night, and it would have provoked him to make an unannounced visit. But if that were the case, wouldn't he just have a hit man do the job? There'd be no need at all to fly down from Sacramento.

The sun beat down on my car and I started to roast. I hung my left arm outside the car and felt the hot August air drift through my fingers.

A thought grabbed me and I couldn't shake it loose. Every notion I had about the case was pure speculation. I had nothing tangible or solid.

The prosecution would have facts and photos. Hard evidence, the knife with Gloria's blood still on it, for example. Bobbi had a witness, a neighbor who would point at Rodriguez, and say, "That's him! That's the man I saw arguing with Gloria Graham just before she was murdered."

What would I do then? Would I stand in front of the twelve jurors, who'd be waiting for solid answers to the prosecutor's claims and say, "Well folks, you see, I have this feeling in my gut."

I glanced across the street. A movement in the window caught my eye. I could see Mrs. Wilson, Bobbi's witness, stealing a look at me through a slit in her Venetian blinds. I walked to her house and rang the doorbell.

Chapter Thirty-Four

A wary eye peeked at me when the door cracked open a few inches. "Are you Mrs. Wilson?"

"Yes," the woman replied in a meek voice.

I slipped my card through the opening. "My name's Jimmy O'Brien. I'm representing the poor man who's wrongly accused of the murder that happened across the street. Could I talk to you for a few minutes?"

"The police said you would try to see me. They told me I don't have to talk to you."

"That's true, you don't–but I'm just trying to clear up a few points. Get the facts straight in my mind. It won't take long."

"They said that you would try to trick me."

I smiled and held my arms out, spread my fingers and twisted my open hands a few times. "I haven't any tricks up my sleeve. I'm just a lawyer trying to do my job, not a magician."

"You seem like a nice man, but I already told the detectives everything I know."

"Mrs. Wilson, I'm sure you did, but it's up to me to make certain they wrote what you told them correctly in the report."

"You think they'd lie?"

"No, not at all," I said with all the sincerity I could muster. "I just want to ensure that an innocent man doesn't go to prison because of a clerical error."

"Well, I don't know..."

"You wouldn't want that to happen, would you?"

"No, I guess not..." Her voice trailed off, and she was quiet for a moment, then she said, "It's hot outside. C'mon in."

She closed the door, released the security chain, and opened it again. Mrs. Wilson, in her late sixties, had gray hair cut short in an attractive manner. She wore a light blue housedress and only a touch of makeup. I stepped into her small living room and sat in a wicker armchair.

"Would you care for a cool drink?"

"Sure."

"*Jamaica*?"

"Pardon me?"

"*Jamaica*, it's a delicious drink. My late husband Raul taught me how to make it. I just brewed a fresh batch. It's served chilled, like iced tea."

Why didn't she brew coffee like everyone else? "Oh, I'd love some."

Mrs. Wilson left to fetch the refreshments and I let my eyes wander around the room. The place was spotless. But a number of modern paintings hung on the walls–if you could call them paintings. They looked like someone's nightmare, dark and gloomy with red streaks running through them. A sick mind at work.

I automatically sat up straighter when Mrs. Wilson returned. "Do you like my paintings, Mr. O'Brien? I never took an art course or anything, just paint what comes to me in my dreams."

"There're wonderful." Okay, I lied.

"You're too kind." She held a platter. On it were two tall glasses filled with ice cubes floating in a reddish pink liquid. She handed me one of the glasses. I took a sip. Delicious! How long has this stuff been around? I asked myself.

"This is a great drink," I said. "What's it made from?"

"Hibiscus flowers. I grow them in the backyard."

I set the glass down on the coffee table in front of me.

Mrs. Wilson sat prim and proper, taking little bitty sips of her hibiscus concoction, smacking her lips from time to time. I asked her about the argument, and she proceeded to tell me what I already knew from the police report. The truck was in the driveway, where it stayed past her bedtime. Gloria and Rodriguez argued, she said, for about ten minutes. She

201

had spotted them earlier in the evening arguing on the driveway. After the argument ended, around six, Gloria went back into the house.

Mrs. Wilson went to bed at ten, took a sleeping pill, and didn't hear or see anything after that.

"Did you hear what they were saying when they argued?" I asked.

"No, I wasn't listening. I just heard a loud voice."

"Whose voice was it? Miss Graham's or the accused?"

"Gloria's. She seemed very agitated. You know, waving her arms around and shouting."

"But you couldn't hear what she was shouting about, is that correct?"

"No, I was too far away."

"What was Rodriguez doing?"

"Rodriguez?"

"The accused."

"Oh, he just mostly listened."

"Didn't he shout back?"

"I couldn't hear. I was too far away."

"Did he look angry or upset in any way?"

"His back was to me. I couldn't tell if he was upset. Couldn't see his face."

"Was he jumping up and down, waving his arms around, anything like that?"

"If he did, I didn't see it," she said, shaking her head slowly.

I didn't want to press too hard. Maybe I should ease up a little.

"I just have a few more questions, Mrs. Wilson."

"You can call me Vera, that's my name."

"Vera, you've been very helpful. You have a keen sense of observation."

"I'm not a busybody or a snoop."

"Of course not," I said. "But you're doing the right thing, volunteering the truth. No one else in the neighborhood came forward like you did."

"I just want to be a good citizen."

"I understand. Now let's see if you and I can figure this thing out, together."

"I'll help if I can."

"Of course you can. Now let's review: Gloria seemed furious and Rodriguez just stood there. He told me Gloria wanted the trees moved. Do you think that made him angry, fuming mad? What do you think?"

"I don't know if he was angry or not."

"Well, it takes two people to have an argument. Do you think maybe it was only Gloria who was upset?"

"She seemed upset."

"Upset about a few trees? Rodriguez moved them. He said it was no big deal."

"Maybe she was upset about something else," she said.

"But not at my client?"

"Perhaps not. I don't know."

"Telephone records show that Gloria called her boss's hotel that afternoon. Sometimes bosses can upset people." I let the last statement hang in the air and waited for Mrs. Wilson to respond.

We just sat, looking at each other. After a few moments, Mrs. Wilson started to fidget. She reached over to the end table and picked up a framed photograph, an older guy. "My late husband, Raul would get calls from his boss here at home once in a while. He'd get upset." She smiled at the picture and put it back.

"Perhaps rant and rave a little, after the call?"

"Oh yes." She had a tender look in her eyes.

"But not really directed at you, of course," I said.

"No. Raul was just blowing off steam."

"Maybe that's what happened with Gloria. What do you think?"

"Yes. Maybe that's what happened," she said.

"So, perhaps Rodriguez and Gloria hadn't been arguing

at all. Gloria could have been just blowing off steam," I said.

"Well, the police said they were arguing."

I almost jumped out of my skin. "The police? They weren't there at that time. Didn't you tell the cops that they were arguing?"

Her eyes opened wide and she said in a startled voice, "No, I just told them what I saw. They said it sounded like an argument."

I sat down. "Mrs. Wilson...I mean Vera?"

"Yes."

"There was no argument, was there?"

"Gloria was just blowing off steam." Mrs. Wilson sat there with a blank look on her face, sipping her red drink, and rocking back and forth ever so slightly.

After leaving Vera Wilson's, I drove around for a while. I was tired of the police and their hard-nose tactics. Tired of lying cellmates. Tired of guys like Fred Vogel selling me out. Tired of getting nowhere. And I was tired of being tired. Without thinking, I found myself going south on the Long Beach Freeway. I instinctively exited at the Willow off-ramp and headed for the airport.

Vogel had lied to the police. I knew for a fact the plane had been flown those extra two hours. Karadimos and his gang of Elvis impersonators had gotten to him, I was sure of it. But how did Karadimos find out so fast that I had talked to Vogel?

I wondered if he'd see me. Probably not. I wanted to knock him on his ass. Maybe he'd knock me on my ass, but I still wanted to confront him face to face. I wanted him to tell me about Karadimos.

I pulled into the Executive Aviation parking lot, sat in my car, and thought. Would it do any good to challenge him? If I got tough with him, would I be accused of trying to intimidate the witness again, making the situation worse? The cops might even start investigating the bribery charge all over again. The way the circumstances stood now, I couldn't call him as a witness for the defense. He'd obviously lie on the stand. I'd look like an idiot and lose the case.

I went into the building. "Vogel here?" I asked the clerk working the reception counter.

"Ain't here," the scrawny kid said. "He's on vacation."

"Don't give me that crap, he was here yesterday. No one starts their vacation on Thursday."

He ignored my statement for a moment. Then without looking up at me he said, "Called in this morning, said he's taking a few weeks off."

I felt my temperature rising, the pressure building. I needed a release. Suddenly, I lost it. I reached over the counter and grabbed the guy by his shirtfront. I pulled him across the ledge. His head snapped back and his eyes opened wide in surprise.

"I want to see Vogel. Now, Goddammit! Get his ass out here," I said through clenched teeth.

"Hey, lemme go!" he shouted. "I'm not kidding, mister. He's not here. Go and see for yourself."

What in the hell was the matter with me? I looked around the lobby; people stared at me. I felt foolish. I was acting like an out-of-control juvenile. I let go of the kid. "Nah, I believe you. If he calls in tell him to get in touch with me." I tossed my card on the counter.

The clerk tried to straighten his uniform shirt while backing away. "Don't bet on it, asshole," he said.

Chapter Thirty-Five

I arrived at the office early Friday morning. Rita wasn't in and I needed a cup of coffee. I saw the new coffeepot sitting there, gleaming with its buttons and lights and all its automatic doohickeys. You'd have to be a mechanical engineer to fire the thing up. I didn't even know where you were supposed to load the coffee. Or even if I knew, how much would I have to put in the thing? Great, I thought, I don't even know how to make a cup of coffee anymore. If I touch the pot, it'd probably blow up in my face like everything else. The hell with it; I decided to head over to Dolan's Donuts. I ordered two glazed and a large coffee to go. I put the bag in my car and shot back to the office.

I was starting on my second donut when Rita came through the door. She had on tight jeans and a T-shirt with a picture of Mickey Mouse, one arm around Minnie. Mickey had his other arm raised, and two of his fingers formed a V. The caption under the cartoon said, *Make love not war.*

I glanced up at Rita's angelic face. She had the type of complexion that didn't require make-up, and she wore very little. It gave me a boost to see her cheery smile.

"Hey, Boss. Want some coffee?"

"I have some, but thanks anyway."

She saw the printing on the cup and arched an eyebrow. "When we have time, I'll show you how to work the coffeepot."

"Thanks, but first we have to prepare a discovery request. We have to find out about Rodriguez's cellmate. I'll need to break him down on cross. Prove he's lying."

"We're out of discovery forms. In fact, we've never had any."

"Yeah, I know, never needed them. You can pick up a

few at the legal stationery store on Firestone. Ask Mike the owner for some carbon paper, too." I reached in my pocket and pulled out my bankroll. I gave half to her. "Here's a few bucks, should be enough."

"I'll make you a deal," Rita said. "I'll fill out the discovery forms, but you tell me what you want to say, what to ask for. Then later I'll show you how to work the coffeepot." She smiled. "Who knows, maybe you'll want to make the coffee now and then."

"You went to law school. Use your own words on the request."

"What about the coffeepot?"

"Forget about it," I said. "Oh, after you've filled out the forms, don't forget to serve them on the DA's office. Then file the papers with the clerk at the court."

She turned to leave. "See you in a bit."

"Wait," I said. "I'll need some cash." I'd need money for the fundraiser at Chasen's. Although the dinner was paid for, I'd still need a few bucks for parking and maybe a tip or two. "Bring me the checkbook. You can stop at the bank on your way back. I'll sign your paycheck now, too."

"I used the balance of the money you gave me from the racetrack winnings, to catch up on the back rent and telephone. And now, after my pay, we'll have less than two hundred in the bank," she said as she laid the book on my desk. "And your car insurance bill is in the drawer."

"The insurance company can wait; somehow they'll make it without my check. Might have to hold off on building a new skyscraper this week, though."

"Boss, you're crazy, but nice." She flashed me one of her world-class smiles.

"Rita, I just thought of something. When I was in the Sav-On the other day, I saw a Phillips mini-tape recorder on sale. It'll fit in my briefcase, and it comes with those new cassettes." She gave me a bewildered look. "Pick one up on your way back from the bank. Okay?"

"How much?"

"Sixty bucks."

"Jimmy—"

"I know, but I'm meeting Welch tonight. It cost Sol a lot of money to set it up and I want to record the interview."

"Do you think the senator will let you tape him?"

"We'll see," I said.

"Are you going to tell him he's being recorded?"

"We'll see."

"You're the boss." She sighed.

I signed the checks. Rita left just as the phone rang. I answered it. "Law office. O'Brien speaking."

"Hi, remember me? Tracy Spencer, Ron Fischer's girlfriend? Remember you talked to me the other day at the apartment?"

"Yes, Tracy, I remember."

"That's my stage name, Tracy Spencer, get it? Spencer Tracy, the movie star. I wanted people to remember my name, but then he died..." Her voice trailed off, probably a moment of silence in remembrance of her fallen namesake. "I guess I'll have to change it again. What do you think of Hoffy Dustman?"

I took a sip of coffee. "What is your real name?"

"Bertha Weems."

"What can I do for you, Tracy?"

I felt sorry for her. I knew her boyfriend, the pilot, was most likely gone for good. I knew firsthand how it felt to be lonely. However, with her looks and her job, I also knew she wouldn't be lonely for long.

"You seemed so nice the other day I thought it would be okay to call you." I reassured her, and she continued: "Yesterday I got a postcard from Ronnie. He said everything is okay. He's got a temporary job, didn't say where, said he had to leave town for a while, but not to worry, he'd be back."

My hand started to shake. The coffee splashed on my desk. I took a deep breath and tried to remain calm.

"Mr. O'Brien, are you there?" she asked.

"Yes, I'm here. By any chance did you notice the postmark on the card?" I tried not to show my excitement.

"No," she said.

My heart sank. "Do you still have the card?" Holding my breath, I crossed my fingers.

"I put it in the drawer. Do you want me to get it?"

I exhaled. "Yes, that would be nice."

A few seconds later she told me, "It was mailed from Las Vegas, but I'm confused."

Las Vegas! I had to call Sol fast and tell him where to start looking. But I tried to remain calm. "Sounds like he's okay. Why are you confused?"

"I came home from work last night and noticed Ronnie's El Camino was broken into. And I think someone went through his apartment too. The door was unlocked. But I know I locked it after I dropped off his clothes. You think I should call the cops?"

Cops, my God! They'd arrest him before I could get the answers I desperately needed. "No, don't call them," I almost shouted.

"Why?"

"Oh, I'm sure it was just kids fooling around." It bothered me that it had become so easy to lie.

"Okay." She didn't sound convinced.

"Remember, Tracy, you said he had some trouble in the past. I don't think he'd like the cops snooping around.

"Yeah, I guess you're right."

"Now listen to me. This is very important. Do not, I repeat, do not tell anyone about the postcard or this phone call. Do you understand?"

"You sound scary. What's going on?"

"I'm not sure, but your boyfriend is hiding out for a reason. We don't want to tip off anyone that might be out to harm him."

"You think he's in trouble?"

"Yes."

"Will you help him?"

"If he asks me, I'll help. But first I've got to find him."

We said goodbye and my hand trembled as I hung up the telephone.

I immediately dialed Sol's office number. It was still too early for him to be in, but Joyce said he'd be there shortly. I left a note for Rita. I told her I was going to Sol's office and she could start filling out the discovery form. I'd review it when I returned.

I ran to my Corvette. If Karadimos found Kruger first, he'd disappear for good. Sol said Kruger had been a bartender before he was a pilot. A bartender, I thought as I drove. Where would we start to look? Las Vegas was the drinking capital of the world. There had to be a million bars.

The trial date was bearing down on me. I was running out of time and I was out of money. I needed Kruger's testimony.

Chapter Thirty-Six

I entered the lobby of Sol's office complex. Telephones rang off the hook, people bustled about with papers in their hands and files and folders under their arms. Their footsteps were muffled by an array of lavish antique Persian carpets. Flaming reds, vibrant greens, and golden silk threads were woven together to form intricate designs that told ancient stories. The rugs didn't mention where I could find Kruger.

"I'm O'Brien, here to see Mr. Silverman," I said to the young man sitting behind the reception counter.

"Yes sir. I was told to expect you. I'll buzz Joyce."

An abstract painting took up the whole wall behind the guy. It was black and white with gobs of paint running down the canvas. I had had no idea what it was supposed to be. Looked like some sort of a shaggy animal.

I strolled to the picture window at the end of the room and peered out. The rich architectural decor in Sol's office clashed with the view of Downey's commercial district–a body shop, thrift store, and a taco stand with a hand-lettered sign that read, *"Carne Al Pastor Con Frijoles."* Maybe the picture on the wall was the goat they used in the tacos.

Joyce appeared. "Hi, Jimmy. You can wait in the conference room. Sol will join you in a few minutes."

I sat at a polished wood table that could have doubled as the deck of an aircraft carrier for a nation of pygmies. I didn't count the chairs, but if the seats filled, the population in this room would have rivaled a small European principality.

A tall man materialized carrying a silver coffee service with two fragile-looking cups. He wore a formal waiter's outfit, black pants, white shirt, and a cutaway jacket. The jacket looked too small.

"Jamaican Blue Mountain," the waiter said.

"What?"

"The coffee, sir. Mr. Silverman's favorite."

I didn't care if it was Purple Mountain Majesty; I needed to speak with Sol. "When will the boss be here?" I asked.

"Soon." He turned and slipped quietly out the door.

I sipped the coffee. No surprise, it was excellent. I was pretty hyped up about Tracy's news that Kruger was alive and most likely in Las Vegas. I drank some more coffee and was pouring a second cup when Sol came bounding into the room. He sat at the head of the table.

"Hope the coffee's okay."

"Sol, you know damn well it's great," I said, a trifle facetiously. I was proud of his success and he knew it.

He poured a cup for himself. "I have a guy who picks out my coffee and grinds it special."

That came as no surprise, either. But I didn't comment. I wanted to tell Sol about Kruger. "I got a call from Tracy, Kruger's girlfriend. He mailed her a postcard from Vegas."

"I guess you could call him a coffee designer," Sol said.

"I think he's a bartender–Wait, not the coffee guy, Kruger. He's probably a bartender."

"Oh, I know about Kruger. I've already had my men up there looking for him."

I leaned back in my chair. "How'd you know he'd be in Las Vegas?"

"One of my informants spotted him on the strip, then he disappeared. But it fits. Kruger wants the action and it'd be easy to find a job bartending. There are more bars in Vegas, per capita, than any place. Don't forget he's hiding out. It's like they say–if you want to hide a book put it in a library."

"With all the places to look, how long will it take to find him?"

Sol set the coffee cup down. "If we just went place to place, showed his picture around, and went back to each bar at every shift change, we'd never find him, not in this lifetime. But we have help."

"Yeah, from whom?"

"Our old friends, Nick La Cotta, Joe Sica, and the boys."

"Oh."

"Look, Jimmy, these *goniffs* know Vegas. The Mafia built the town. Not much goes on up there that they don't know about and we need all the help we can get. Remember, we're not the only ones looking for Kruger."

"Yeah, I know. Karadimos is after him. Not to mention the FBI. He skipped on the drug thing."

"If the FBI finds him first, they'll hustle him off to Houston on the fugitive warrant and you'll never get to him. Even if you did, he'd clam up. You wouldn't get anything out of him. But, that's not the worst of it–" Sol stopped in mid-sentence for a beat. "I don't even want to think about Karadimos finding him before we do."

"When we find him, we'll still have to get him to talk," I said, thinking out loud.

"He'll talk," Sol said.

"Sure he will," I said, knowing it'd be up to me to get Kruger to tell us what we had to know.

I stood and walked to the large arched window at the far end of the room, wondering how I'd get Kruger to talk if Sol and the mobsters actually found him. I looked out at the traffic on Florence Avenue. There were only a few cars parked at the curb and none of them had goons sitting behind the wheel. I figured Karadimos's men were still keeping close tabs on me, but I hadn't seen anyone tailing me for a while. Could it be that Big Jake had scared them off?

"Good luck at the fundraiser tonight," Sol said.

I turned around. "Right now I'm worried about finding Kruger."

"We'll find him and he'll talk. Quit worrying."

"He'll talk if he's alive."

Chapter Thirty-Seven

"Rita, you did a marvelous job on this discovery form. All it needs is my signature and it will be ready to file. How'd you know what to request?"

I sat across from Rita at her little desk in our outer office. She had handed me the discovery request form. I signed it and handed it back to her.

"Three years of law school, Jimmy," she said. "I know enough about the case to figure out what to request."

"Well, it's perfect."

"When I was at the store, I bought a copy of *The Legal Secretary's Handbook*. I used my own money to get it for you. Everything is in the book, how to fill out forms, make a will, all kinds of stuff. You'll need a secretary when I'm gone. I'll be getting my bar results soon. And...well, you know."

"With that book and a rubber stamp for my signature I wouldn't even have to show up at all. The secretary could do everything," I said, half laughing.

"Yes, that would work; a signature stamp. Good idea, Jimmy. I'll still be your secretary for a while, anyway. I could pay the bills, file the forms, and take care of things when you're not here. You're not here very often, you know, and you always send me home early."

I realized that Rita needed to be more useful and wanted to expand her skills. She had to be bored sitting around waiting to answer a phone that rarely rang.

"If the stamp is only used with my prior authorization, I guess it would be okay. Call the bank. Find out what we need to do to set it up."

"Done." She snapped to attention. "I put your money and the tape recorder on your desk."

I stepped into my office, and Rita followed. I tucked the

money in my pocket and started to fool around with the cassette machine.

"I'll go back to the bank and get the forms for the stamp." She moved toward the door.

"Rita," I shouted after her.

She looked back at me over her shoulder.

"While you're at it, have some new cards printed. You're now the new office manager, that is until you pass the bar, and then..." I paused; I didn't know how to ask. "Maybe we could work something out."

"I've had a few good offers, Jimmy. I've been meaning to speak with you."

"Yeah, I know." I knew the day would come when Rita would leave, and that day was close at hand, but knowing didn't make it easier. I'd miss her terribly.

"Hard to turn them down," she said. "Don't have to make the coffee at those fancy law firms."

"Rita, I'll make the coffee."

"I've tasted your coffee." She paused. "But I'll stay anyway." She flashed a smile that lit up my heart.

"You will?"

"Yes," she said. "I admire you, Jimmy. And I respect you for what you're doing for Mr. Rodriguez, especially doing it for no money when we're practically broke. I like you a lot and love working here and I want to do what I can to help."

"It's a deal then. As soon as the bar results are in, you're my new associate."

"Oh, wow!" Rita rushed over and threw her small arms around me in a warm hug. She stepped back and looked up at me with a solemn expression on her face. "One condition, Jimmy."

I knew what was coming–her salary. I really hadn't thought it through. I didn't know where the money would come from, but I wanted her to stay with me. I needed her, and not just for her skills; I needed someone I could talk with, someone who liked me for who I was. "Aw, Rita, I think I can come up with something–"

She cut me off. "I still make the coffee. I don't want you messing with our new pot. Deal?"

Our eyes met, and hers sparkled. We both laughed, and it felt good. I wanted to hug her again, and I wanted to tell her how much she meant to me, but the words wouldn't come.

I turned and picked up the mini-recorder. "Now, Miss Associate, show me how to work this damn machine."

She took the recorder from my hands and started to take it apart. "Thanks for the promotion, boss. Office manager, not bad." She nodded. "From secretary to office manager in six months. And soon I'll be an associate. Not bad at all."

"If this keeps up," I said. "In another six months, you'll be the senior partner."

"You bet, and I haven't even passed the bar yet."

We both laughed again.

Rita patiently taught me how to work the recorder. I fiddled with it while she prepared the proof of service for the discovery request. She would file it at the court and serve a carbon copy on the DA's office after she returned from the bank with the papers for the signature stamp. In addition to the discovery, I'd need a motion *in limine* to exclude the testimony of Rodriguez's cellmate. I planned to spend the weekend working on it. I wouldn't file it until I received the discovery response from Bobbi. I might have to make a few changes depending on the documents she produced.

I stuffed the cassette recorder into my briefcase and left the office a little after five p.m., in time to stop at the dry cleaners before they closed. I thought about the small fortune Sol had paid for the tickets and I didn't want some officious doorman at Chasen's turning me away just because I wasn't wearing a suit and tie.

216

Chapter Thirty-Eight

The simple white structure at 9039 Beverly Boulevard had an elegant look. No garish signs–*All you can eat, one thousand dollars*, nothing like that. Just the name Chasen's, in raised gold script, floating on the front next to the canopy-covered entrance.

I pulled into the lot next to the restaurant and tossed a buck to the parking guy. After checking the crumpled dollar bill, he hurried off to greet the Rolls that had pulled up behind me. I parked my own car.

A discreet six-inch square sign hung on the front door, *Private Party. Re-elect Senator Welch, Invitation Onl*y. I had never been to Chasen's and I was surprised by the old-fashioned décor. The restaurant, with its plush emerald green carpeting, had that warm clubby look that was big in the thirties. Tufted leather booths and tables draped in immaculate linens, with enough silver to deplete the Comstock Lode. I liked it.

I presented my ticket to the *maître d'*. He snapped his fingers; a waiter appeared. "Oscar, take Mr. O'Brien to the Siberian room." He gave me a curt nod and turned to greet the next arrival.

The waiter escorted me to a small table in a dark alcove, close to the kitchen. I set my briefcase on the chair next to me. Rita told me the tape would record for forty-five minutes on each side. We'd tested the device in my office and the recorder picked up our voices while tucked out of sight in my briefcase.

I strolled over to the bar, ordered a Coke, then made my way back through the cigarette and cigar smoke swirling in the air and again sat at my table, waiting. I scanned the restaurant–at least the part I could see–and noticed Judge

Johnson standing among the crowd in the front. He had a drink in his left hand and he seemed to be giving the once-over to a good-looking blond standing close by. Johnson's wife stood next to him, clutching her arms tightly across her chest.

After fifteen minutes, the *maître d'* approached my table. "Mr. O'Brien, Maude Chasen said it would be all right to use her office for your meeting with the Senator. Please follow me."

I got up and spotted Karadimos standing in the middle of the crowd, glaring at me. I could almost feel the hatred that flowed from his blazing eyes. When I raised my glass in a mock toast, he turned and walked away.

The *maître d'* took me through the busy kitchen to a small office off to the side. The plain office held a desk, two leather armchairs, and a sofa. The *maître d'* said he'd inform Welch that I was waiting. When he shut the door I opened my briefcase, took out the tape recorder, turned it on and put it back. I snapped the briefcase shut and placed it next to the sofa. Leaning back, I folded my hands in my lap.

Of course I wouldn't tell Welch he was being recorded, and because of that little detail I couldn't use the tape in court. In fact, I would be fudging the law just recording him without his permission. But what the hell, I was defending a murder case. Anyway, I'd just use the tape for my notes and then quickly erase it.

A few minutes later, Thomas French entered and held the door for the Senator. Welch had a slender build, stood about six-foot-one and had an immaculate tan, like a movie actor. I wondered if it came out of a bottle. When would a guy like him have time to hang out at the beach? His dark, slicked back hair glistened as it caught the light of the wall lamps when he moved farther into the office. I stood, and he came over to me. We didn't shake hands. Instead, he nodded toward French and told me, "I hope you're not going to have a problem with my attorney being here."

"Nope, I have a few questions for him too," I replied.

French waved his arms in front of his chest. "Oh no, just the Senator. That's the deal and you've only got ten minutes." He glanced at his watch, then pointed a finger at me. "Starting now."

Welch sat in one of the armchairs and crossed his legs. "I think I can save some time here." He tugged at his pant leg a little so as not to wrinkle the razor sharp crease. "I did not kill Gloria. That's why you're here. That's what you wanted to ask me."

"I have other questions, as well."

"I was in Sacramento in a room full of people at the time she died."

"I think you were sleeping with her, having an affair."

French waved his hands again. "What kind of remark is that? He wasn't involved with the girl. The very idea."

"God knows I tried. What a gorgeous body." Welch began to pick a piece of lint off his suit jacket. "I couldn't get anywhere. I think she was hung up on someone else."

I thought I saw a flicker of truth in his eyes. I didn't think he'd lie about *not* having an affair and then admit that he made a move on her.

"Didn't you send her a letter? She got it Saturday. You dumped her. I found the envelope at her house, handwritten. The cops could check your handwriting."

"Let them check. I've nothing to hide."

He didn't seem to be bothered about the envelope. Perhaps he wasn't involved with Gloria after all. Maybe the envelope was nothing. His denial carried a ring of truth. "Are you saying you were not having an affair?"

"Asked and answered," French shouted.

"Shut up, French," I said. "This isn't a courtroom."

"Nope, I'm sorry to say," Welch said. "Jesus, she was hot stuff."

I could feel my theory about the case slipping away, but I continued: "Did she call you the day she died? Between four and five in the afternoon?"

"No, she didn't." Welch glanced at the ceiling. "The only call I got on Saturday was from Phil Rhodes, our PR guy. He'd hired a comedian for the dinner and the prick cancelled at the last minute. Phil wanted me to ask Goulet to sing an extra set to cover for him."

"Graham called the hotel and talked to someone for twenty minutes," I said.

"Not me." Welch glanced at his buffed fingernails. "Let's see. Yeah, between four and five, I was in the bar with Tom Brokaw; he's the news guy on Channel 4 here in L.A. He's doing a piece on the 1974 governor's race. He'll verify it. He paid the bar tab. I'm sure he put it on his expense report."

French jumped in. "Why don't you get off the Senator's back? It's obvious that he had nothing to do with Miss Graham's unfortunate death."

"Why did you pressure Judge Johnson to force my client to plead guilty?"

"That's enough, O'Brien!" French snapped. "You're crossing the line with these insinuations."

"It's okay Tom. I'll answer him." Welch started to climb out of the chair. "It's true I had lunch with Johnson on the Monday following the murder, but I didn't pressure him. My assistant had been murdered. They caught the guy who did it, and I wanted to make sure they got the right person, that's all."

"It was in your best interests to have the case closed as soon as possible," I said.

"Okay, that's it, O'Brien. He told you he didn't pressure anybody." French shook his head. "Interview's over. Goodbye."

"Thought I had ten minutes. It hasn't been that long."

"You're questions are inappropriate. The senator hadn't agreed to be slandered." French started to move toward me.

I looked into Welch's eyes. "What about Hartford Commodities and Karadimos? I know you're connected with him. You too, French?"

That caught their attention. Welch raised his eyebrows slightly and his mouth opened as if to speak. No sound came out, but French piped up: "The Senator's business interests are in a blind trust. Karadimos is a large contributor. He just wants quality government. Now, this meeting is over. Please leave."

"Welch, I think you're in up to your neck with the Greek."

"You're outta here, O'Brien."

"Senator, answer my question."

"Don't say anything, Berry." French stepped quickly between Welch and me. "Now, do I have to call someone, or are you leaving?"

I moved to the door and put my hand on the knob. Turning back, I looked at Welch and French. "I know about the cantaloupes," I said and left the office.

Chapter Thirty-Nine

"Mack the Knife" reverberated from the bar as I walked back into the dining room. The crowd was whooping it up for all they were worth. I found a spot where I could see the kitchen passage, and waited. Waiters scurried in and out, and after a long while–at least it seemed like a long while–French and Welch emerged. They brushed by me without looking and joined the group in the main dining room. I glanced around. The coast was clear. I raced into the kitchen and maneuvered around the prep counters, chefs and busboys nearly slipping on the tile floor, then darted though the double doors, heading back toward the office.

When I reached for the knob, I paused, I hadn't planned to leave my briefcase with the recorder running in the office after I left. I told myself I didn't actually mean to eavesdrop on Welch and his lawyer. But I knew better. And I'd have been a fool not to take the opportunity when it popped up. The remark about cantaloupes came to me in a flash–imports from Mexico. If the produce business was on the up and up, Welch and French would pass the remark off as a non sequitur. But if they responded to it, I'd know for sure that they were partners, engaged in some sort of illegal activity.

I opened the door and dashed into the office. Grabbing my briefcase, I darted through the kitchen again. I just wanted to get out of the restaurant–fast. Go somewhere and listen to the tape. I headed toward the front and pushed my way through the crowd. When I got closer to the main room, I saw Karadimos shoving guests aside as he elbowed toward me. Our eyes locked. I saw his fury and knew he must have figured something wasn't right. He charged at me like a raging bull, bellowing; even his nostrils flared.

A shout from the crowd rose above the clamor, "Andy,

wait!"

Karadimos jerked his head to the side and I followed his gaze. French shook his hand slightly, and nodded toward the small group with a TV camera in a circle of lights gathered around Mayor Sam Yorty. Karadimos would draw unwanted attention if he kept coming at me.

He stopped. Looking around, he snapped his fingers at a couple of heavyweights leaning against the wall by the entrance. He pointed at me, and then made furious jabbing motions with his finger toward the front door. The hoods came alive like puppets on a string. They sprinted past the *maître d'*s station and pushed their way outside.

I backed up a few feet, turned, picked up my pace, and retraced my steps through the kitchen, running for the rear. The back door opened onto an alley littered with trash containers and empty boxes. I shot around the corner of the restaurant and entered the parking lot. My Corvette was parked close to the front near Beverly Boulevard.

One of the parking guys ran toward me. "Hold it. What are you doing back there?"

I pulled the car keys from my pocket, holding them in the air. "Going to my car." I pointed to my Corvette. "I came out through the back door." I kept moving. The valet turned and walked back toward the front of the lot.

Karadimos's men loitered on the sidewalk by the street. I spotted them and they spotted me. I made a dash for my car. I got there fast, but too late.

One of the thugs grabbed my shoulder and spun me around. He came back with his right hand and took a roundhouse swing at me, but I blocked it with my forearm. The other guy tugged madly at the briefcase. I held on, jerked it free, and took a swipe at his head with it. I missed. Suddenly, out of the corner of my eye, I saw a fist coming at me, heavy and fast, like a freight train. I whipped my head back. The punch grazed my jaw.

All the color drained out of the night and the darkness

turned white. I staggered, but I hung on to the briefcase when the other guy grabbed it again. Suddenly, I heard loud yells coming from everywhere. The noise reverberated in my head like shouts in a tunnel.

"Watch out–"

"Jesus! Crazy bastard–"

"He ain't slowing down."

"Get outta the way!"

The tugging on my briefcase eased. I didn't know how I was able to hang on to it, but I did. I shook my head. My vision cleared enough to see Big Jake's Cadillac bounce over the curb, hurtle toward us, and screech to a stop right in front of Karadimos's men.

Before the thugs realized what was happening, Jake bolted from the Caddie. With his left hand, he grabbed the briefcase guy and flung him into a parked Bentley. The guy struck it hard and stayed down. Jake's right hand was a steel fist that exploded violently into the other goon's nose. It burst like an overripe tomato and blood pulsed out in a sickening stream. The guy dropped. He was down for the count.

Jake turned and ran back to his car. "Get outta here, O'Brien, 'fore the cops come."

A crowd started to form. But they scattered when Big Jake stomped on the gas, screaming backward, without looking, at about ninety miles an hour right out of the lot and onto the boulevard. He whipped the car around, made a skidding U turn, and disappeared down the street. The whole thing was over in a matter of seconds.

I pulled my Corvette onto Beverly, turned right, and headed west. In my rearview mirror I saw two squad cars, red lights flashing, swerve into Chasen's parking lot. I glanced at the briefcase resting on the passenger seat, and my jaw didn't hurt so much anymore.

Chapter Forty

At Sunset Boulevard, I turned left and drove west to the PCH. I followed the coastline north and cruised past the Palisades, then Malibu, and soon I was beyond Point Mugu. A jade green florescence shimmered on the breakers as they rolled onto the shore fifty feet to my left.

I merged onto US 101 and drove until I came to California Street in Ventura. I exited and stopped at the first motel I saw. After checking in, I dead-bolted the door. I had to get away and wanted to go away from Downey. I figured someone at Chasen's might have gotten my license number, and I didn't want the police pounding on my door. I wanted time to analyze the tape and plan my next move.

The motel was typical for a beach town: a dozen or so tiny cottages, built in the 1940s, surrounding a gravel parking lot. The neon sign in front by the office flickered and buzzed like fireflies gone mad. Each cottage had a double bed with a single thin blanket, a lamp with a forty-watt bulb that barely cast enough light to read by, and a black and white TV resting on a veneer-covered plywood dresser. The room was perfect.

I aet my briefcase on the bed, sat down, and removed the recorder, anxious as I rewound the cassette. I hit the play button and skimmed the first part, where I was in the room.

At the point where I made the remark about the cantaloupes, I hit stop. I stood, walked around the room, went into the bathroom, and splashed water on my face. Why was I stalling? I told myself to get in there and turn it on. I took a deep breath, sat down, and pushed the play button again.

I listened to ten or fifteen seconds of silence. Then Welch's voice erupted, *"What does he know?"*

"Nothing, he's fishing, that's all."

I'd been holding my breath, and when I heard what

Welch and French said, I exhaled. Goddamn, I knew it. I stood, flexed my hands, and paced as I listened to the rest.

"What do you mean, fishing? Did you hear him, the cantaloupes? He's not fishing; he's off the boat and on the shore. I'm telling you he knows what's going on, and I don't like it—"

"Calm down, Berry. Karadimos has everything under control, but what was he talking about when he said something about a letter to the girl?"

"Who knows? I don't give a shit about that. But, damn it, I'm concerned. Listen, French, you're in this too. I thought you guys were gonna get rid of him."

"Look, it isn't that easy. We've tried. He's got help from Sica's gang."

"Can't you blow up his car or something? Jesus Christ Almighty!"

"Berry, we don't want any more bodies lying around. We're in enough trouble with Graham's murder. We've got to snatch O'Brien and get rid of him in Mexico. Turn him over to our partners down there. Nobody will know what happened to him and I doubt that anyone will care."

Thanks a lot, French, I thought. We'll see who cares about you when all this comes out.

"What about that other guy? What's his name, the pilot?"

"Kruger. We're looking for him now. He won't be back."

"He knows all about it. He helped set it up. Are you guys sure you're going to find him? I'm worried as hell."

"Come on, Senator, get out and do your thing. There are important people here tonight. Karadimos is counting on you to stay in office, so you can win the big one down the road."

"I want out. You guys can keep the money. I'm going to be the fucking governor of California in two years for Christ's sake. You listen to me—I want out now!"

"It's not healthy to talk like that, Welch. How do you think you got here?"

"Did I hear what I think I heard? Are you threatening me?"

"No. No, of course not. It's our partners south of the border. They're pressing us, but we have to keep things closed down until it blows over. So let's not say anything about quitting right now."

"Let's get the hell out of here."

The tape continued. I heard the office door open, slam shut, then nothing. I snapped off the recorder and stared at the machine for a long time. Now I knew for sure what I only suspected before. Karadimos was importing drugs, and French and Welch were in it with him.

I quit pacing and sat on the edge of the bed. A minute later, I heard a noise outside. My heart thumped. I darted to the window, pulled back the skimpy curtain, and peeked out. It was nothing, some guy and his frumpy wife banging their luggage as they checked in the cottage next door.

I thought about French and Welch and the image they projected. Concerned citizens, stalwarts of the community.

I shook my head. Thomas French, the Boy Scout, the winner of the good citizen award, the speaker at Downey High's commencement last June. Excerpts had been reprinted in the *Downey Enterprise*. The title, *'The Challenges Facing Youth in Today's Changing World.'* Next year he could update it a bit. *'The Challenges Facing Youth in Blowing up a Car.'* It would get more than a write-up in the *Enterprise*, might even make the *Times*. I was sure it would.

I listened to the tape again and realized just how hot it was. I could get burned just touching it. It'd blow everything wide open. But if I turned the tape over to the court, I'd lose my license when they found out what I'd done. Was I willing to sacrifice my career, and possibly go to jail, to save Rodriguez? That's a question they didn't answer in law school.

Chapter Forty-One

Sitting in the motel room, I heard the ocean waves pound the shore as I played and replayed the tape. I listened carefully to the words, the hidden meanings and inflections. I'd hear something, stop, rewind the tape, and play it again. I listened to the words that weren't there and tried to connect the dots. The most incriminating thing on the tape was the part about blowing up my car.

My wild remarks about Karadimos and the cantaloupes had paid off. Welch had become rattled and started spilling his guts. French mentioned that Karadimos had "partners in Mexico." I drew the only possible conclusion: his drug-smuggling operation was based somewhere south of the border. The fact he was involved with drugs would explain the mob war and the money. I tried to figure out what French would say if the conversation ever became public. How could he and Welch explain it?

I knew the tape–even illegally recorded–would ruin Welch's political career. But there was nothing on the tape to prove that Rodriguez was innocent. If even a modicum of evidence appeared on the tape hinting at his innocence, then a copy would already be on the *L.A. Times* editor's desk. I'd lose my license but my client would go free. As determined as I was to see Welch and his cronies face a court of law, I didn't think I could destroy my career to ruin Welch. No; my obligation was to Rodriguez, and I wasn't a crusader. I dismissed the thought of sending the tape anonymously to the *Times* or the police. Too many people would know where it had come from: Phil Rhodes set up the meeting, the staff at Chasen's saw me with a briefcase, and even Rita knew. I wouldn't allow her to commit perjury if it came to that.

The sun was rising by the time I dropped on the bed and

plunged into an exhausted sleep.

I woke up a couple hours later and for an instant didn't remember where I was. I jerked up and wiped the sleep from my eyes. The cassette recorder sat on the bed next to me.

My face hurt and I was a mess, wrinkled and disheveled from sleeping in my clothes. I hadn't planned on being away from home and didn't pack anything; no toothbrush, razor, not even a comb. I glanced around the room, saw the phone, and lunged for the receiver. Dead, no dial tone. What the hell was this place, the Bates Motel?

Using the bathroom, I threw water on my face, tried to comb my hair with my fingers, and slowly rubbed my sore jaw. A bruise had formed. I thought it fit in with the rest of my look.

Leaving the motel room I started walking, going nowhere really, just walking and thinking. I wanted to turn the tape over to the DA's office immediately. I wanted to see Welch and French rot behind bars, but my mind told me hold off. The tape had been illegally obtained; I'd be charged with a crime and might even go to jail if it came out. I'd have to find another way.

A marine layer, low clouds and fog had rolled in from the ocean, and the sky was overcast and gloomy. I walked slowly past shops lining California Street, typical for a beach resort: a surfboard store, and a place selling souvenirs, stuff to send to your Aunt Tillie back home in Grundy Center, Iowa. She'd love a printed T-shirt, a mug; *I heart Ventura*, or some such bullshit on it.

I walked all the way to the ocean; the tide was out along the wide beach. At the waterline I took off my shoes and waded in the cold water rippling at the edge of the hard wet sand.

I figured Karadimos knew about the tape by now. He's smart, and his instinct would have told him something was up. The way I clutched the briefcase when he goons attacked me would've clued him in about the recording–he would've questioned French and Welch thoroughly–but he wouldn't tell anyone, that's for sure. I turned and headed back to the motel, the Cozy Corner. I had only one chance–find Kruger before Karadimos found him.

I checked out of the room, shoved the recorder into my briefcase, and stashed it behind the driver's seat of my car. I drove to a nearby Denny's coffee shop, wondering whether the police had hit my apartment last night. I'd ask Sol to check his sources and see if there were any warrants out on me because of the fight.

After ordering coffee and eggs I called Sol at his home from the pay phone, but he wasn't there. He wasn't at his office either. I left a message, and then called Rocco's. They hadn't seen him since lunch Friday. I called Joyce back, told her to try Sol's mobile car phone. No luck.

"It's urgent, Joyce," I said. "Keep trying."

"Sure, Jimmy, I'll stay on it. Where will you be if I reach him?"

"I'm laying low. Cops might be looking for me. But I'll check back."

I went back to my table and the waitress appeared with my breakfast. She also handed me a copy of the *Times* a customer had left. I glanced at the paper while I ate and found a small article buried deep inside the middle section, near the obituaries: *Drunken Brawl in Parking Lot at Gala Fundraiser.* The article went on to say, *Two unidentified men were taken into custody Saturday night after a brawl erupted in the parking lot of Chasen's restaurant. The posh Beverly Hills eatery was holding a private fundraiser hosted by the Re-elect Welch Committee. According to Philip Rhodes, the event chairman, the incident in the parking lot was not related to the affair going on inside at the time. The two men involved were released and no charges were filed.*

The article gave me some comfort. I didn't have to worry about the police, so I drove back to my apartment. On the way I constantly checked my rearview mirror. If Karadimos's thugs had followed me last night, I'd be dead meat. I didn't see them now either, but they could be out there just the same.

I thought about Karadimos's two goons and the battle in Chasen's parking lot. The image of Jake's Cadillac bouncing over the curb and charging in like the Seventh Calvary made me chuckle. I thought, what the hell, maybe it didn't hurt having him on my side. And when I parked in front of my apartment building, I felt doubly glad to see him sitting in the Caddie across the street, giving me a thumbs-up.

Upstairs, I bolted the door, stashed the tape recorder in my closet, and spent the rest of the day calling around trying to find Sol. Nobody had seen him.

I fell asleep before dark, rolled over twenty-four hours later, made some kind of weird noise and fell back to sleep again.

Chapter Forty-Two

Monday morning; how in hell had that happened? Was I asleep or unconscious? Must've needed it.

A ringing phone would have woken me up. That meant I still hadn't heard from Sol. I cleaned up, grabbed the tape recorder and drove to his office. I wanted to find him and go over the tape. Joyce met me in the lobby again.

"Jimmy," she said. "I know you're worried, but sometimes Sol has to get away and relax, escape the pressure of running a large concern. He's done this before. He'll turn up. He's never gone for more than a few days."

Christ almighty, this is not the time for him to run away and relax. "He would've called, left a message, something."

Joyce just looked at me for a moment before she spoke. "You know Sol. Expect the unexpected." She smiled.

I couldn't wait around any longer. I had to do something. I called Rita at the office and told her I'd be tied up for a while. She reminded me about the motion to exclude the jailhouse witness. I was supposed to work on it over the weekend. I hadn't, of course. To my surprise she'd already typed it up on pleading paper and filed it with the court.

"Rita, I'm proud of you. You'll make a fine lawyer."

"Ah, boss, I knew you'd say that. But I haven't been tested yet, haven't had to make the hard decisions. I don't know how far I'd go to protect my clients..." Silence filled the line for a moment, then she said in a low voice, "...like you're doing for Mr. Rodriguez."

I thought about the tape. Would I really make it public? Would I do that even to set Rodriguez free? Would I be willing to sacrifice my career, and be convicted of a crime? Did I have that kind of courage?

"Wait for Sol's call, okay? I'll check back on the hour."

"I'm sure he's okay. He'll call. Don't worry."

I shot north on Firestone and drove past Harvey's Broiler, the drive-in restaurant where we cruised in our hot cars when we were high school kids. My buddy's father owned the Chevrolet dealership in Downey, and one night the kid drove though the drive-in, sitting smugly behind the wheel of a brand new '54 red and white Corvette. The convertible top was down as he slowly glided between the rows of parked cars. He was like the Pied Piper. Even my date jumped out of my jalopy and chased after him.

I arrived at the South Gate Police Department and walked to the front desk. "Who's the graveyard shift dispatcher?" I asked the cop working there.

"Who wants to know?"

I handed him my card. "O'Brien, criminal defense lawyer, investigating the Graham homicide."

Yeah, I remember you," he responded, tapping the card on the counter. "Mitch is the graveyard guy."

"Is he here? I need to see him for a moment."

The officer glanced at the clock hanging on the wall behind him. "His shift's over. Got off at nine, but let me check, might still be in the locker room."

He retreated to one of the battered steel desks, pushed an intercom knob and spoke into it. A few seconds later he came back and said Mitch would be right out.

"You waiting for me?" Mitch looked more like a surfer than a cop. He had on a Hang Ten T-shirt, cut-off Levis, and open-toed sandals. His hair was streaked blond from the sun.

"You're the officer who took the anonymous call involving the Graham murder?"

"Yeah, what about it?"

"Got a minute? I need some information."

"Who in the heck are you?"

I reached out to shake his hand. "Name's O'Brien. I'm a lawyer now, but used to be on the LAPD, worked night watch out of Newton Street." I figured I'd toss out the cop routine, maybe develop some rapport–just one of the boys. "I've got a couple of questions. Won't take long. Can I buy you a cup of coffee, some breakfast?" I wanted to get him out of the station before Hodges spotted us talking.

"Newton, huh? Tough division. How long on the job?"

"Since before the Watts Riots."

"Wow, I was in junior high at the time. Must've been rough. What was it like?"

"C'mon, I'll tell you over breakfast."

"Sure, why not?"

We took separate cars to the Pancake House, a down-home type of place on Atlantic, south of Firestone. The tired, clapboard restaurant had been there forever. The place had Formica tables, sticky with syrup, the wooden chairs didn't match, and the overweight waitress was probably named Flo. It seemed all these diners had a waitress named Flo.

The waitress came and poured coffee into cups that were already on the table. "The special this morning is pigs-in-a-blanket, two eggs, dollar-ninety-five," she said as she passed the menus to us.

Mitch ordered the special. She looked at me.

"I'll just have coffee, Flo," I said.

"Who's Flo?"

I laughed at my slip of the tongue. "I'm sorry–"

"The name's Jacqueline, but you can call me Jackie." She turned her head slightly to the side and lifted her chin. "Some people say I look like my namesake, Jackie Kennedy."

She looked more like Jackie Gleason than Jackie Kennedy. "Yeah, Flo–I can see it, except she has dark hair. Otherwise, dead ringer," I said.

She smiled and rushed away to fetch the food.

Mitch shook his head and laughed. "Did she say Jackie Kennedy? *Jesus.*"

"Ah, Mitch, maybe she looked like Jackie O thirty years ago, who knows. I think when we get older we still see ourselves as we were when we were in our prime. Nothing wrong with that."

"You're all right, O'Brien. I like your attitude."

"Can I ask you about that call?"

"Well, I guess so," he said, hesitantly. "What do you want to know?"

"Can you describe the voice?"

"Male, adult, no accent or out of the ordinary characteristics, just a voice," he said slowly, obviously thinking.

I already knew the time that the call was made, around four in the morning, and I had the exact words the caller had said. The information was in the police report, but I confirmed it with Mitch just the same. It would've made things easier if the South Gate Police Department had recorded the call, but unlike the LAPD and Sheriff's Department, they weren't equipped to do so.

When Jackie arrived with the food, I remained silent. After she left, I asked, "Would you recognize the voice if you heard it again?"

"Yeah, I think so." He thought for a moment, "I might be imagining this, but the guy had a familiar voice, like I heard it before, just can't place it. It'd help if he said some of the same words. You know, *dead girl–gardener did it*, stuff like that."

Mitch could've heard Welch's speeches on television a few times, and that could be why the voice had sounded familiar. I thought about the tape. I made a mental note to call him at the police station tomorrow night when he'd be on duty and play a small portion of it to see if he could I.D. Welch's voice as the anonymous caller.

"You must get a lot of calls," I said.

"Quite a few, but this is the only one I've had involving a murder. The caller's voice is still ringing in my ear. When he said *dead girl*, I froze for a second. Yeah, if I heard the guy's voice I'd recognize it. Why? You got a recording of a phone call, or something?"

"Nah, just thinking ahead. Trial coming up, you know."

"Guess you lawyers have to cover all the bases. I'm thinking of going back to school someday, become a lawyer like you."

"How long you been on force, Mitch?"

"Three and a half months. Not counting the academy."

He wouldn't make it to four months if Hodges found out he'd talked to me without his authorization. "A regular veteran," I laughed. "I think it would be a good idea to keep this discussion between ourselves."

"Think so? Why?"

"Because I'm going to solve the case and when I do, I'll let you have the collar. Boost your career. Don't want Hodges hogging all the glory."

"Thought they already had the guy."

"Got the wrong guy. Anyway, what do you have to lose? If I find the real killer, you got the collar. If I don't, well, so what?"

"Nothing to lose. Okay," he said. "I'll keep quiet."

We stopped talking for a moment, then he added, "You know, there's one more thing about the call that night. I just remembered...I don't think it's important." Mitch took a sip of coffee and wiped his mouth with a napkin. "Think I should tell Hodges about it?"

"Mitch, at this point, I wouldn't tell him anything. He'll just get pissed and make it hard on you. But, anyway, what about the call?"

"It was long distance. When I picked up the phone, the guy was putting the last of the coins in the slot, quarters. I could hear them drop." He nodded and took a bite of his sausage. "Now tell me about the riots."

Chapter Forty-Three

I made it back to the office from South Gate in record time. "Sol?" I asked Rita as I opened the door and walked in.

"Sorry," she said. "Haven't heard a word."

Now I was really worried. I grabbed the phone on Rita's desk and dialed Mabel at the answering service. No calls. I phoned Joyce, Sol's secretary. She hadn't heard from him either. We'd just have to wait.

"I've got something else for you to take care of," I said to her. "Can you check with the phone company, the one that handles the Sacramento area? I need to see if any long distance calls were made to South Gate from a pay phone, probably somewhere near the airport. Can't be too many calls, it was made about four in the morning, the morning after the murder."

"Okay Jimmy. I'll have to use an associate from that area. It'll take a day or so."

I put the receiver down and glanced at Rita. "What are you typing?"

"A memo to the landlord."

"Oh?"

"The air conditioner needs to be repaired; it rattles. Can't have that kind of racket when we're interviewing clients," she said.

Clients. "Okay," I said and went to my office. I had nothing to do now but wait. So I messed around with the Rodriguez file, looking for some sort of revelation that might come to me. Some speck of information that I may have overlooked. Nothing. An hour later, I asked Rita if she wanted to have lunch. She called Mabel at the answering service and told her to pick up the calls. We'd be back in an hour.

We left for Foxy's at noon. We had a pleasant lunch, hamburger combos for both of us. It was good to laugh a little and to let the tension evaporate. Rita was wide-eyed and excited about going to a lunch with an *older man,* she said. And she was excited about becoming a criminal defense lawyer some day. We returned from lunch at one-ten. Rita went to the bank to pick up the signature stamp, and I called the answering service again.

"Any calls, Mabel?"

"Just one, long distance," she said. "I'll read it: 'I'm in Las Vegas, call as soon as possible.'" She rattled off the number. "It's from Sol Silverman."

I immediately dialed the number. Perhaps Joyce was right. Sol is in Las Vegas, so maybe he has a lead on Kruger.

"Good afternoon, the Sahara Hotel," a perky female voice said.

"Sol Silverman, please."

"One moment, please. Mr. Silverman is in the casino. I'll connect you now."

I waited less than fifteen seconds and Sol came on the line.

"Jimmy my boy, how you doing?"

"Jesus, Sol! Are you okay?"

"Yeah, I'm fine. Why?"

"Where in the hell have you been? I've been worried sick."

"I'm doing *your* work, Jimmy. That's where the hell I've been."

"*Christ*, you could've let me know."

"What? You're my mother now? Shut up and listen."

"Okay, Sol. I just–"

"Forget it. Now listen, you've got to get up here, fast."

"You got a line on Kruger?" I asked, holding my breath.

"Joe Sica's brother, Freddie, found him. He's bringing up some boys from L.A. and they're going to snatch him tonight when he shows up at his job. When they nab him, they want

238

us here, in town."

The butterflies in my stomach were beating their wings to the *1812 Overture*, fireworks and all. "I'm on my way."

"Better go pack a bag first. Don't know how long we'll have to hang around. They're going to take him to a secret location, and then they'll call us."

"Where will I meet you?"

"Here at the Sahara. Johnny Hughes, head casino guy, comp'ed our rooms. You won't need to stop at the bank to cash a check. Everything's on the house. You'll only need money if you want to gamble."

Gamble? Was he nuts? My whole life was a gamble.

I looked at my watch. "It's almost two. I'm leaving now. I'll see you up there at about six, six-thirty."

Before hanging up I told Sol about the tape. I wanted him to listen to it. Maybe he'd pick up a new slant, the way a word was said, something like that, maybe something I missed. Maybe I could call Mitch the cop from the hotel and play the tape.

Rita returned and I briefly explained the situation.

"Don't worry, boss. I'll run the store while you're gone."

"I'm sure you'll do a fantastic job."

She flashed a sunny smile, but then a cloud darkened her pretty features.

"Please be careful, Jimmy."

I shot home, tossed the tape recorder and a few clothes into a duffel bag and was on the road in minutes.

It's a three hundred mile drive to Las Vegas through the blazing hot Mojave Desert. I felt uneasy about driving that far when the temperature on the highway was over a hundred degrees. I stopped to check the oil and water at the Union Oil station before charging out on the Interstate.

The 605 ended at the San Bernardino Freeway and I headed east toward Barstow. The Corvette ran smooth. The temperature needle stayed in the green, but I kept the speed below eighty. Why take chances? I told myself. If I kept the speed down, everything would be okay.

The Cajon Pass loomed before me, a five thousand feet summit. My car climbed steadily, reaching the high point of the pass, then rolled smoothly down the backside of the mountain. The temperature needle stayed in the green. I shot past Hesperia, Apple Valley, and Victorville. In Barstow, I made a pit stop at a Standard Oil station. Out of the corner of my eye I noticed Big Jake's Caddie idling at the curb as the attendant filled the Vette's gas tank.

I pulled out of the station and saw a sign on top of the Barstow First National Bank building, *103°*. It could've been worse; it could've been 104.

I pulled back on the highway and in about forty-five minutes, I raced past a sign on the side of the road that read, "Zzyzx Road, One Mile." *Zzyzx*, what in the hell did that mean? In the rearview mirror I caught a momentary glimpse of Jake's car darting in, out and around other cars about a quarter-mile behind me. It felt good knowing he was back there.

I pulled under the elaborate portico of the Sahara at exactly six-thirty. Valet parking guys were all over the car. Just as I climbed out, Big Jake's Caddie pulled in behind my Vette. I waved off the parking guys and walked over to him.

Jake rolled down the window. "Karadimos's goons would've reported to him by now."

"Reported what?"

"He knows you're in Vegas and he knows why," Jake said.

I didn't like the sound of that.

"I'll have to warn Freddie. Karadimos is sending hoods lookin' to shanghai Kruger. Could be trouble."

"I thought the big guns back east didn't allow gang violence in Vegas–bad for the tourist trade."

"That's just PR crap," he said. "See ya around, O'Brien."

"You're not coming in?"

"Against the rules. I'm in the book."

"I understand." I said. "Thanks for the escort."

The "book" was a list of gangsters that the Nevada State Gaming Commission circulated to all the gambling establishments in the state. No individual listed was allowed to enter any hotel with a casino, at least not through the front door.

I walked back to my car, still parked in front of the hotel, and took out a dollar to tip the parking valet, standing there at attention. The kid shook his head.

"Can't take it, Mr. O'Brien," he said.

Mr. O'Brien? Guess I was expected.

Chapter Forty-Four

"Yes sir, we've been waiting for you," the parking guy said. "The boss says you're to get the treatment."

"The treatment?"

"High-roller treatment. Full comp, friend of one of our honored guests, Mr. Silverman. By the way, Mr. Silverman said to tell you he'll call your room after you get settled. He also said to tell you, 'No word yet.' I guess you know what that means."

"Yeah. Thanks."

"Here, let me take your luggage, sir." He reached out for my duffel bag.

I wasn't about to part with the bag, not with the recorder in it. "Don't bother. I'll carry it myself."

A blast of cold air hit me in the face when the valet opened the hotel door. The contrast of the scorching heat outside and the hotel's artificially conditioned air perfectly mirrored the contrast between my real life and the fantasy world I now entered.

He ran to the registration desk to get my room key while I watched the patrons wandering about without a care. Some were dressed in formal eveningwear, others in terrycloth robes and swimming suits. Women who looked as if they belonged on the cover of *Vogue* strolled arm in arm with men whose pictures would have been more at home on a wall at the post office.

"Your key, sir," the valet said. "It's a twenty-two suite. Compliments of the hotel, friend of Mr. Silverman," he said again.

After he explained how to get to the room, I took a private VIP elevator to top floor. I opened the door, and the polished marble entry of the suite gleamed in the sunlight that pervaded the room. The west wall was all glass and the view was stunning. I held my breath for an instant and sidled into the room. A full-size bar that would rival the one at the Bistro Gardens in Beverly Hills lined the north wall. Built into the other wall were shelves that held a large TV and a stereo.

I dropped my duffel on the couch and walked into one of the two adjoining bedrooms. I wasn't surprised to see an oversized fruit basket filled with all kinds of goodies and a bottle of Dom Pérignon chilling in an ice bucket on the table. I expected that, but what I didn't expect was the ravishing blonde who sat on the round bed, her long and gorgeous legs crossed.

"Hi, I'm Candi," she said.

"I bet you are," I replied.

She had on a black, low-cut number with spaghetti straps that strained under the stress of the load. "The hotel sent me," she said. "Thought you might be lonely. Can I fix you a drink, Jimmy?"

"A Coke, for me. Fix yourself anything you want. We'll have our drinks in the other room."

Candi stood. The spaghetti straps held. Amazing. We moved into the living room, and she fixed the drinks at the bar. I took the Coke from her. She set her glass on the table and moved to the stereo.

"Jeez, they must have a bazillion tapes here. I'll put on something romantic."

A moment or two passed. Sinatra's voice warbled from the stereo speakers.

She turned back to me. "All you guys like Frank Sinatra."

I let the *you guys* remark pass. "Candi, sit down for a minute. We have to talk."

She picked up her drink, took a hard pull, and eased over to the couch. A lot of thigh showed when she sat and crossed her legs again. "You don't like me?"

"I don't know you, but you're very attractive."

"Nancy with the Laughing Face" filled the room. Candi could stay and have a drink, but after one more song, she'd have to leave.

"You don't like what I do for a living?"

"I don't care what you do," I said. "But I care what I do."

The phone rang. I took a sip of my Coke and answered it.

"Jimmy, they told me you checked in."

"Hang on, Sol. I'll take the call in the other room." I put him on hold, moved to one of the bedrooms and shut the door behind me. I grabbed the phone next to the bed and punched the blinking button. "Sol, what about Kruger?"

"Clean up and change, we'll talk in the bar. I'll meet you in the Casbar Lounge in twenty minutes."

"Did they snatch him yet?"

"It's a long story. I'll explain when I see you downstairs."

"Okay, but I'd like you to listen to the tape. I want you to tell me what you think. Later, when the cop comes on duty, we can play a portion for him over the phone. Maybe he'll recognize Welch's voice."

"Sounds good. But, Jimmy, I don't want to use the hotel phones for that. Don't want to go through the switchboard. Know what I mean? Bring the tape with you to the bar. We'll find a payphone."

"See you in twenty minutes."

I walked back into the living room. Candi was still there, sitting on the couch, sipping her drink. "Thanks for stopping by, Candi. It's been fun," I said.

She stood. "Maybe I could come back later? There's a hot tub here in the suite, we could light some candles, sip some champagne."

"Tempting, but no thanks."

She tossed back the remainder of her drink. Her hips did a little rumba as she strolled toward the door. She stopped about halfway, turned her head, and peered at me over her shoulder. "I guess I won't see you again."

"We'll always have Paris."

She left the room. The lock clicked as the door swung closed after her.

I thought about Candi as I showered. Did all high rollers–and friends of high rollers–find a cold bottle of champagne and a hot blonde in their rooms after they checked in? I dressed, grabbed my duffel bag,and left the suite.

So this is what it's like to be rich, I thought, as the VIP elevator descended: first-class service, and everybody addressing me by my name. It obvious they knew Sol. He's a true high roller; but how'd they know my name? They must have one hell of a system.

At the Casbar Lounge, I stood behind a horde of people clamoring to get in. Hands from the crowd waved twenty-dollar bills. The Asian *maître d'* and a few of his assistants held their ground, like sentries at the palace gate, staving off the barbarians while the royalty dined sumptuously inside the walls. The *maître d'* charged through the crowd, grabbed my arm, and propelled me toward the entrance.

"Mr. Silverman is waiting," he screamed.

Waiters zipped around the barroom with drinks and plates of mouth-watering appetizers balanced on their arms. It was exciting. Bursts of laughter and jubilant conversation all but drowned out the jazz combo in the background.

Sol, a napkin dangling from his neck, sat behind a table heaped with a potentate's assortment of hot and cold hors d'oeuvres. He stood to greet me with a baby back rib in one hand and a tall multi-colored drink in the other.

"Jimmy, my boy, sit and enjoy."

"What about Kruger?" I asked.

"He didn't show at his bartending job, called in sick. Might have to stick another night. Sica's boys will grab him the minute he arrives."

"Oh, *Christ*. Are you sure he'll show up?"

"He'll show. Quit worrying."

"Can't they pick him up at his apartment?"

"He gave a phony address on his job app. Nobody knows where he lives. I got my guys trying to find his place. But there are no listings anywhere for the guy, utilities, phone, nothing in either name, Fischer or Kruger. We'll have to cool our heels for a while."

"In the meantime," I said, "let's go someplace quiet where you can listen to the tape."

"Sure, as soon as I finish my drink."

"Mitch–the cop I told you about–might recognize Welch's voice." I looked at my watch: ten to seven. "We can call him as soon as he gets to work, the graveyard shift."

"Then we have plenty of time." Sol finished his drink and ordered another one.

A tall middle-aged man in an expensive suit walked up to our table, leaned down and whispered in Sol's ear. Sol nodded once and the guy left.

"Who was that? What did he say? News about Kruger?"

"No, afraid not," Sol said. "I should've introduced you. That was Johnny Hughes, casino manager–the real boss around here. The guy's been in the gambling business since the early days. As a kid he worked for Capone in Chicago. Knows how to take care of his customers."

"What he say?"

"Said the staff is alerted about the call. They'll let us know the minute it comes in."

We talked some more about Kruger, and the Sica boys. He laughed when I mentioned Candi, the blonde, in my room. I also told Sol about Big Jake following me up here.

"It's good to have him around," Sol said. "He's a bulldog. Once he gets his teeth into something he won't let go. Now let me have that tape recorder. I'll keep it safe until we phone the cop."

"Don't trust me? Think I'll lose it? Cost me sixty bucks," I said facetiously as I pulled the recorder out of my bag and handed it to him.

Sol turned it over in his hand a couple times. "It's small, isn't it? Not much bigger than a pack of smokes. 'Course, in my business, they have professional recorders, much smaller. We have a few. Cost *beaucoup* bucks." He flipped it open.

"Yeah, well this one did the trick–"

Sol looked up. "Okay Jimmy, where's the tape?"

"What do you mean?"

"The goddamn cassette is missing."

Chapter Forty-Five

At 10:30 the next morning, Sol and I sat in the Sahara Hotel coffee shop going over the details of the night before. We discussed the mystery women and the stolen tape.

Candi had told me that the hotel sent her. But after Sol discovered that the tape was missing, he'd summoned Johnny Hughes and asked him who the looker was that the hotel had sent to my room. Hughes knew nothing about her. The hotel hadn't sent anyone.

"I'll say this: Karadimos had balls, sending her to room to snatch the tape," Sol said.

"How'd you figure out she worked for him?"

"If the hotel sent her, Johnny would've known about it, and if she'd lied about that, what else did she lie about?"

"Why didn't he just send one of his goons?"

"His men would have been noticed by hotel security. They know all the wise guys–part of the job. Besides, you might've been a little concerned if you'd discovered some big ugly gorilla with a reptilian brain lounging on your bed instead of a blonde bombshell."

"You figured it out real fast, Sol."

"It was easy, a looker like that shows up in your room and doesn't ask for money up front? C'mon, my boy. You're not that good, are you?"

"Thought I was."

Sol laughed. "Actually, Jimmy, hotel security caught the bellboy who gave her the key to your room. Candi went down on the poor schmuck in the employee locker room and he was putty in her hands, so to speak. The whole lascivious scene was captured on one of those new video cameras that the hotel had installed a few weeks ago. I saw the tape: disgusting!" Sol grinned.

"He copped out about giving her the key?"

"Yeah, spilled his guts. Once caught, he knew if he didn't come clean, he'd be in one of those unmarked graves out in the desert."

Even with everything I heard about the plan to steal the tape, I still hadn't gotten over the fact that I'd been an idiot to let it out of my sight. I told Sol I felt terrible about screwing up so badly.

"Jimmy, it wouldn't have been a good idea anyway to tell the cops about the tape. Remember, rule number one."

I knew what he was going to say. "That's rule number two."

"All right, rule number two: Don't put yourself in the slammer to get your client out."

"Yeah, I know. But I wasn't going to turn over the tape. At least, I don't think I would've."

Before he could reply, the bar manager rushed to our table with a telephone. "Phone's for you, Mr. S.," he said as he plugged it into the jack.

"This is it, Jimmy." Sol grabbed the phone and, after a few grunts and okays, he slammed the receiver down. "Let's go. Sica's men have Kruger stashed at the Lake Mead Lodge. Bungalow number six."

I shot out of the booth and made a dash for the exit, Sol beside me. "How far is it?" I asked on the fly.

"About thirty miles."

My Corvette was parked under the canopy. Someone had washed it during the night. "The keys," I hollered to the valet, pointing at the car. He tossed them to me. I caught them and jumped into the driver's seat. Sol got in the passenger side. He boomed directions and held on as I weaved through traffic. I hung a right onto Boulder Highway, then punched it. The Vette fishtailed through the turn, but it held the road tight. I straightened out and accelerated to ninety. I ran a red light in Henderson and screamed through the town.

I heard the sirens before I saw the flashing red lights in

the rearview mirror. *Damn*, I thought, *cops on my ass*. Glancing over my shoulder, I saw two police cruisers bearing down on us, closing fast.

"Better pull over, don't make it worse," Sol said.

"Yeah, guess so."

I did as he said, but the cruisers didn't slow down. They closed the gap and blew by me going about a hundred.

"What the hell?" I said.

"What's that's all about?" Sol asked.

"Did you see the markings on the squad cars?"

"Yeah, Clark County Sheriff's Department."

Just as I was about to pull back onto the road, a third cop car zoomed past us, going in the same direction as the others.

"Something's up, Sol."

"Yeah, don't like it."

We drove through the quiet town of Boulder City at a respectable speed. I turned off the thoroughfare at Lakeshore Road. To the right I saw the intense blue expanse of Lake Mead shimmering in the afternoon sun. We wound down the desert slope to the valley below and onto a road that fronted the recreational area. Close to the lodge entrance, a sheriff's cruiser with its red lights flashing straddled the gravel road. A deputy–a large economy-sized guy–leaned on the hood. As the Vette crawled closer, the deputy raised his chubby hand, palm out. I stopped the car.

"I'll see what's up. Wait here." Sol climbed out and walked toward the cop. "What's going on?" he asked the guy.

"Road's closed."

"Why?"

"Police activity at the lodge."

"What do you mean?" Sol asked.

"Just what I said, police activity. What are you doing here anyway?"

Sol flashed his PI credentials. "We've got business at the lodge."

The big cop stood straight and tugged at his john brown.

Without taking his eyes off Sol, he reached into the squad car and pulled out the radio mike. "Okay buddy, stay right there. Don't move." He keyed the microphone. "Roy, it's me, Wally. I got a private dick over here. The guy says he's got business at the lodge. Might have something to do with the shootout."

When he said *shootout*, my stomach knotted.

The radio crackled. "Hold him there. I'm on my way."

I scrambled out of the Corvette, my shoes crunching on the gravel as I walked toward them. "Sounds like there was a gunfight at the lodge," I said.

"Yeah, a bad one," the cop said.

We turned toward an approaching patrol car, which roared up and stopped, sending sand and gravel flying. A tall, officer wearing a crisp uniform with sharp creases climbed out. The lieutenant bars on his collar gleamed in the sun.

"What have we got here?" he asked.

"These guys were going to the lodge." Wally, the deputy, pointed at Sol. "That one's a private peeper."

"What went down at the lodge, lieutenant?" Sol asked.

"About twenty minutes ago, three or four men approached bungalow six, and shooting started. We think the four men inside the unit were the targets. That's all we know right now." The lieutenant shrugged. "Could be a drug thing."

"Anybody hurt?" I asked.

"Yeah, two guys. One fatality."

"Any names?"

"You guys know anything about this?" the lieutenant asked. "You seem mighty interested." Sol and I didn't say anything. "Okay, let's see some ID."

We handed him our identification. He studied our licenses, then peered at Sol over the rim of his Ray-Bans. "You're Sol Silverman, the investigator?"

"Sure am." Sol pointed at me. "And this is my friend, Jimmy O'Brien, criminal lawyer."

The lieutenant glanced at me. "Never heard of you, but I've heard a lot about you, Mr. Silverman. I'm Roy Garza.

Good to meet you." Sol shook his hand. "Sheriff Lamb mentions the big case every now and then. Remember, back in the sixties, the singer's kid who'd been kidnapped?"

"Yeah, it was pretty basic. Just a day's work."

"You working on a case that has something to do with this, Mr. Silverman?"

Sol was quiet for a moment. He glanced around and seemed to focus on a hawk circling over a rocky hill in the distance. He turned back to Garza. "Look, Roy, Jimmy may have a conflict of interest talking to you about this, but I'll make you a deal. You tell me what you know, and if I can fill in any details without compromising Jimmy's client, I will. You know I'm a straight arrow."

The lieutenant thought for a moment, then nodded. "We don't know a lot. A few witness reports, but as I said, four shooters approached cabin six, and shots were fired. When the smoke cleared, one guy inside was dead and another wounded. Fat guy took four hits, but he's still alive. The wagon hauled him to the emergency room at Valley Hospital in Vegas. Everyone else split before we arrived on the scene."

"Can you give me the names of the two guys who were shot?" I asked with some reluctance.

"Yeah, just a minute." He retrieved a notebook from his car. "The wounded guy had a gun permit." The lieutenant fingered through a couple of pages of his pad. "Name's Cohn, Jacob Louis. Let's see...oh yeah, the fatality was Fischer, Ronald."

Fatality. The words hit me like a Winnebago. I slumped against the cop car. Sol looked at me for a moment, and then turned back to the lieutenant.

"The dead guy's real name was Kruger," he said.

Chapter Forty-Six

A jackrabbit jumped in front of my Corvette as I turned the car around to head back to the hotel. The creature froze in the middle of the road and stared at me, its ears straight up, as if to ask, *What now, Jimmy? Without Kruger there's no case.* I had no answer and the rabbit bounced away, disappearing into the scrub.

We were quiet on the drive back to the hotel.

At the Sahara, Sol and I walked slowly through the entrance doors. In the lobby, before we parted ways, Sol said, "So long, Jimmy. See you back in Downey." He paused and put a hand on my shoulder. I guess my anger and disappointment showed. "Can't win them all, my boy. But quit with the long face. We'll come up with something."

"Yeah, I know. We'll come up with something." But I knew how hopeless it would be to develop a new angle now, especially with time running out. Karadimos had won.

Sol said he'd drive to the sheriff's office and give them a statement. He would tell them what we knew. It wasn't much. Karadimos's men gunned down Kruger to keep him quiet, but we had no proof to offer the law. The shoot-out would go into the books as another gangland dispute, or a drug deal gone sour. That would be that, case closed.

Later that afternoon I checked out of the hotel. The valet gave me directions to Valley Hospital, and I drove there. The white concrete building was awash in the bright Nevada sun, and the hot blacktop in the lot was soft underfoot as I walked toward the entrance.

In the stark lobby, people slouched in functional furniture, waiting the endless wait for news of loved ones engaged in life-or-death struggles. In here the shameless fantasy of the Las Vegas pleasure palaces ended and the harsh reality of life played out. Like the gambling tables, there are winners and losers, but there are no comp'ed drinks or show tickets. They even have clocks on the walls.

A young woman with curly short hair and blue eyes greeted me at the information desk. "May I help you?" she asked politely.

"I need to see Jacob Cohn."

She thumbed through a large Rolodex. "I don't see anyone with that name here. When was he admitted?"

"Sometime earlier this afternoon. Gunshot wounds."

"Oh yes, the police brought him in. Are you a relative?" The woman studied me with raised eyebrows. "Or an associate?"

I handed her my business card. "I'm a lawyer. I need to see him."

She sighed. "Of course. He hasn't been assigned a room yet; still in surgery." She leaned over the counter and pointed to the right. "You can wait in the waiting room down the hall. I'll tell the authorities you're here."

I hadn't eaten anything since the previous night. "Do you have a cafeteria around here?"

"Yes, go to your left and follow the arrows painted on the floor."

The hamburger was dry and lifeless. The patty must have been made with oatmeal and lard. The fries were limp, the coffee cold and weak. Welcome back to reality. I thought about checking to see if my Corvette had turned into a pumpkin.

After finishing my meal, I wandered to the waiting room and browsed through a six-month-old issue of *Modern Maternity*. It was that or a medical journal with no pictures. Time passed slowly, but eventually a man in a wrinkled brown suit came in. His collar was unbuttoned, his tie loose. He looked like a cop who could use some sleep

"You the lawyer?" the man said. "Here to see Cohn?"

"Yeah."

"I'm Anderson, homicide, sheriff's department."

I stood and handed him my credentials. He took a quick glance at my bar card and gave it back. "Follow me," he said. "You'll only have a few minutes."

"How's he doing?"

"Doc says critical. Might not make it."

I entered the small, cold intensive care unit. There were six beds lined up against the wall. Big Jake lay in the second bed from the door, an array of tubes stuck in him, supplying painkillers and life-giving fluids, I figured. Yet they had him cuffed to the bed rail. It seemed absurd. He wasn't going anywhere.

The cop stared at Jake over my shoulder. I turned to him. "Detective Anderson, this conversation is privileged. I could use a little privacy."

He backed away. I leaned close to Jake's face.

In a raspy voice barely above a whisper he said, "Sorry kid, I let you down."

"What happened?"

"Surprised us, shotguns...one guy had an automatic rifle. Door burst open, shots fired...everybody ducked, dropped to the floor. Kruger...tied in a chair, I tried to block the shots, got hit a few times...went down. Kruger nailed. Ten seconds...all it took–"

Jake's body convulsed. He grimaced, coughed, and let out a deep moan.

"Take it easy, Jake."

He tried to roll on his side but the handcuffs held him tight. "You were right, O'Brien...about Kruger. He knew what was goin' on."

"Kruger talked?"

"With a little...persuasion."

My mind reeled. "What'd he say?"

"Welch and Karadimos...in business together. Drugs, money laundering, phony companies...teen prostitutes. Welch got Karadimos a bank license to handle the cash. Has some stooge in Downey front it for him–" He stopped talking and coughed again, twice.

"Has a place in Mexico...farm or ranch, something like that. Grows cantaloupes, front for drugs, has...partners down there. They hollow some of the cantaloupes...fill 'em with smack. Karadimos and Welch...they got an import company in the states. They import the cantaloupes." Big Jake paused, closed his eyes, and swallowed hard a couple of times. "Yeah, okay, we're bad guys...I'll admit, but this asshole...rotten, like his cantaloupes."

"Did he tell you why they killed Gloria?"

"She got whacked...had information, papers, files, records. Payoffs to her boss and other pols. She was the bag lady, carried the cash to Welch and his buddies. She...stole from them. Skimmed a little off the top, got caught, threatened to ratfink on Karadimos and Welch. She was gonna...call the cops."

"What happened then?"

"After the fund-raiser, Kruger...he was supposed to work her over and get the files. They figured she had the papers at her house. One of Welch's workers saw her take...big aluminum case from the office...Friday night."

Jake arched his back when another wave of pain hit. "Funny thing though," he gasped. "Kruger said he didn't fly...plane back that Saturday night. But Karadimos got the fuel bill and called him Monday about the flight...Kruger knew he was in trouble. Figured the Greek wouldn't believe him. So...he took it on the lam."

I could see Big Jake was starting to falter; his eyelids were closing and his voice grew weaker. But I needed more information.

Detective Anderson put his hand on my shoulder. "Time's up."

"I have one more question–"

"C'mon, let's go." He pulled me back, but I twisted free.

"Jake, can you hear me? Did they find the files?"

His monitor beeped rapidly. The nurse rushed into the room. "Please, you people must go," she ordered.

"O'Brien, the guy's dying. Leave him alone." Anderson grabbed my shoulder again.

I turned to leave. "*No*," Jake boomed. I dashed to his side and leaned down again. He whispered in my ear. "Kruger never went over there. After the murder...cops was all over the place. And Monday he did a rabbit."

Anderson pulled me away, but when I got to the door, I turned back again. The nurse hovered over Jake. His eyes were shut, his breathing shallow and intermittent. "So long, friend." I hoped he heard me.

As I started through the door I heard Jake say, "Be careful...Jimmy. I won't be there...to protect you." I stopped for a beat, then left.

Chapter Forty-Seven

I left the hospital, my nerves stretched so tight that I was afraid I'd snap. I walked slowly to my Corvette. But before I got in, I walked to the edge of the deserted parking lot and looked out across the city, thinking about Jake. He took four bullets trying to keep Kruger alive for me. Did I feel any guilt? No, I thought, after mulling it over. I felt a deep sorrow for him, of course; but he had chosen his life–a life of violence.

I reflected on Kruger's confession, trying to make sense of it. The bank that Kruger told him about had to be the one that Joyce had mentioned: the Mutual something or other. The import company could only be Hartford Commodities. The stooge, the front man for these companies, had to be Thomas French.

I knew it would be impossible to prove in court that Karadimos had an overwhelming motive to murder Gloria, based on Jake's statements. Even if Big Jake lived, he wouldn't testify. He'd be liable for all kinds of charges if he did. I couldn't use his testimony anyway. Kruger's statements were obtained under duress and a judge wouldn't allow them, even under the dying-declaration exception to the hearsay rule. No, I wouldn't be able to call Jake to the stand.

That wasn't the worst of it. In his confession to Big Jake, Kruger stated he hadn't flown the plane back from Sacramento that night. He had no reason to lie. So that meant I didn't have anything to tie the flight to the motive, and I had no leads as to who flew the plane that night. Anyway, without Vogel, the mechanic, I couldn't even prove that the plane had *been* flown.

I climbed in the Vette, started the engine, and eased out of the lot. In downtown Las Vegas, I drove the full length of

Fremont Street. Vegas Vic waved his neon arm slowly from side to side. I waved back. "Adios, Vic," I said as I passed the Golden Nugget, heading for Highway 93 and home.

At Baker, I turned into the Standard Oil gas station, filled the Corvette with Ethyl, and went inside the attached café for a cup of coffee. The place was packed. It was easy to tell the difference between the motorists going to Vegas and the ones returning. Those on the way were full of life, happy and joking. The poor folks heading home were glum and ordered aspirin with their coffee.

I got back onto the highway, wondering about Gloria Graham's file. If Karadimos didn't have it, and the police hadn't found it at her house, where could it be? She hadn't sent the papers to Bonnie Munson, her friend in Kansas. Bonnie would've told me if she had. She could not have rented a safety deposit box. She took the documents out of Welch's office Friday night after the banks were closed, and banks weren't open on weekends.

I'd run out of ideas and didn't know what to do next. I turned on the radio and twisted the dial until I picked up a Barstow station that played standards from the '30s and '40s. I was about to turn it off when "Easy Street " came on. The line at the end of the song summed up exactly how I felt: "*I've got nothing to do, Sam, and I'm doing it tomorrow.*"

About ten miles east of Barstow I saw flashing lights strung across the highway in the distance. I started to slow. A sign said, *Agricultural Inspection Station, One Mile Ahead.*

I rolled to a stop under the station canopy and rolled down the window. A female inspector leaned down. She had a pretty face, a warm smile, and even though she wore a drab green outfit, I could see she had a nice figure. Even in my dark mood, it felt nice to be greeted by a government official like her.

"Welcome to California, sir," she said. "Where are you coming from?"

"Las Vegas."

"Are you carrying any fruits, vegetables, trees, or plants?"

"Nope."

The inspector stepped back and motioned for me to move forward. I gave her my best winning smile, but she didn't jump in the car with me.

I edged slowly back into traffic. Off to the side of the highway, three CHP cruisers stood ready to charge out and run down anybody attempting to smuggle a Florida orange into the Golden State.

I made my way through Barstow, keeping my speed at forty miles per hour as I drove down Main Street. It seemed like walking after traveling at seventy on the highway. I passed the Red-Spot Café and thought about stopping for a hamburger, but I wasn't hungry.

The good-looking inspector at the Agricultural Inspection Station played into my mind. She had long black hair, high cheekbones, and beautiful dark eyes. She spoke with a southern accent that I was couldn't place: Georgia, Arkansas, something like that. She asked about fruits, she pronounced vegetables with only two syllables, and when she'd said–

It came to me like an epiphany. I saw white, almost a flash. I stomped on the gas and roared through town. She'd said *trees!*

I pictured Rodriguez's shovel lying on the grass at Gloria's house next to the patches of dirt where he'd dug three holes for the trees, which he'd later moved. Gloria could've buried the files in one of the holes in a waterproof case. A case like the one filled with money that she'd sent to Bonnie Munson. I was sure of it. That's why she wanted the trees moved. It gave her an opportunity to bury the package in one of the holes Rodriguez had dug. She could do it without anyone noticing.

I knew I couldn't sleep until I checked out my theory. I wrapped my mind around the idea and thought about it some more. Yeah, it was a long shot, but I had to find out tonight if she'd actually buried the files there.

I pulled up to the curb in front of Gloria's house on Rosewood Avenue after midnight. The police tape was still stretched around the perimeter. There was no moon out and nothing moved in the dark silence; no dogs barked, no footsteps, no late night TV—nothing, just dead quiet.

Switching on the small emergency flashlight that I kept in my car, I swept a dim cone of light around the backyard. I found the shovel and began to dig. I picked the middle patch of dirt for no logical reason. After digging down four feet, I gave up. I then started on the bare circle of dirt to my left. At two feet, I hit something solid. My heart raced.

I dropped to my knees, took a deep breath and held it. I reached into the hole and dug with my hands, like a dog after a bone. I tried to free the case. It wouldn't budge. Digging frantically, I finally loosened the case and pulled it out.

After wiping the dirt off it, I sat the aluminum briefcase upright on the grass. I jammed the shovel's edge into the seam where the two halves came together. It popped open.

I knelt down next to the case, which overflowed with documents. Holding the flashlight in my mouth, I rifled through the papers, spilling some on the grass.

"*Holy Christ*," I said out loud. I set the flashlight on the grass, scrambling to scoop up the papers and put them back in the case. I didn't need to study the files right now. I knew what I had found. I felt like Alfred Nobel. I had discovered dynamite!

"Freeze, asshole," a voice said. "Don't make a sound." I felt a gun barrel jammed against the back of my head and heard the ratcheting sound of a hammer being cocked.

Chapter Forty-Eight

"What the hell–" I began.

"I said keep quiet." His voice sounded unstable. "I'll drop you right here, motherfucker!"

"Okay, okay. I'm cool."

"Stand up."

With my hands in the air, I struggled to my feet.

The gunman rammed the barrel into the small of my back. "Pick up the case and walk slowly to the car. It's on the street."

I bent over, closed the briefcase, and tucked it under my arm. We left the backyard and moved down the driveway, then marched toward the blue Buick sedan parked a couple of houses away.

"You're not a cop," I said.

"No such luck, O'Brien."

"You know me? Karadimos sent you?"

"We've been following you since Vegas."

"Vegas?"

"Almost lost you when you stomped on it in Barstow," the gunman said, "but the Buick Electra with 455 cubes and a McCulloch supercharger held its own against the Vette. Too bad you have small block in your machine. Should've coughed up a few bucks more and got the big 427."

"Lousy gas mileage," I said.

"You're a riot, O'Brien."

Christ, this was no time to chat about cars. I broke out in a sweat and tried to think of a way out, but nothing came. This wasn't like TV or the movies; this was real. If I made a move on the guy, he'd shoot me dead before I could turn halfway around.

As we approached the Buick a guy the size of the

Goodyear blimp jumped from the driver's seat. Another gorilla climbed out of the passenger seat. They called him Angelo. I remembered Jake mentioning Angelo, said he was one of Karadimos's best persuaders. From their conversation I learned that the other two were Gus and Lenny. Angelo *looked* like a persuader, mean and ugly with a nose spread all over his face and small knotty protrusions on his forehead. He'd been a professional fighter once, and I had no doubt he could hurt people without a care. I recognized Angelo, he was the goon who followed me around in the Buick.

Lenny took the case from me and placed it in the Buick. Angelo patted me down. He took the car keys from my pocket and tossed them to Lenny.

"Get that Vette out of here, 'fore someone sees it."

"Hey, you sonofabitch, nobody drives my car–"

Angelo hit me in the right kidney. I doubled over.

"No one asked your permission."

My Corvette disappeared down the street. I wondered if I'd ever see it again.

Gus, the gunman, backed up, still covering me, and opened the rear door.

"Get in, O'Brien," he said. "Angelo you're driving. I'll watch him."

We climbed in. Angelo, the heavyweight, started the car, drove around the block, and turned right on Firestone Boulevard. We pulled up next to a phone booth at a closed gas station.

"Tell the boss about the briefcase, Angelo," Gus said without taking his eyes off me.

Angelo made the call and was back in the Buick in less than a minute. "The Greek wants us to take O'Brien to the yard. He'll meet us there."

"Looks like you're going to taste a little garbage. You like rotten cantaloupes, O'Brien?" Gus asked.

I clenched my fists. "Yummy," I said.

About fifteen minutes later we pulled into Karadimos's

trash yard on Atlantic Avenue. Angelo parked the Buick next to a black Mercedes in front of the old stucco office building. A dim yellow light highlighted the shade-covered window in front. Someone was inside. Had to be Karadimos.

"Get out and head for the door." Gus pointed to the office. "I'm right behind you."

I reached the door, felt the gun against my back, and heard him say, "Open it."

I did what he said. He pushed me hard, and I stumbled into the building.

Karadimos sat behind his beat-up desk. "Well, Mr. O'Brien, what a pleasure," he said in his nasal wheeze.

I glared at him. "Can't say the same."

"Now, O'Brien, let's keep a positive attitude."

"Okay, I'm positive it's not a pleasure."

"I see you came back to my yard. Do you enjoy the ambiance?"

"It's not a rose garden, but it does have a distinct odor."

"Glad you like it. Because it appears you'll be spending the rest of your life here."

"This place is crawling with scum and germs. I haven't had my shots."

"Don't worry. You won't be alive long enough to catch anything. Angelo, bring me the briefcase. Gus, keep the gun on his head and shoot him if he moves an inch."

Angelo obeyed, and Karadimos started rummaging through the case. "This is what I was looking for. You're to be congratulated, O'Brien. A shame you didn't listen to me; you would have been amply rewarded."

I remained silent, thinking. The only way I'd leave this place would be dead, or with the briefcase. I had to control my anger, not make any stupid moves, or I'd be history and Ernesto Rodriguez would spend his life behind bars.

Karadimos tossed Angelo a roll of duct tape he pulled from the top desk drawer. "Tape his hands behind his back. Don't cover his mouth. We're going to have a nice little chat.

Aren't we, O'Brien?"

"Nothing to talk about."

"Turn around and put your hands behind you," Angelo demanded.

With my arms behind my back and my wrist bound, Angelo shoved me into the chair facing Karadimos, who said, "I'm gonna ask you a few questions. If you cooperate, tell me what I want to know, then we won't have to use extreme measures. Am I making myself clear, O'Brien?"

I started to shake. I didn't like the sound of *extreme measures*. But I wondered what I could tell him. He already had the cassette tape; he already knew what I knew about his operation.

"Why don't we start with the obvious question? How many people have you told about the unfortunate conversation you'd taped at Chasen's? Illegally, I might add."

Illegally. He had to be kidding. The guy runs drugs and teen prostitutes and he talks about what's legal. I glanced around. My left brain told me that I'd never get free. My right brain still tried to figure out an escape route. Gus stood behind me with the gun pointed at my head, Angelo, the monster, hovered off to the side. Other than the revolver in Gus's hand I saw nothing in the office that could be used as a weapon.

"Come on, O'Brien, speak up. Don't be shy."

I remained silent.

He paused for a beat, then his voice changed, became hard. "Angelo," is all he said, but the way he said it made my skin crawl.

Angelo stood and flexed his fingers as he moved toward me. He backhanded me twice across the face. I tasted blood.

"Goddammit, I haven't told anyone about the recording."

"You expect me to believe that? You're working with Sica. You would've told him right off the bat."

"Yeah, I told Sica. I forgot." Let him take up the issue with the Sica gang. I didn't give a shit.

"Who else?"

"No one."

"What about that fat Jew you hang around with?"

Oh Christ! No way would I tell him about Sol's involvement. "He's just a friend. We don't talk about business."

Angelo whacked me again, three times in rapid succession. I could feel my face pulse as my mouth started to swell. Blood ran down my shirt. He hit me again, harder.

"I know you've discussed the tape with that cute little piece of ass you have running around your office. We'll be chatting with her too."

Oh God, no! What have I done? Shit, not Rita.

"She knows nothing, goddammit. She's a filing clerk, that's all. I don't confide in her about anything. You told me yourself the tape is illegal. Believe me, she knows nothing."

"You're protesting too much. She's in on it, all right."

I squirmed, wanting to get my hands around his fat ugly neck and squeeze until his eyeballs popped out of their sockets.

"God damn it! I told you she doesn't know anything!"

Angelo hit me with his fist this time. My head snapped back and my vision blurred. I shook my head, spraying blood around the room.

"You're a lying sack of shit, O'Brien. But we have ways." Karadimos reached in his desk drawer again. This time he pulled out a syringe and held it to the light. A drop of viscous fluid oozed out of the tip of the needle.

Chapter Forty-Nine

Angelo jerked me out of the chair and dropped me onto the old, ratty car bench seat that Karadimos used as an office couch. I didn't dare resist, not with Gus keeping the gun trained on me.

"Lay him out and tie his arms and legs down." Karadimos tossed Angelo the roll of duct tape. He came around from his desk, holding the syringe. "Don't try anything, O'Brien. Wouldn't want to have Gus shoot you here and mess up the upholstery."

I realized what he was going to do: pump me full of Sodium Pentothal or Amytal–truth serum. Early in my LAPD career, I'd seen a detective use the stuff on a prisoner. It wasn't pretty. The cop gave the guy too much and he convulsed and almost died.

"No, you sonofabitch–"

Angelo backhanded me across the face again. The blow loosened one of my back teeth. I pressed it with my tongue and felt it move. My face must look like hamburger.

"Shut up, and do as you're told," he snapped. "Or I'll whack you again, harder."

Now I couldn't move. Angelo had tied my legs too tight, cutting off the blood flow to my feet, and Gus stood over me with the business end of the revolver pressed against my forehead.

Karadimos held the syringe up to the light; a tiny stream of liquid shot out of the needle. "Two milliliters should do the trick, don't want to knock you out entirely."

He jabbed the needle in my thigh, right through the fabric of my pants.

The hell with Gus and the gun. I twisted and bucked, tried to kick my feet. No good, my legs were trussed like a

Thanksgiving turkey. I struggled harder.

As Karadimos slowly depressed the plunger, he shouted, "Hold still, O'Brien. You'll break the goddamn needle. Angelo, for chrissakes, pin his legs!"

Angelo's two hands were like vice grips, clamping my knees against the seat. But it didn't matter. There was nothing I could do now. The fluid coursed through my veins.

I'm weak, muscles like Jell-O and warm, very warm...pain in my face, disappeared...a nice...wonderful... euphoria coming over me. I'm floating...drifting in the air...*eyelids; heavy...vision closing in...a circle of light, getting smaller, smaller in the darkness...*

"Wake up!" a faraway voice said. I felt a slap across my face...didn't hurt, and I didn't care. Someone slapped me again. Just want to sleep, such a beautiful sleep...

I felt another slap. "Wake up!" the voice...closer this time, almost in my ear. "Can you hear me? Wake up, you son of a bitch!"

A sliver of dim light...eyelids heavy, each weighed ten pounds. I floated on the car seat, weightless...Karadimos, floating too...his face inches from mine.

A blur, a hand whipped across my face...why...what have I done? The Greek...mad...not floating anymore... My tongue is thick...hard to breathe...*focus focus try to focus.* Nothing hurts. He said to relax...relax...

"I could've given him too much." Karadimos's voice.

Have to talk...tell him how I feel. "Good morning...what a wonderful day." My voice is strange. I said that?

"Wait, he's coming around. In a few more seconds he'll jabber like a cockatoo. I want to hold him in twilight. Gus, get me the black satchel by my desk. Has more juice in it, in case we need it later."

"I like juice...like coffee better, but my coffee tastes like piss." I heard myself say and had no idea what I was talking about. "Rita makes good coffee...Goddamn, she's pretty...fucking beautiful...I'm her boss. Wouldn't be right..."

"Welcome back, Jimmy. How do you feel?"

"Fucking great, thank you very much."

"We're going to have a nice little talk. Do you feel like talking to me?"

"Yeah, a nice talk. What do you want to talk about?"

"Tell me about the tape recording."

Tape. "*Hey, Jude don't make it bad. Take a sad song...song...song...*"

"Jimmy, listen to me. Did you tell anyone about the tape?"

"I lost the tape...my favorite, the Beatles. They don't perform anymore, you know..."

"Not that tape. The one you recorded at Chasen's."

"Lost it, too...let a hooker steal it...she gave it to you...Sol said she worked for you."

"How much does Silverman know about my business?"

Sol's smart...he's my friend." I could hear my voice echo in my brain. *Don't talk. Don't talk about Sol.* I shouldn't..."Sol doesn't like you."

I rolled my head. So confused, hazy, but I couldn't stop talking. "Sol wants to put you in jail." *Christ, keep your trap shut.*

"Did you tell the police, or the district attorney, what you heard on the tape?"

"She hates me..."

"Who hates you?"

"Bobbi."

"Why?"

"Thinks I lied about your airplane."

"You did, Jimmy. You lied to her. I didn't kill that girl."

"Bobbi's pretty too, I'd like to–oops, not going to say that. We have a Chinese wall..." *Is this a nightmare?*

I wanted to throw up.

"What's he talking about, boss? What's this crap about a Chinese wall?"

"Shut up, Gus! He's talking, that's what counts."

It became quiet for a moment. Tired...I felt tired, but not as tired as before. The shadows in my mind started to brighten...I'm coming back. I remember now. *Oh Christ!* He gave me Pentothal!

Karadimos slapped me again. "Tell me about Rita, your secretary. What does she know? Had she heard the tape?"

"Fuck you, Karadimos!"

"Gus, get me another syringe out of the bag."

Do something, and do it fast. Sing, act drunk, something. Act like someone who'd overdosed on Pentothal. "*Hey, Jude don't make it bad, take a sad song, and make, make it...*"

"Hold it. I think he's still under the influence. If I give him any more he might black out or croak. We won't get shit from him."

"*Lady Madonna, children at your, feet...feet, sweet feet...*" I slurred my voice. The Beatles would shit if they heard me sing their music.

"O'Brien, tell me about Rita. What does she know?"

"Aw, sweet little Rita. Dumb as a box of rocks. I only keep her around because she's got a cute ass..."

"O'Brien! What does she know?"

"She doesn't know her goddamn name...but she can sure swing that sweet little tushy. Good night, Karadimos. I'm going to take a nice li'l nappy."

I closed my eyes and pretended to pass out. I had to control my breathing, relax, let my body go limp. It was my only hope at staying alive.

Karadimos slapped me again. But I just lay there with my eyes closed, trying hard to keep from slipping back into the simmering fog.

"O'Brien, wake up! Goddammit, I need more information." Karadimos's voice echoed in my head.

"What the hell was that all about, boss?" Gus asked. "The guy sounds like he's drunk. I don't think your joy juice worked."

Jeff Sherratt

"He may be faking," Karadimos said. "Hand me that lighter on the desk."

A moment later someone grabbed my arm. I head a click then felt a searing pain on the back of my hand. If it weren't for the lingering effect of the Pentothal, I wouldn't have been able to stand it. But the pain would help keep me alert. I clenched my teeth and didn't move.

"Maybe you gave him too much," Angelo said. "Looks like you knocked him out."

"Sometimes it happens like that. We won't get anything more out of him. Besides, he's getting nowhere in his chicken shit investigation of our organization. He's nothing; I've got him blocked at every turn. It's that bastard Silverman I'm worried about."

"Maybe he'll quit the case if O'Brien should happen to disappear."

"No way. He's a fucking bulldog. We'll fight him if we have to. But I don't want the cops finding any more bodies. There's too much heat coming down now, because some asshole whacked that Graham bitch before Kruger could get to her."

"What do you wanna do with him?" Gus asked.

"You two get him outta here, right now. Get him outta my sight! Throw him in the garbage pit. Then turn on the grinder."

Chapter Fifty

Angelo and Gus cut me loose from the couch, grabbed my arms and legs and carried me out the door. With my eyelids slightly open, I saw everything in a hazy blur. My mind was back in focus, but my muscles won't function. I felt like a sack of wet mush. I couldn't resist, could hardly move, but if I didn't get control of my body, I'd soon be dead. As we got closer to the garbage pit, the stench made me want to gag, but I couldn't even do that.

The dim yard was spotted with circles of yellow light coming from floods mounted high on posts. The two goons carried me between a dump truck and a huge diesel tractor with a scraper blade toward an area about fifty feet behind the office. One of the floodlights illuminated the pit, a metal-lined rectangular hole in the ground with a chain guard rimming the perimeter.

They dropped me on the hard ground close to the edge, and I tasted dirt.

"Go turn on the grinder. I'll roll him into the pit," Angelo said.

"Yeah, the machine has to be up and running or he'll plug it up," Gus replied. "I'll have to feed him in slow and easy with the rest of the crap. You sure he's out of it?"

"Hell yes." Angelo let out a mirthless laugh. "The boss thinks he's a smart son-of-a-bitch, but he ain't no doctor. He shot him so full of joy juice it practically killed him. That shit never works. I could'a told him. But he never listens to me."

I turned my head a fraction and saw Gus hand Angelo his gun. "Here, use this if he comes to."

Angelo jammed the gun in his belt. "He ain't coming to. Be more fun if he did. I'd like to hear the bastard scream as he makes a nosedive into the grinder."

In my mind, I saw a large garbage disposal ripping chunks of my body to shreds as I was being fed into its gaping maw. Not pretty.

Gus dashed off into the dim light toward a tall iron platform twenty feet away. Beyond the platform loomed a cluster of heavy-duty machinery.

I had to act. But I was still too weak to put up a fight.

Angelo pulled one of the metal pipes, a stanchion connected to the thin guard chain, out of a small hole in the ground and cast it aside, leaving a section open. He grabbed my legs and dragged me close to the edge. I heard Karadimos, probably standing somewhere outside his office, shout, "Angelo, for chrissakes, dump him in the goddamn pit already and get your ass back here. I need help going through these records."

"Aw shit, boss. I wanna watch him get chewed up in the grinder."

My body teetered on the side of the pit for a second or two. Then, Angelo rolled me the rest of the way in.

As I twisted and started to slide into the hole, I grabbed the chain lying on the ground and held on for dear life. The chain snapped and the pipe stanchion followed, hitting me on the head as I tumbled into the pit and landed on a pile of rotten cantaloupes. My head hurt and blood ran down my face. But after what I'd been through, it didn't seem to matter.

Suddenly I heard a loud whirring noise, like a jet engine firing up. The grinder! I felt a vibration, and the rotten cantaloupes under me started to move. I was sinking into the morass. I had to do something fast. Gus must have also switched on the conveyor that fed the giant garbage disposal. It moved under the refuse. I didn't give a damn about the putrid smell, the viscous slime oozing into my pores, or anything else. I just had to get the hell out of there. Adrenalin pumped through my system, eliminating the Pentothal effects, and my body came to life.

Holding the pipe in one hand, I reached out with the

other, feeling for the side of the pit. Like a gator swimming through a river of shit, I squirmed and kicked and made it to the side, but I continued to sink deeper. The side of the pit was slippery with sludge; no foothold. I scraped and clawed and only slipped farther down into the muck.

Looking up, I saw stars in the night, but I also caught sight of the edge of the pit, maybe five feet above my head.

Above and to my left, an angle iron brace crisscrossed the opening. I ran my hand over the chain that was connected to the pipe—rusty and thin. It'd snapped before when I held it as I rolled in, but I had to try again. It was my only hope.

Holding the end of the chain, I tried to loop the pipe around the brace. No luck. It fell back and I sank deeper. The grinder made crunching, gnawing sounds as it gobbled up the refuse being fed into it.

I had one more chance before being sucked down under the garbage heading for the grinder. I brought my arm back like a spear thrower and snapped it forward. The pipe shot upward; it didn't fall back. It circled the brace and dangled there. I quickly looped the other end of the chain around the angle iron and started to climb out of the pit, hand over hand. I prayed Angelo hadn't disobeyed his boss and hung around to watch, and I prayed that the chain would hold my weight.

My prayers were answered. It held.

I crawled over the edge of the pit, exhausted and covered with rotting garbage, but alive. Sprawled on the ground for a moment, I gasped for air. The pigs in Saugus would have to make do without ground lawyer on the menu tomorrow.

I shot a glance around the yard: no Angelo. In the shadows off to my right, I could see the tall platform. I made out the dim outline of Gus standing atop it. He stayed busy feeding garbage that came up an inclined conveyor into a hopper above the giant grinding machine. I also spotted an enormous steel cylinder beyond the grinder and could smell the ground slop being cooked in the long rotating tube.

Undoing the pipe looped around the brace, I scrambled

to the bottom of the platform. I had to get Gloria's aluminum case before Karadimos destroyed the evidence, and I needed a weapon. Gus had given his revolver to Angelo, but he probably had another gun tucked away.

The deafening cacophony of the machinery concealed any sound I may have made as I scurried to the top of the platform. Gus turned and faced me, eyes wide, just as I wound up and bashed his head with the pipe stanchion. He fell where he stood. He wouldn't be getting up anytime soon. Quickly, I went through his pockets and felt around the rim of his pants. I also patted his legs looking for an ankle holster. Goddammit, no weapon of any kind. What kind of asshole gangster didn't carry a hidden gun, or even a knife?

Back down on the ground, I glanced toward the lights burning in the office. Karadimos and Angelo were still there. It'd be suicide to walk in unarmed. But soon they'd wonder about Gus, and they'd come out to look for him.

Hunched down, I made a dash for the big D7 Caterpillar parked close to the office and climbed atop the bulldozer. I knew about these beasts from working summer construction jobs during high school. Pushing the button, I started the pony motor–the small motor that starts the big one–and waited a few seconds, then pulled the lever in front of the instrument panel, engaging the main engine. The diesel coughed once, belched smoke, and turned over. I feathered the choke, and it ran smoothly. I pulled the throttle out a hair, put the dozer in gear, and jumped off the monster. It crawled away, moving in a circle like a lumbering ogre at about two miles an hour. The dozer's racket was deafening, drowning out whatever noise came from the grinder.

I darted to the old house Karadimos used an office and flattened myself against the wall next to the front door. Holding the pipe like a baseball bat, I waited. I figured when Karadimos heard the tractor start up he'd assume Gus was messing with the machine. After all, I should be dead by now.

I didn't have to wait long. He immediately sent Angelo

to find out why Gus would be driving the tractor around in the middle of the night. When Angelo came through the door, I was ready. He stuck his head and shouted, "Gus! Hey, asshole, what the hell is going on?"

He ventured a little farther into the yard, closing the door behind him. I took my best swing with the pipe, and he toppled to the dirt. He fell in a heap, not making a sound.

I quickly grabbed the .45 from his waistband and darted back to my place near the door, where I took a few deep breaths. Sweat ran down my face and mingled with the caked blood. The .45 felt heavy in my hand as I held it up. I couldn't wait any longer; I had to get the drop on Karadimos. He'd likely be at his desk, going over the files. I kicked the door open and jumped in, gun leveled. No Karadimos. My eyes swept the room. Nothing. Behind me, the dozer continued to rumble. Where the hell was he? Taking a crap?

I backed up and turned, holding the gun out in front of me. Karadimos stepped out from the corner of the building. He held his revolver straight out, aimed at my chest.

I flinched. "What the hell—"

His finger was wrapped around the trigger, the gun cocked. "Say goodnight, O'Brien. It's time to turn out the lights—"

We both heard it at the same time: the loud crunching shriek of metal chewing metal.

"Shit! My goddamn car! The fucking dozer is running over my Mercedes—"

As Karadimos flicked his eyes toward the metallic carnage, I shot him in the head.

I dropped the .45 as the distant sound of sirens wailing in the night came closer.

Chapter Fifty-One

Light streamed in from the hospital room window. It was Friday, almost thirty hours after Sol and the cops found me staggering around Karadimos's dead body. When he noticed my bloody face and dead eyes, Sol had one of the deputies rush me to the emergency room at St. Frances in Lynwood.

Dr. Kaufmann, a plastic surgeon, did what he could to heal my facial wounds and improve my appearance. He told me I should feel better soon and could be released in a day or so. Other than a few small scars, I'd look the same as before the trauma. I told him I'd slip him an extra fifty bucks to make me look more like Robert Redford. "No dice," he said, "not enough to work with." But for twenty-five, he could make me look like Phyllis Diller. I passed on the deal.

I remained in the recovery room for hours after the surgery, then a couple of gurney jockeys wheeled me into a private room with a view. I couldn't get out of bed to see the view, but they assured me it was nice. During Dr. Kaufmann's most recent visit he indicated I was healing fast and could now have visitors. People had been waiting to see me, he said. He'd let them know I was awake.

Soon after the doctor left, Rita slipped quietly into the room. When she noticed my eyes were open and saw me smiling, she rushed to my side and took my hand.

"Oh, Jimmy, we've all been so worried. Sol has been here the whole time. He just went to get some coffee. He said you were almost killed. I don't know what I'd do if anything happened to you."

"You could take over the firm."

"Don't say that!" She tapped me playfully on the arm. "Sol told me some of it, but not how he knew you'd been kidnapped, or what happened at the yard."

I gave her a sanitized version of the story, omitting the fact that they threw me into the garbage pit. But I did tell her about the shootout in Las Vegas, my discovery of Gloria's briefcase, and my showdown with Karadimos and his thugs. Then I explained how Sol and the police found out I'd been captured and taken to Karadimos's facility in Cudahy.

"Late Wednesday night Sol drove back from Vegas and stopped at Rocco's for a quick drink before going home. He recognized a thug named Lenny parking my car in the lot and followed him into the bar."

"I thought you didn't let anyone drive your car," Rita said.

"You're right, and Sol knows that too. The guy took it after Angelo and Gus kidnapped me. Anyway, Sol grabbed Lenny and threatened to beat him to a pulp if he didn't tell him what happened to me. It didn't take long for the guy to spill his guts. Sol called the cops and they made a beeline for the refuse yard. They got there just in time. I'd lost some blood and was ready to pass out. Angelo had come to and was crawling around looking for a gun."

"Wow!"

"I have to ask you a question."

"What, Jimmy?"

"I know they found Gloria's briefcase in the office, but what happened to it?"

"Oh my God! I didn't tell you. The Sheriff's Department turned it over to the DA's office. You were still recovering from surgery and couldn't be disturbed, so I called Bobbi Allen to remind her to make sure the charges against Rodriguez were dropped. After she's goes through the stuff and does a preliminary check, she promised me she'd file a motion to dismiss all charges against him. Also, at the coroner inquest she's going to recommend that the Karadimos shooting be ruled self defense."

I took a deep breath. It had all been worth it. Rodriguez would go free. Still, I felt something wasn't right.

"You won the case, Jimmy! Without even going to trial, you won the case." Rita bent down and kissed me on the cheek. "I'm so proud of you."

Sol appeared, carrying two cups of take-out coffee. He handed one to Rita. "Where's mine?" I asked.

"Aw, Jimmy my boy; you've been lying around here being pampered long enough. You'll have to get your own."

I made a move to get out of bed, "Oh, damn," I said, and lay back down. "Not today, Sol."

"I'll get you a cup," Rita said. Before I could stop her, she dashed out the room.

Sol pulled a tape cassette out of his pocket. "Found this before the cops did on Karadimos desk."

"*Jesus*, is that the missing tape I recorded at Chasen's?"

"Yes it is, my boy, and when you get out of here, we're going build a little fire."

"Maybe roast some marshmallows."

"I'm thinking hotdogs."

I became serious. "Sol, you saved my life..."

"Yeah, we do that for each other. Don't we?"

I just smiled.

"Hey, the story's all over the news. Someone leaked it to the media." Sol flashed a mischievous grin. "The cops are rounding up the rest of Karadimos's bunch as we speak, and they've just arrested French. Welch seems to have skipped."

"Probably heading for the Galapagos Islands," I said.

"Here's something you might want to know, I called the hospital in Vegas. It was touch and go, but Big Jake will survive. Be back kicking the shit out of people in no time."

We heard a soft knock. Sol and I turned toward the door. Bobbi peered inside. "May I come in?"

"Sure," Sol boomed, "why not?"

Bobbi stepped cautiously into the room, carrying a gift basket of flowers with a red balloon attached. "Hi, Jimmy. I brought you these." She held out the flowers.

"Thank you," I said. Sol placed the basket on a table

against the wall.

She sat in the chair across from me, folded her hands in her lap, and glanced around the room. Just then, Rita returned with my coffee. She said hello to Bobbi and asked about the Rodriguez motion of dismissal.

"I filed it an hour ago. He'll be released today."

"That's wonderful," Rita said.

No one said anything for long seconds, until Sol broke the silence. "C'mon, little girl," he said to Rita. "I'm going to buy you the best damn lunch you've ever had." He slipped his arm around her waist and started moving her toward the door.

"Jimmy," Bobbi said after they left.

"Yeah?"

She walked to the window and stood looking out at my nice view, then turned. "I'm sorry I doubted your integrity."

"Well, it's your job, I guess."

She sat down again. "Fred Vogel, the jet mechanic from Long Beach, talked to Sergeant Hodges. He told him about the hidden meter. You were right. I'm really sorry."

"I guess it doesn't matter now," I said.

"You brought down a massive criminal organization!"

"Rodriguez has been exonerated. That's all I wanted."

"That's all?"

"That's about it."

"Maybe, when you're feeling better... Well, maybe, we can take in that movie we'd talked about."

"Saw it already."

I waited in the uneasy silence, then Bobbi stood and dusted off her skirt. "I have to go, Jimmy. But if you want to talk, I'm available."

I nodded. "Thanks for stopping by."

Bobbi left. The nurse soon came around and checked my blood pressure, the doc popped his head in the door and waved, and a candy striper bought me a pasty meal. I wasn't hungry and the food needed salt, but I ate most of it anyway.

A messenger walked in carrying an enormous wreath

with a wide ribbon draped across it. I opened the card: *I know you won't forget our favor*. It was signed, *Joe Sica*. Did I now owe the mob a favor? Wasn't getting rid of Karadimos enough? I glanced again at the wreath and wondered if the resemblance to a funeral arrangement was intentional.

Friends from long ago and people I didn't know sent cards and gifts. Later in the day, I even received a handwritten card from Judge Bob Johnson. It said our "little misunderstanding" about the case was forgiven, and the schmuck even asked me to endorse him in the next election.

After reading the get-well cards, I put them on the nightstand next to my bed and took a nap. That night I turned on the TV mounted high on the wall. A comedian on the Dick Cavett show, a guy named Foster Brooks, was hilarious. He did a drunk bar patron routine.

I turned off the TV and glanced at the stack of gifts. My gaze landed on a leather-bound copy of Walt Whitman's *Leaves of Grass*. Picking the book up, I fiddled around with it, absently flipping through the pages. I put it down and stared at the ceiling. I couldn't concentrate. I felt restless, as if I had missed an important detail. *What was it?*

I drifted off again, and after a half hour of restless sleep, I bolted up in bed. Thoughts and ideas came to me at a mile a minute. I shuffled through the stack on the end table and found the envelope I was looking for. Of course! The handwriting matched the envelope that I had found at the murder scene.

The pieces began to fall into place. I'd make one phone call, and it would finally be over. I couldn't do anything until I got out of the hospital. But it could wait, I guess.

I rolled over on my side and fell sound asleep.

Chapter Fifty-Two

On Sunday afternoon, two days later, we gathered at Rocco's for a luncheon that Rita had arranged in my honor. Half of Downey turned out, including Judge Bob Johnson, Joe DiLoretto, the mayor, and Richard Conway, a reporter for the L.A. Times. Rita had even invited Mabel, our answering service lady. At the last minute, I'd asked Rita to invite another guest. He hadn't arrived yet.

I worried about Rodriguez and Bobbi being at the same lunch. However, when Bobbi arrived, she rushed over and apologized to him. Out of the corner of my eye, I caught the smile on his face as he shook her hand.

When Rita invited her to the luncheon, Bobbi had called and asked if her presence would make me uncomfortable. Knowing I'd been harsh with her at the hospital, I said it would be fine.

Sol, being Sol, made sure that Rocco's was well stocked with Dom Pérignon and Beluga caviar. He even brought a few pounds of his special blend of Jamaican Blue Mountain Coffee and arranged to have the restaurant's spunky piano player entertain us. Everyone howled at the guy's fractured song routine.

Bobbi approached me with a bewildered smile on her face. "Alone again, *Ralph*?" she asked.

"Could be our song," I said.

"It would be charming," she said, "but when are we going to have that talk?"

"Soon."

Sol worked the room with Rodriguez under his wing. Joyce followed with a pen and notebook in hand. I asked Rita what the heck was going on. "It's wonderful," she said. "Sol is lining up gardening business for Mr. Rodriguez. He's already got him the City of South Gate contract and he's now working on Downey."

Mabel, the answering service lady, stopped by my table. "How's it feel to be a big shot?" she asked.

I'd never met Mabel in person. She was just a voice on the phone that nagged me from time to time. She had dyed red-orange hair and her make-up was over done. "Mabel, I'm not a big shot. I just do my job and try to survive like millions of people do every day."

She turned to walk away, but then stopped. "You big shots are all the same, full of bullshit." Her grin belied her words.

"You know, Jimmy," Rita said a few seconds later, "Mabel came by the hospital, stuck around while you were in surgery, but she had to leave to handle her business. She's a good person, you know."

"Yeah, it was nice of her to be there."

"When I pass the bar and become your associate, we should hire her."

"What?"

"Those new answering machines are wiping out her business. And we'll need someone to answer the phones."

"Where's the money going to come from?"

"It'll work out. Someone or something is watching over you. You've got that little halo above your head."

"Does it glow?"

She laughed. "Oh, boss."

At one-thirty, my special guest arrived. I pulled Bobbi aside, told her what was on my mind, and asked her to stick close to Mitch the cop for a while. I introduced Mitch to a few guests, then I took him to meet Sol.

"Mitch, say hello to my best friend. Sol, he's the officer who took the anonymous call that morning. Been on the force less than four months, but his career is about to skyrocket."

"Good for you, Mitch," Sol said, then turned to me. "How's he going to do that?"

"You'll see." I glanced around the room. Bob Johnson sat alone in a booth in the back of the room, his hands wrapped around a tall drink. I saw Bobbi and Mitch sit in the booth next to his. "C'mon, Sol, lets go talk to the judge."

"Jimmy, it's always a pleasure to see you," Johnson said when we slipped into his booth. "You too, Silverman."

"Not always, Bob."

"Excuse me?"

"I got your card, in the hospital. Wrote it yourself, very thoughtful."

Johnson paused for half a beat. I felt he sensed something was up. "Figured you'd like it. Now, what's the matter? Don't want to endorse me?"

"I don't endorse murderers."

"What!"

"You were having an affair with Gloria Graham. She was sleeping with a married man who was running for re-election. That's you, Bob. You're on the ballot in November, too. But two weeks ago, you sent her a Dear John letter. Was she going to expose you, Bob? Is that why you killed her?"

"Have you lost your mind?"

"You flew to the fund-raiser with Welch and Karadimos that weekend."

"That's right, you dumb bastard. I was in Sacramento at the time—"

"You weren't at the Saturday night dinner."

"Of course I was—"

"Saw Robert Goulet and the comic, Foster Brooks? He did his famous drunk routine. Remember, you said he was hilarious. Isn't that right, Bob?"

"Yeah, very funny, like you are right now. Are *you* drunk?"

"Foster Brooks wasn't there, Bob. He cancelled at the last minute. You wouldn't know that because you were flying the jet back at the time."

"The pilot flew the jet—"

"Death bed confession: he didn't fly it."

Johnson gulped his drink. Sol sat there in shocked silence. He knew this was my play, a little grandstanding, but he would know I deserved a little payback for what I went through because of Johnson.

"Get out of my booth, you goddamn bastard–"

"You flew jets in Korea, Bob. You were the only one on the trip who knew how to fly a jet, and you flew down Saturday, killed her, and searched the house. You found the letter, but couldn't find the envelope."

"Karadimos searched the place–"

"He couldn't fly a jet. Karadimos didn't even know it was flown that Saturday night until he got the gas bill on Monday. He didn't make the anonymous call. I talked to the police dispatcher when I was in the hospital and had him listen to the police tapes of Karadimos's voice. Wasn't him."

"You crazy bastard–!"

"You even sent thugs to trash my office. They stole the Rodriguez file. But worse, they tore up my 1951 Angels team photo. They didn't have to do that, Bob."

"I don't know what you're talking about."

"You shouldn't have pressured me to plead Rodriguez out."

"You can't prove anything."

"You killed the girl, Bob. Had to get back fast, didn't have time to do a thorough search, and the envelope was still there, sitting on her dressing table."

"God almighty–"

"I saw it. It's in your handwriting, just like the card you sent me."

"Jimmy, listen to me–"

"And the gift–Walt Whitman's *Leaves of Grass*–must be your favorite. I saw the card you sent her, with the quote from *To a Common Prostitute*. Is that how you saw her, Bob?"

"For chrissakes, O'Brien!"

"You called the police from Sacramento that morning.

Shouldn't have done that, Bob. The call was long distance and it's obvious, whoever made the anonymous call was the killer."

"Wasn't me!"

"I've got proof."

"Karadimos... Welch..." he stammered.

"Give it up, Bob."

There was a long pause, Johnson glared at me, his chest expanding and deflating erratically, as if his body tried to adjust to what his mind already knew.

But he didn't give up. He shook his head and said, "Listen to me, God damn it! Your client, that guy walking around free over there? *He* did it! The gardener did it!"

My eyes locked on Mitch in the next booth. He nodded and mouthed the words, "It's him."

Johnson bolted up. Mitch grabbed him and slapped the cuffs on his wrists.

Johnson looked over at me, his eyes pleading. "Jimmy, we were friends..."

"What's a little murder between friends?" I said. "Goodbye, Bob."

Jeff Sherratt was born in Los Angeles, California on September 22, 1941. When he was in grade school his father bought a cattle ranch and moved his family to Utah. But after a few years the family returned to Southern California and settled in Downey where Jeff went to high school. In his senior year he met Judy and soon after graduation they were married. They've been together for over forty years now and have three daughters, Kristin, Karen, and Holly. They also have seven grandchildren.

For most of his adult life Jeff had been in business for himself. He owned companies that made and sold food related products. But as a lark, he once became a partner in a political public relations firm. 'Some of the characters in my books are based on the candidates we've handled. I guess that's why we folded the tent and sneaked away. Our guys were losers and we weren't good enough to make them look like winners,' Jeff said, recalling his experience as a political spinmeister.

After selling his business, Jeff devoted his time to writing mysteries, which soon became a full time career. His first Jimmy O'Brien mystery novel, 'The Brimstone Murders' was released in February of 2008 by Echelon Press.

Jeff Sherratt lives in Newport Beach, California with his wife, Judy. He is a member of Sisters in Crime, an organization combating discrimination against women in the mystery field, and the professional association, Mystery Writers of America. Jeff is currently working on the next book in the Jimmy O'Brien series.